Michael Poeltl

FIRST EDITION

978-0-9813168-6-4

The only way to learn is to survive the lesson.

HER PAST'S PRESENT

By Michael Poeltl

CHAPTERS

Michael Poeltl

Chapter One
September 15th, 2:00 am

It wasn't your fault. These are healing words, something Tess's therapist had her write out a thousand times when she was twelve. It became her mantra, a reassurance that what had happened to her baby brother could in no way be her fault.

Today, fifteen years after the suicide that had devastated her life and the lives of her parents, she finds power in those words once more.

"I'm sorry," says Sam, her husband, standing stock-still before her. All that separates them is the granite-topped island in the middle of a kitchen under renovation. It is the only working surface to lean on should he confirm her fears.

"Please," she pleads. "Please just tell me it doesn't mean anything. Tell me it was just the one time, and I can forgive you." She isn't hopeful for this outcome but can't bear the thought of the consequences of such an admission. To be a single mother amidst all the renovations, bills, contractors, and sleepless nights has overwhelmed her the past few days, and her already pale complexion is rapidly fading to a sickly, almost translucent white.

Sam's head drops slowly, his eyes studying the grout lines framing the new tile at his feet. His heart isn't in this. He was far from ready to tell his wife of five years he'd met someone else; he'd been seeing another woman since the last month of her pregnancy. Sam's decided that is a significant amount of time, and he is very much committed to this new woman. But not at all ready to tell his wife.

"Tess," he struggles with her name. His chin is beginning to tremble.

"Please, tell me it will be okay." She begs. "Tell me that you love me."

"I *do* love you, goddamn it," he manages through clenched teeth. His fist falls with a weak thump on the black granite counter while his other hand finds his face, defending Tess from his diminishing façade. He jerks and cries into his shield, turning away from Tess.

"Then why?" Tess begs, slowly sinking to her knees, coming to rest on the dusty tile, her back landing against the island's cupboard.

"I don't know why." Sam turns and slides down the opposite side of the island. "I don't know."

"Please don't leave me with nothing," she begs.

"If I had an answer, I'd give it."

"*Please.*"

"I don't have an answer for you. I haven't an answer for *myself.*"

Her voice cracks. "If you love me, be with me."

"Don't you think I want that? Don't you think I *want* to be happy here?"

"You're not happy?"

"You know I'm not."

"I'm sorry if I haven't had the time to put into you. We have a baby."

"Jesus, I know we have a baby, and I love her, but I feel like the walls are closing in on me."

Tess shifts uncomfortably, the thin fabric of her pajama pants offering little insulation from the cool tile. "It's okay to feel trapped, but you need to talk to me."

"It's not *you.*"

"Then what?"

"*Me.* It's me."

It's not your fault. She tells herself. *It's not your fault.*

Chapter Two
October 15th, Monday

Tess is up with her daughter. It's 3:30 in the morning. It is the second time tonight, and she only put Emilia down at ten. At six months old, Tess had hoped Emma would have gotten into a pattern of sleep that would take her through the night. Even if she weren't going to bed until later in the evening, at least sleeping through the night would be a blessing. But neither was happening, and now that she no longer has Sam to lean on, her days and nights seem to run together, one bleeding into the next.

Sitting in Emilia's room, rocking gently to the soothing sounds of her daughter feeding at the bottle, Tess wonders, as she does every night at this time, what next? It has been a month since Sam left. It was nearly that long since she'd heard from him, too. He left her with everything, including the bank account. She could complete the renovations on their apartment and live comfortably for the remainder of the year if it came to that. Still, Tess missed him endlessly: his presence in her bed, his turn with Emilia overnight, dinners, anticipating his return from work, adult conversation.

Tess cries silently over the baby, now convulsing to repress this reaction to her life. Every feeding ends up like this now - Tess crying over her infant daughter, a myriad of what-ifs tormenting her. *It wasn't your fault,* she reminds herself. *There is nothing you could have done to change the outcome.* Emilia is now sleeping, so Tess lays her in the crib. Careful not to make a noise, she sneaks out of Emilia's room.

It's now that the exhaustion of the day, both physical and emotional, hits her. With the last feeding of the night over, the long stretch of wakefulness begins until the morning light. Tess has not been able to sleep past four in the morning since Sam left, and with the relentless barrage of scenarios attacking her at her most vulnerable, there is no point in trying. Even lying in bed is a challenge. Reading a book is a lost cause; nothing silences the onslaught of questions. So, like every morning before sunrise, Tess drags her weakened spirit across the bedroom and into the nearly finished kitchen to begin her day.

After she makes a pot of coffee, Tess sits in front of a pile of bills she has had no time or inclination to pay. This spurs another panic attack. The first had happened the night after she and Sam had confronted his decision to leave. The experience was frightening, and this was no different. It comes without warning and starts in her left hand, travels up her arm, and attacks her shoulder. The feeling resembles a description Tess had read on heart attacks so closely that she immediately moves her right hand to her chest. Sure enough, the pain enters her chest, and Tess grips her left breast, willing the pain away.

Nothing can make you feel more confident that you're having a heart attack than a substantial panic attack. Even a heart attack either takes you within seconds or goes mostly unnoticed. A panic attack, on the other hand, goes on and on, and with each passing minute, your heart fills with dread that, this time, it really is a heart attack!

Tess fumbles with her tablet and punches in a search for panic attack symptoms. This technique settled her nerves enough to allow the attack to subside three days earlier. Finding the page again, she scrolls down, reading hungrily in anticipation of the pins and needles sensation in her arms dissipating. Breathing in and out slowly also assists in alleviating the building panic. Each breath is an exercise in concentration.

After ten minutes, the symptoms left as suddenly as they'd appeared. Feeling one hundred years older, Tess sits, bent over the dining room table, head in folded arms. Then, the baby cries.

It seems that she will be given no quarter today, and with the men coming to complete the kitchen in just a few short hours, Tess predicts a difficult day of electric drills and skill saws buzzing in her ear while she and Emilia shut themselves into her bedroom to watch cartoons.

* * * * *

As nine o'clock approaches, the buzzer sounds, and Tess lets the men in with all their noisy equipment. She's happy to know the work will end after today, or so she's been told, but the barrage of questions concerning the job's specifics is more than she can handle. This is their sixth time at the house, and Tess is well-versed in making small talk. She points out the coffee maker with a full pot brewed on the counter and relays her plans with the baby for the day.

The foreman assures Tess they will finish today and be out of her hair for good, barring any unforeseen difficulties. Tess nods and realizes she's been staring at the man. He looks inquisitively at her and asks whether there is something else. Tess, embarrassed, shakes her head.

"Sorry. Just tired, is all."

"If I have any questions, I'll knock on your door." He smiles and turns to accept a coffee from his apprentice.

Tess turns around and walks quickly to her room with Emma on her hip. It had been a long time since she'd even considered the company of a man, but fixed in that gaze, she suddenly yearned for the unshaven foreman dressed in a white tee, beige overalls, and steel-toed boots.

In her bedroom, Tess catches herself in the vanity mirror and stops. Studying her reflection, she chastises herself.

"Look at you. Nobody would want *you*." Her hair is in knots, and her face is blotchy from the embarrassment she felt from breaking eye contact with the foreman. She had done nothing to fix her appearance since waking up in preparation for their arrival, never even considered it. How could she have let herself go like this, she wonders. Glancing over at the collage of wedding photos still adorning her wall, she sets the baby down on her bed and pulls them down, lobbing them into the corner pile of laundry. The glass shatters on one of the frames, and she again berates herself. She had thought leaving them on the wall served one of two purposes: Either Sam would return, and everything would be as it was, or she was steeling herself against him. Nothing had changed, though. Not in the month since he had disappeared. He hadn't returned to them, nor had she felt stoic against the black-and-white memories. She lives in a Mausoleum, she decides, a sad memorial to a marriage that didn't work.

* * * * *

That afternoon, the work is completed as promised, and as the apprentice cleans up, the foreman knocks on Tess's door.

"All done," he says. Tess opens the door and smiles at him. She'd made herself up, put on something more appropriate than the tights and loose sweater she'd been wearing to greet them, and walked to the kitchen with Emilia, again resting on her hip.

"Wow, that looks really nice," she tells them. "I couldn't imagine it finished for the longest time."

As the men clear out of the apartment, tools in tow, the foreman hangs back a moment to collect his check. Tess places Emma on the floor in front of the TV and writes the remainder of what she owes him. She pauses, wondering whether she could ask him out for a drink sometime. She feels she needs to recover from the verbal beating she gave herself earlier in the day. A date would do that.

"Say, Remy, right?" She keeps her eyes on the check while she addresses him.

"Yes. Tess, right?"

"Yes, um, I was wondering if you wanted to; I mean, maybe you'd like to get a drink sometime?" Tess feels her face flush. Her gaze remains on the counter.

"Oh, uh, I can't, but I would like to." He pulls a ring from his pocket and places it back on his finger. "I, uh, I take it off when I'm working."

Tess glances over to see that his ring finger now wears a gold band. She stands up straight and hands his check to him, red-faced. "I'm so sorry. I mean, for me, not that you're married. I loved being married." She smiles awkwardly and walks to the door. "Listen, I'll, um, give you good references if you need them. Great work. Thanks again." She can't stop talking now, wishing the moment away.

"Hey, I'm honored, really," he tells her from the hall, quickly studying her decorated ring finger.

"Oh, you don't have to say that. I'm okay, I understand." She runs a hand up and down her arm nervously.

"Well, you take care and enjoy your new kitchen." He bows out and heads towards the elevator where his apprentice is waiting. Tess closes the door and sinks to the floor, humiliated.

Chapter Three
Tuesday, 3:00 am

Tess wakes with a start. Her heart is pounding, and she feels a chill on her back as she sits up. She's soaked through her nightshirt, and her hair is matted to one side of her face. She peels her shirt off and ties her hair back, lifting it off her neck. Looking at the alarm clock, she sees it's nearly time for Emilia to wake up for her feeding. It's not particularly hot in the house; in fact, it's quite cool, *so why all the sweat?* Bad dreams, she faintly recalls.

Tess moves to the other side of the bed, avoiding the sizeable damp circle, and lies down again. *Pathetic,* she thinks, that she still practices sleeping on her side of the bed, while *his* remains vacant. Then, the dream that woke her reveals itself in sporadic scenes; flashes of memory dance behind her eyelids.

There was a war going on outside her home. Not her current home, but her home all the same. It was dark save one electric light flickering with each vibration. Plaster fell on her each time a sound more threatening than thunder exploded overhead. The last thing she remembers of the dream was searching helplessly through the rubble of her home for her children, crying out to them, panic-stricken, wishing her husband was there.

I can't even escape into my dreams anymore, she tells herself, placing both hands over her face. The idea that she may find no peace in sleep now devastates her. Tess refuses to take anything to induce sleep for fear of not waking when the baby cries. She surrenders to the anxiety and turns to sob into the pillow, a pillow that still carries Sam's scent.

Emilia does not wake for her 4 am feeding on this night, and Tess manages to collapse back into sleep after an exhausting hour of crying. At 7 am she rolls over to look at the time. The house is silent. Tess is suddenly overcome by fear. *How could Emilia not be awake if she hadn't eaten in the night?* Tess hurries out of bed and rounds the hallway to her daughter's bedroom. She rushes in and finds Emilia on her stomach in her crib. She is still. Tess is afraid to touch her. She's afraid to know. She's heard of crib death in infants; she's heard of all kinds of awful ways a child might die.

Emilia coughs and Tess's heart leaps. She reaches down and pulls Emilia up to her chest. The baby is blurry-eyed and begins to cry. Tess savors the moment, hugging her and tearing up.

"Oh, Emma," she says over and over. "I love you. I love you. I love you."

Emilia settles down, and Tess walks her to the kitchen, opens the fridge, and retrieves a formula bottle. She had tried to breastfeed early on, but after a month of aggressive pumping, she became discouraged and decided to go with formula. This did nothing to encourage her that she was a good mother, and she scolded herself each time she prepared a bottle of store-bought baby formula.

Once the bottle is warmed, Tess sits on the couch and thumbs at the television converter for a children's show. Emilia is happily feeding on the bottle when the phone rings.

"Hello," she answers, more enthusiastically than she'd meant.

The other end is silent, so she repeats herself, this time with a hint of irritation.

Still, there is nothing from the caller. Tess listens attentively, furrowing her brow as she leans into the earpiece. The caller hasn't hung up. They haven't done *anything.* Emilia lets out a satisfied burp and goes back to feeding.

"Sam?" She waits for some response. "Sam, is that you?" The phone drops at the other end. Tess jerks back from the receiver and hangs up. She looks down at her daughter.

"Your Daddy says hi." She smiles sadly and brushes her thin fingers through Emilia's short blonde hair.

The phone rings again, and Tess checks the call display this time. *Unknown number.* Well, maybe it was, and maybe it wasn't.

She would take some comfort in believing it was Sam and let it ring.

Chapter Four
Tuesday, 1:00 pm

That afternoon, Tess keeps a lunch date with a friend from her office. Amanda asked Tess more than once to bring Emilia in so everyone could ogle over her, but Tess found one reason after another as to why she couldn't. Now, a month into her separation, she couldn't imagine facing the humiliation of an explanation.

Sitting outside a trendy café, Emma rests comfortably in her stroller beside her. Tess waits for Amanda to arrive. Tess waves as she watches her friend approach from across the street. She stands to meet her, and the women hug.

"You look fan-*fucking*-tastic!" she tells Tess.

Embarrassed by the compliment, Tess waves it off, shaking her head as she sits.

"Shut up," Amanda continues. "I have to starve myself for a week to look like you. This is unfair. *I'm* having a baby!" She rounds the table and crouches next to the stroller. Looking up at Tess, she covers her mouth with one well-manicured hand. "Oh, she's *gorgeous.*"

Tess has always liked Amanda, who would often include her in group situations, pulling her into a debate and offering Tess up as an expert on something she barely knew anything about. It was all at once fun and frightening.

"Thank you." Tess tilts her head and smiles.

"So this is Emilia! I love the name too!" She reaches out to cup Tess's hand, and Tess closes her other hand over Amanda's. "Are you sure you won't bring her to the office?"

Tess shakes her head, her lips sealing into a tight, thin line. "Not a good time for me right now to face everyone."

Amanda's expression falls, but her beauty never diminishes. Just then, the waiter asks if they are ready to order drinks. Amanda asks for the house white, and Tess follows suit. Menus are left, but Amanda's gaze is too engaging for Tess to ignore.

"Sam left me," she puts bluntly. Amanda pushes back from the table, her brows nearly meeting her hairline. "About a month ago."

"Tess." Her friend is speechless. Her impossibly large eyes grow in size while her hands cover her mouth.

"It's okay," Tess tries to reassure her, shaking her head. "I'm okay, Emma's okay." She reaches into the stroller and pulls the blanket level with her sleeping daughter's bare neck. Tess had decided to share this information with Amanda, saving her the painful and repetitive discussions when she returned to work in a few months, knowing her friend would relay the data systematically.

Over lunch, Tess shared most of what she knew about what had happened and why. They break to eat quiche and sip their wine, but her sad news dominates the meal.

"You know, I have a friend who just went through something like this, and he went to a counselor and swore it saved his life." Amanda waves the server over and asks for a refill. Tess nods to another glass when asked and considers what her friend has suggested.

Looking past Amanda, Tess's eyes are drawn to the hospital, which sits atop the hill bordering the city's southwest end. "I hear the hospital has a new wing dedicated to psychiatry. I hear they design programs around a person's specific needs."

Amanda follows her gaze and then looks back in surprise. "You're not *crazy*; you don't need to go to a *hospital*. Just look into a counselor; they're a dime a dozen."

Tess smiles and nods, never taking her eyes from the hilltop. "Yeah, it costs like eight hundred dollars a day, but my insurance would pay a portion if my doctor signed off on the stay." Tess finds comfort in the building's architecture, and the idea that she could stay there for a time intrigues her.

"That's a LOT of money! Just consider counseling." Amanda cleans the lipstick from the rim of her glass. "This is one of those things that can play on your mind - you guys were together a long time."

Tess listens with a blank stare, watching Amanda's lips form word after word. She could never understand how anybody could talk so much about anything. Even in her career, Tess only spoke when absolutely necessary to get a point across or give direction. She nods as Amanda continues, undeterred, about how to deal with this challenging time in her life.

As Amanda gets up to return to work, Tess decides that therapy is how to approach the scenarios she's been suffering from lately and tells her friend that she will get help.

"It couldn't hurt."

Chapter Five
Tuesday, 3:00 pm

Tess walks Emilia back to the apartment after lunch. The October sun is warm on her face and feels invigorating. Waiting at a light, she closes her eyes and faces the blue sky, allowing the sun's healing properties to brighten her mood.

Since Sam left, she's been taking vitamin D, which promised to lift her depression, but she put little faith in herbal remedies and had always shied away from prescription drugs. Now, with the idea of therapy on the horizon, she can see an alternative to both.

But the pessimist in her finds new arguments regarding a shrink messing around in her head. She wrestles with the idea and confirms that it has worked for her in the past. When her brother had died, she was inconsolable. Therapy was right for her.

Deep in thought, Tess moves forward as a crowd passes her, indicating the light has changed and it is safe to walk. Unbeknownst to her, the group picks up their pace midway, as the light had gone from 'walk' to 'stop.' A car speeding toward the intersection, anticipating the green light, rushes through a red and strikes a van, making a right turn.

The sounds of crashing metal and squealing tires shock Tess, bringing her to a standstill in the middle of the crosswalk. The van careens into the light pole behind them, skidding within a few inches of her and Emilia. Tess's hair and dress lifted with the powerful gust accompanying the van's near hit.

A man rushes out to pull Tess and Emilia away as the van spills fluid from under its hood. Tess is frozen in place, but she completes the crossing at the man's urgings, her hands tightly gripping the stroller.

"Lady, if you had nine lives," the man tells her, breathless. Tess barely acknowledges him, staring at Emilia, still sleeping, secure in her stroller.

The crowd surrounding them moves to assist those involved in the accident while others direct traffic away from the scene.

"Thank you," Tess manages in a stunned whisper. The young man looks Tess up and down and guides her further away, distancing them a block or more. She allows him to lead her.

"Thank you," she says again, but the man does not release her arm. Tess finally looks at him and suddenly doesn't feel any safer than when she was standing in the middle of the street.

"I'm fine," she tells him, her grip on the stroller loosening should she need to defend herself. He looks at her and smirks. She wonders what's happening. *This isn't normal.*

"I just want to get you to a safe place," he explains. "I know a spot I can take you."

Despite her shock, Tess knows something is very wrong. Now she is frightened. Looking back, she sees they have traveled more than two city blocks from the gathering crowd.

"I'll scream," she tells him under her breath.

"You don't want to do that," he explains, showing a long knife at his belt, hidden behind his jacket. Tess can't believe her bad luck.

"What do you want?"

"Just to get you to a safe place."

"Is it money you want?"

"Yes, I want money," he continues to lead her along the broken sidewalk. "But I may ask for something more than money." A wink follows.

Tess is in no shape to fight a man with a knife. It is a seemingly impossible situation, and she is becoming increasingly alarmed as they travel into a less populated section of the street.

The man's hold on her arm is beginning to hurt, and she struggles weakly to shrug him off. He won't have any of it.

"I'll give you what you want; I will just promise me -"

"I don't make promises," he replies. "Too hard to keep."

"I have a *baby,* for Christ's sake!"

"So do I. Two, in fact, and they like to eat," he says matter-of-factly.

"So take my money," she pleads.

"I will," he assures her. "But you see, I like to fuck."

Tess goes cold. She was going to be raped. She was going to be raped, she says again and again to herself. But if that was all, then she could survive this, she rationalizes. If she cooperates, then he will let Emilia and her go.

As she tried to process what the next few hours might be like, two police officers rounded the corner and headed towards them. His grip on her arm increases tenfold, and she winces at the pain as his filthy fingernails dig into her pale, soft flesh.

He leans toward her and whispers a threat. "Say anything, and I'll cut your throat, I swear."

"HELP ME!" Tess cries to the officers, pushing the stroller out in front of her. They eye the man and pull their weapons. He releases his grip and flees into the street. There, a tractor-trailer plows into him, sending his body dozens of feet forward as the driver slams on his brakes.

Tess watches on in horror as his corpse skids along the asphalt, and the truck runs him over a second time, pulling him under the right tire. The sound, the bursting and crunching, is unimaginable. Tess falls to her knees and crawls to the stroller where Emma is now stirring.

One officer rushes to Tess's aid while the other calls in the gruesome scene.

"Are you alright, Miss?" he asks, kneeling to meet her gaze. Tess pulls Emma from the stroller and hugs her tightly, leaning against a building to steady herself. She's nodding to the officer, her mouth open and debating whether or not to lose her lunch. Hiding behind the baby's carriage, Tess shields herself from the mess in the street. Two close calls, she thinks. *What's happening? Why is this happening to me?*

Chapter Six
Tuesday, 6:45 pm

Tess gives her account of the afternoon's events at the police station, relating lunch with her girlfriend, the car accident, and the man who died so violently.

"Have you ever seen the man before?" asks a female police officer seated on the opposite side of a cluttered desk. Emma, who is now alert and irritable, plays with her mother's hair.

"I haven't, no," the image of the man crushed under the wheel plays repeatedly in her head. A new reason to go to therapy, she thinks, as if she needed one.

"This looks to be a random event, Mrs. Seager. He saw you in distress, standing in the middle of the street while an accident was happening around you, and took his opportunity. You're fortunate. These attempts happen constantly, and we seldom get involved until after the fact."

"He said he had two children," Tess supplies, to her surprise.

"Did he?" the tight-faced woman asks.

"Yes, he said they were hungry; I just - I hate to think of two children waiting for him at home wondering..."

"You're a sweet woman, Mrs. Seager." But Tess knows she means naïve. "I can assure you he has no children. I didn't tell you this before, but we identified him from his fingerprints a half hour ago and know who he is. He has a mile-long rap sheet but no kids."

Tess is satisfied with this explanation, grateful for the police intervention, and ready to visit the option she and Amanda discussed over lunch if only to gather more information.

* * * * *

Tess lays Emma down for a nap at home and takes a long shower, washing away the day's drama. She surprises herself at how well she seems to be dealing with the surreal events. *Who survives an accident like that, only to be abducted and then survive that without so much as a scratch?* As the thought lingers, she lifts her left arm. Looking down, she noticed bruising where the man's grip had tightened when the police appeared. A strange idea occurs to her: the ghost of a dead man's hold exists even after he is gone.

She feels nothing for the man, confident he'd had it coming: Preying on people like that in vulnerable situations. She shakes her head at having thanked him for pulling her from the crosswalk.

Stepping out of the shower, she pulls her bathrobe on and slips into bed. It's now eight o'clock, and she and Emma hadn't had dinner. A coffee and a bagel at the station for her and two yogurts for Emma probably weren't enough, but Emma would be up in a few hours to eat again, so Tess allows herself to drift off.

Chapter Seven
Wednesday 8:30 am

Surprisingly, Emma woke up just once to feed, and equally shocking, Tess slept soundly, even following the feeding.

Strangely, she considers, she hadn't suffered any terrible nightmares or visions connected to the accident or the abduction or the violent death of the man whose grip she still bears. She wonders whether she should force herself to cry over it, to cleanse herself of the scene, but feels no need.

"I must be tougher than I thought," she tells her daughter. "Maybe I'll call Lucy today and have her come over to watch you for a few hours while Mommy goes and runs some errands."

Tess grabs the phone and calls her babysitter. Once they set a time, she takes a deep breath, runs through a list of things to do in her head, and decides she'll visit the hospital.

* * * * *

It's a short drive from her apartment, and as the new wing of the hospital comes into view, Tess feels a spike of anxiety rise in her chest. Despite her fear, she resolutely parks her car, opens the door, steps out, and starts the long walk. Tess is hyper-aware of every movement and each decision to push onward. Finally, she enters. The wing is so new Tess can't decide whether the smell upon passing through the front doors is that of new laminate flooring and paint or the usual sterile smell of disinfectants one can expect in a hospital setting.

Either way, it beats the last time she was in a hospital, in Emergency at two in the morning with her daughter, and the smell of blood and vomit permeating the place. Tess flashes back to that experience. It's mostly a blur. But the anxiety she felt bringing her baby into that circus stayed with her. She's never much cared for hospitals. In truth, the weak attempt to revive her brother and the resulting bad news her family had received following his suicide had something to do with that.

She takes a deep breath and moves away from the rotating doors towards the information desk, where three attendants are either on the phone or typing madly at their keyboards.

"Hello," she says, placing her purse on the counter. One of the attendants raises a finger to signal she'll be with her in a moment, and Tess smiles and pans the foyer's interior. A snack bar and gift shop adorn the right side, while several rows of plastic molded chairs linked together by a steel bar occupy the space to her left. Two double doors with security access panels adorn the wall just beyond the chairs. Children play against the windowed wall, which overlooks the parking lot, while their parents sit reading magazines. Tess wonders whether they are waiting to hear the diagnosis of their eldest child and go home to contemplate leaving him here for the rest of his life.

"How may I help you?" The woman's voice is pleasant enough, but Tess imagines she isn't thrilled with her position.

"I'm, um, I'm here to enquire about -" She freezes, wondering what must lie beyond those locked double doors. Did they still practice lobotomies and electric shock therapy?

"Yes?" The overweight woman behind the counter interrupts, now perturbed.

"Well," Tess turns back to meet her gaze, "I read that you take people voluntarily? I mean, what do you call it?"

"You want to sign yourself up for in-patient care?"

"I would like someone to see me. I think if I stayed here a couple of weeks, maybe," Tess trails off as a young man is escorted into the foyer by what appears to be an orderly. The parents seated in the plastic chairs stand up, and the boy walks past them to his sisters playing at the window. The orderly introduces a man, who could be the resident psychiatrist, to the couple. Tess wants to hear how the story she dreamed up ends, but her attention is forced back to the fat lady whose cheeks are becoming flush.

"Yes," she nods absently. "I think I would."

The woman sighs as if this were the most challenging part of her day. She places a small booklet on the counter and asks Tess to take the paperwork home, fill out all the necessary fields, have her doctor sign off on it if going through insurance, and bring it back when she is ready to enter the program. She also offers a brochure on the facility with doctor bios and amenities.

"We will set you up with a counselor first for an evaluation, and then once accepted, you'll be interviewed by one of the doctors on staff to assess what sort of program they will create for you."

Tess thanked her. She is still watching the drama play out in the waiting room. The doctor is nodding. The parents look confused.

"I'll be back," Tess tells the woman, who nods and picks up her receiver.

As Tess walks toward the front door, she focuses on the family as they shake the doctor's hand and gather their children. Tess waits outside the door a moment, hoping to catch a conversation between the boy and his parents to get closure on this story she has stumbled upon.

"You see, Mom," says the teenage boy, pushing through the rotating door. "It happens." He takes each of his sister's hands and charges forward. "I'm not *crazy!*"

"Oh, Paul, I never said you were," his mother pleads, fidgeting through her tiny purse.

"I told you this was a mistake," the father tells his wife as he takes the car keys from her.

Tess begins walking with the couple, keeping a respectable distance but still hearing the rest of the conversation.

"*Cutting* isn't something everyone does, Jim. There's nothing *normal* about it."

"I'm not saying it's normal; I'm saying this was a mistake. Bringing Paul here and embarrassing him about it like this." He thumbs at the button on his keys. "Where the hell did we park?"

"So you'd rather we ignore it?" she huffs. "You know he's ending up with scars all over his forearm because of it."

"We'll discuss the doctor's points with him tonight."

As the family moves toward the car with the flashing lights, Tess veers off to the right and gets into her car, an Audi from the late nineties.

What is cutting? Tess wonders as she pulls up to the parking gate. *Is it actually physically cutting yourself? What benefit could that offer a confused teen?* She pulls onto the road and sees the family's hybrid pull out in her rearview mirror behind her. No one's lips are moving. She envisions a hard night for the teenager and a sleepless night for the parents.

Chapter Eight
Wednesday, 5:30 pm

Returning home, Tess is happy to see Emilia playing with the babysitter. Lucy is sixteen and has been a great help to Tess the past week. The sleepless nights and long days of entertaining a toddler vastly differ from her 9-5 lifestyle before Emilia came along. Upon looking back, even the pregnancy was comparatively easy.

Tess looks Lucy up and down and decides that she and the boy at the hospital are roughly the same age. Tess sits on the couch and addresses Lucy, kneeling on the ground, engrossed in a tug of war with a stuffed elephant.

"Lucy," Tess starts. "Could I ask you a question?"

Lucy looks up, offering a genuine smile, brushing the red curl from her forehead. "Sure, Mrs.Seager."

Tess leans forward, her elbows digging into her thighs, hands tightly locked together. "Have you ever heard of *cutting*?"

"Like where you cut yourself?"

"I guess so," Tess wasn't surprised to hear her initial assumption was correct but was taken aback by the immediacy of her babysitter's answer.

"I know like three kids at school that do it. It's so gross."

"Huh," Tess leans back. "But why do they do it? Have any of them said why?"

"It's supposed to relax you or something. I don't get it. I couldn't relax if I were putting a razor on my arm. What if you went too deep? You know?" Lucy's face contorts as she shakes off the thought.

Tess laughs ironically, relieved her babysitter isn't a practicing masochist.

"Why, is someone you know a cutter?"

Tess doesn't quite know how to answer this question. No one she knew, but she also didn't want to tell her she is now considering it as an alternative to anxiety. "Oh, I just overheard a conversation today. I hadn't heard of cutting before that."

"Well, I guess I'll go if you don't need me anymore." Lucy stands up and walks toward the door. "Love your new kitchen, by the way."

"Oh, thanks. Hey, do you want to stick around for dinner?"

"I should get home before it gets too late. But thanks."

Tess smiles hands Lucy the twenty dollars she promised for the afternoon, and opens the door for her. "Thanks again for being so available. Could you manage the same time tomorrow?"

"Yup! My afternoons are all spares," Lucy says as she walks the short distance to the elevator. Tess waves and closes the door.

Cutting. She thinks. Then she thinks better of it and goes back to Emilia.

Wednesday, 10:15 pm

After the cutting, Tess finds she is hopelessly lost - curled up in the corner of her living room, the television running some old film in black and white, and her daughter fast asleep on the couch. The feeling isn't foreign to her. She hasn't felt herself since Sam admitted his deception, leaving her to fend for herself and their baby. Never mind the nightmare of the day before, being abducted in plain view. She is confused and does not feel the endorphins cutting was meant to release. Maybe she shouldn't have had so much to drink in anticipation of running the razor across her arm.

She sobs uncontrollably. Once driven by purpose and encouraged by progress, Tess feels she has become unhinged by the separation. Looking down at her arm and the seven bleeding cuts inflicted on herself confirms her fears.

I am lost, she tells herself, standing and falling into the wall. She didn't think she'd had so much wine that she could fall over, but the bloodletting is likely partly to blame. She isn't a fan of blood, to begin with.

Tess stumbles over to the couch and kneels before her beautiful child. She feels embarrassed and ashamed to have done this tonight as she looks over the innocent features of her sleeping angel. *I'm sorry*, Tess tells Emilia. And she is. She is very sorry for so many things. Sorry she was so stupid to have missed Sam's growing discontent in their marriage, sorry she didn't do anything more to make him stay, sorry she was so weak and has done this to herself. Sorry, she has lost her focus.

"I was happy, Em," she whispers to her sleeping daughter. "I don't understand what happened." She kisses her baby lightly on her soft cheek. Tess looks down at the damage she's inflicted on her forearm, crawls to the kitchen, and pulls herself up to the sink. She turns on the tap and runs warm water over the cuts. They sting to life, and she bites her bottom lip. The pain is sobering. She watches the dry blood mix with the water as tributaries run down her white skin. Satisfied, she wipes her arm with a dishtowel.

Leaning back on the island and drying her arm, she notices the self-inflicted wounds have virtually disappeared. She grimaces at this and runs her fingers over the tiny imperfections.

The ringing phone snaps her out of her trance, and she rushes to pick it up before it wakes Emilia. *Shit, shit, shit.* Tess looks at the time on the stove and wonders who would be calling so late.

"Hello?" She waits for the caller to return the greeting. Nothing. "Hello?" she repeats. Still nothing from the other end. "Who is this?" Tess demands in as angry a voice as she can muster. "I have a baby who is sleeping. Why are you such an asshole?!"

"I – I'm sorry." It's Sam. Her heart leaps out of her chest at the sound of his voice. It's husky tonight. He's been drinking.

"Sam?" Tess whispers his name, not knowing how to continue.

"I'm sorry," he repeats.

"So am I," she tells him.

"I'm a bad father and a worse husband." He coughs violently. "You must hate me."

I don't," she begins. "I don't know how I feel about you."

"I don't know how I feel about me either, babe. I don't know who I am or what I'm doing."

Tess thinks *about how sad she is for him* and then shakes her head. "Why are you telling me this, Sam?"

"Because you're my wife." Tess listens as a lighter snaps a flame, and she knows he's in deep.

"You're smoking?" She listens as he inhales, and he answers a moment later, affirmatively, dishearteningly. Tess takes some comfort in this; he's so upset that he would light up again after five years. A pang of guilt stopped the sensation, and she moved to the bedroom to not wake the baby.

"What is her name, Sam?" She picks up where they left off when Sam stormed out of the apartment.

"What does it matter? She's obviously not right for me. I'm lost here, babe."

Tess flinches as he refers to her like that for the second time. It's too familiar now. She sits on her bed and looks at the empty space beside hers. She moves her free hand over the cold sheets.

"I don't know what you want me to say. I wanted us to work. *You* left me, us, your *baby*, how could you?"

Sam is silent.

"Sam?" Tess halfway regrets scolding him. He's hurting, and to compound that hurt with more hurt isn't who she is.

"I'm sorry I messed this up so bad. I'm sorry. Tell Emma I love her."

Asshole! Tess thinks as he hangs up on her. She punches in his cell number and listens. Voicemail. *Asshole!* She rings him again and waits. Nothing. Now she's frantic. Sleep will not come easily tonight.

Chapter Nine
Thursday, 2:30 am

Hours later, lying in bed, staring at the shadows crossing the ceiling from intermittent vehicles traversing the street below, Tess recalls the dramatic scene that sparked Sam's disappearance moments after Sam had blamed everything on himself.

September 15th, 1:30 am

All the color had left him. He was caught in a terrible lie, his pale complexion contrasting starkly against Tess's fiercely red face, burning with humiliation and anger.

"You're everything to me," he admits.

Her delicate features twist into a pained expression of disbelief. "How can you say that? I'm nothing to you. *Nothing!*" Tess is spitting venom.

"Please, don't say that." His legs give out, and Sam crumbles to the tile floor, his head shaking. "Please don't say that."

She, too, settles on the floor a few feet from him, the island between them, their backs to each other.

"I should have known. Jesus, I *did* know." The adrenaline is difficult to control; her toes shake inside her slippers.

"Forgive me, my weakness. I couldn't do this alone."

"But you're okay with me doing this alone?" Tess points out, an ironic smile forms on her face, baring teeth.

"I'm so sorry." His forehead rests on his forearms, which rest on his knees.

"So stop seeing this other person. I can forgive you if you stop."

"I'm not doing this to cause upheaval or drama. I don't know where this is going. I *don't*. I'm suffering through this, too." Sam's not ready to give up on this new woman.

"Well, that's called consequence. Stings, doesn't it?"

"That's not fair."

Tess turns, places her hands against the cupboard door of the island, and shouts through it. "Fair?! You've just decided the whole of the rest of my life with your infidelity, and you're going to tell me what's not fair? You're a classic asshole!"

Sam's voice rises to meet his wife's. "Don't do that. Don't try to classify me. I hate when you do that."

"No? Why not? You won't."

"You don't know me at all."

"Right, well, that's because it's *impossible* to know you. You're a *psychopath*."

"That's great! Now I'm *crazy* because *we* weren't working." He stands and places both hands on the sink. Tess rises to meet his gaze.

"When did you decide we didn't work? I'd be interested in knowing that."

"Years," he spits out, assuming a more passive-aggressive position.

"How many years? Three? Four?"

"More."

"So you fell out of love with me more than four years ago. Explain then why you had a *baby* with me! I mean, do the math!"

"I wanted a baby with you."

"Jesus Christ. Are you listening to yourself? Do you hear how *selfish* that sounds? So you *tricked* me into making a baby."

"No, I mean, we were good then."

"But you didn't *love* me!"

"I wasn't *in love* with you, but I loved you. I still love you."

"Jesus, the garbage that comes out of your mouth." She spins away from him and pulls at her black hair. Turning back to Sam, she makes eye contact. "Do me a favor. *Stop* loving me. *Hate* me for all I care."

"I could never hate you."

"Say *goodbye* to me!"

"I can't."

"What do you mean you can't?" She paces the small kitchen. "Why can't you? Isn't that what this is? You've chosen someone over me. You've made your choice. You don't get to have it all, and I have nothing. You don't get *that!*"

"I can't *not* be your friend."

"That's," a chortle escapes her throat, "listen to yourself. We'll never be *friends* now. You've lied to me for months. *Years.* I can't trust you anymore. That's not how friends act. You can't lie to me, sleep with someone else, destroy our marriage, and think we'll be friends."

"None of this was done to hurt you." His voice lowers to a pained whisper.

"Wow, and how did you think I would feel when I found out?"

"You weren't -" he stops a moment. "You weren't supposed to find out."

"Well, what, do you think you're on a *game show* or something? You think you're the fucking *bachelor* or something?"

"I couldn't do this alone."

"Poor you, couldn't do it alone. You make a decision that affects the rest of my and our daughter's lives and expect us to do it honorably, but not you, huh? *Not you.*"

"I'm sorry you feel like this is so easy for me."

"It *is* easy for you. You made the decision well into a new relationship. Jesus, I'm a fool. I guess you and your girlfriend have been laughing at my expense! *'What an idiot, I'm fucking this girl's husband behind her back.'*"

"She only knows what I've told her."

"Fine, you're the *whore* here. I get it."

Sam loses what's left of his composure and breaks down. "Jesus, Tess."

She turns, recognizing Sam's limits have been reached and backs down. Leaning against the opposite counter, she sighs heavily.

"Tell me *why* you're doing this."

"I don't know!" Sam whimpers.

Michael Poeltl

"You need help. *Jesus,* I need help." Tess runs a hand through her hair and sits on the countertop. Feeling a strange calm overcome her, she asks, "So, what's her name? What does she look like? Is she younger than me?"

"This isn't about her. It's about us. Always has been."

This is not the answer Tess wants, and so the anger resurfaces. Feeling suddenly cruel, she lays out a future for Sam.

"At least we know whoever is unlucky enough to end up with you will suffer the same fate I have. Or maybe next time, it'll be your turn. That's karma. Either way, you'll end up alone."

The baby wakes in her room, and Tess runs to fetch her. Upon returning with Emilia, she finds that Sam has fled. This was the last time she would ever see him.

Chapter Ten
Thursday 11:00 am

The morning after the surprise phone call from her husband, Tess has no idea where even to begin to look for Sam. His private life the past year had been just that. When he went out, he was off the radar. When he went on business trips, he was incognito. When he ran out to get a beer with a friend, she didn't hear from him again until he dropped himself in bed beside her.

She runs through their friend base, wondering who she could call. They had two couple friends; one was an old college friend of Sam's and her husband, and the other was a friend Tess had made at work and her partner. For the most part, Tess's other friends had moved away from the city they'd grown up in while she remained. Other work-related friends pretty much existed only during working hours. Sam had the lion's share of friends between them. His buddies, work and otherwise, were many, but Tess hadn't bothered with them, or at least Sam rarely had them over to the house, so she had no idea of their contact numbers or even where any of them lived. Sam's online presence had been all but erased.

Tess calls the numbers she has and finds no one has heard from Sam in months. Some didn't even know he'd left her. This put the difficult task of telling them what had happened and accepting their sympathies for her. She is drained of energy afterward and left to wonder where all her friends are during this time of need.

Tess had always cherished her time with Sam above all others. Family first, she thought. Once she was married, she dedicated her personal and free time to him. Something he seemed to appreciate in the beginning. *Marriage deconstructs love*, she thinks to herself. That pretty much sums it up. Hindsight is 20/20. Tess has been meditating on her marriage lately. She wondered why I poured all that love and effort into someone who didn't appreciate it.

Wasted time, she thinks. *What could I have done differently with all that lost time?*

But here she is, baby-napping and on the phone with mutual friends, looking for the man who'd left her. How could she make such a mistake and marry someone who wouldn't stay? Why? Tess is getting angry at the universe now, questioning everything, her whole life up to this point. *Was Sam asking himself the same questions?*

Tess turns on the couch, reacting to Emma's shifting weight. Emma is the reason, she tells herself. This beautiful child is the culmination of every moment Tess has ever lived and every decision she has ever made: Emma, her baby, her angel. She wonders for a moment if Sam would share her views. Does he see his life only as his own and now a failure? Or does he see the bigger picture, that his daughter is here now because of him? Too early in the day for such cumbersome thoughts, she reasons and decides to call her mother.

Tess's parents moved to an adult living community three hours north a year earlier to enjoy their retirement. Not so far away from their daughter and new granddaughter to never see them in person, but far enough that they had a buffer. Tess had no problem with this arrangement at the time either. She loves her parents but had Sam to help with the baby. What had been bothering Tess the past month was that she had yet to tell her parents about Sam leaving. She wasn't sure she could handle the coddling, pity, and flurry of activity it would invite.

She punches the numbers to her parent's house and lifts the receiver to her ear. It's ringing, three, four times, and then her mother's voice.

"Hello, Tess!" She greets her daughter with a smile Tess can hear across the void.

Call display, Tess thinks. She had hoped she'd have the option of hanging up if she chickened out, but now she's committed.

"Hi, Mom," she replies, wondering whether she sounds as weak as she feels.

"And how's my baby granddaughter?"

"She's good, Mom. She's napping."

"Is she on her back? You know what I read last year about putting them on their stomachs. Imagine, that's what they told us to do when I had you, place them on their stomachs, they'd said. Now look, they're finding all these things about infant deaths and such, and it's because of what they were telling us to do!"

Wow, Tess thinks. Mom can talk a blue streak. She smiles at the thought, shakes her head, and waits for her to finish.

"Yup, on her back." Tess turns to look at Emilia on the couch, sleeping on her side. She walks over and rolls her to her back.

"Good. You're such a good mom, Tess. You know, I always knew you would be. When we had Thomas, you know, you used to put him in your doll stroller and take him all over the house."

"I remember," Tess lies. "Mom, I wanted to call to tell you something."

"Okay, is everything alright? Do you need us to come for a visit? I know we're overdue, but your father's heart has kept him from driving, and you know I can only drive a short distance now."

"Mom, I know, I know. Listen, Sam has decided to leave me."

No response.

"Mom, it's okay. It happened over a month ago, and I'm okay; Emma is okay. He's left us everything. Mom?"

Her mom seems suddenly lost for words. "You're okay?"

"I am."

"Well, what happened?" Exasperation comes through loud and clear through the receiver.

"He was just not happy. At least, that's the story I got."

"Oh, that's such bullshit!" Surprised at the language, Tess takes the phone from her ear and reads the display number. Yes, it is her mother.

"I don't want you to be upset about it, Mom."

"Tess, whatever you want, you tell me now, okay? Your dad and I are happy to come and stay with you or bring Emilia up to see us and stay awhile."

Tess rolls the idea around in her head, realizing this may be the opportunity she needs to take a break to get away for a week or two. Gather her thoughts. Then it hits her, the hospital. She could fill out that submittal form and take the leap.

"I'd love it if you could come and stay for a while."

"We'll start packing. We can be there in two days. Your father has an oncology appointment tomorrow, but we'll come the following day. What is it today? Thursday? Okay, so we'll be at your place Saturday, honey. Don't you worry. If you need to get your head straight, you do whatever you need to do, and we'll be more than happy to watch that beautiful daughter of yours."

Tess had expected this kind of over-the-top support from her parents. It's why she didn't call immediately, as much as she'd wanted to. A person must be ready to embrace the unique brand of support that would arrive on Saturday. Tess is ready now.

Chapter Eleven
Friday

The next day, Tess busies herself in the apartment, cleaning madly in anticipation of her parents' arrival. It's a free day at the high school, so Lucy is there to watch Emma and take her for walks while the work gets done.

Tess notices she has made it through two hours without thinking about Sam and her current situation. No thoughts of sadness hurt feelings, or unnerving flashes consumed her. The work kept her mind on the task at hand, centered on the now. Though exhausted, she feels more alive than she has in a long time.

Stepping into the shower, Tess catches a glimpse of her naked body in the vanity mirror. She doubles back slowly to look herself over. She has lost weight, no question. Her eyes carry dark circles under each, and her forehead is creased with worry. Her hair looks lifeless, which she hasn't done more than tie up in a ponytail in the past few months. She places both hands on her rib cage and allows her fingers to run lightly up and down them, envisioning strings on a harp.

Her stomach is a hard mass of muscle, tense and not showing the trauma of childbirth. She is lucky, she surmises, she won't be marked all her life with the stretch marks and sagging skin many women are left to endure. Though very small, her breasts map the ordeal of pumping milk five or six times a day in the first month. But then, she's never been fond of her breasts.

Her legs look thin but strong. Tess turns to look at her profile and sees that her ass has also shrunk and appears less taut. She also notices a slight hunch in her posture. Her skin is very white, and the dark hair on her head and pubic region plays up the washed-out appearance.

She places her hands on her sunken cheeks; her fingers wander to her thin lips and slide down her neck. Suddenly, her hands dropped like weights to the countertop, and Tess sobbed. She has lost so much now, so much of herself that it shows in the landscape of her body. How could she hide this from her mother? She couldn't. And her father is so protective of her that he will have difficulty seeing his baby like this. She hoped he didn't bring his sidearm and started searching for Sam. *Maybe I should cancel their visit*, she wonders but thinks better of it.

Tess takes a deep breath and avoids the mirror on her second attempt at the shower. The warm water doesn't feel warm enough. She fingers the cold water tap back until she feels the bite of heat on her flesh. She soaks her hair and begins to wash. She soaps up for a long time, and after rinsing, she soaps up again. She picks up her razor and shaves her legs and under her arms and pelvis. She wrings out her hair. It's too long, she decides. Tying tight, she picks up a pair of scissors and cuts it off at the shoulders.

This is transformational. This is necessary. As Tess stepped out of the shower, the bathroom filled with steam. She wipes at the mirror where her face is reflected and ruffles her hair. It falls just below her ears. She smiles. "I like it."

She picks up the scissors once more and cuts herself bangs. She plucks her eyebrows and waxes her upper lip. "I should get a massage," she whispers to no one. Her nails are next. Clipping, trimming, and painting. Tess riffles through her lingerie drawer in her bedroom and finds the perfect bra and panties. Then she sits at her dresser and pulls out her make-up. Next, she rummages through her closet for a sexy little number and tries on a few options. Many are too big for her now, but she settles on an outfit without allowing herself to be discouraged. A nice heel would complete the look, and she finds a pair of four-inch stilettos. She pulls a comb through her hair while applying hair spray and runs her fingers through it.

When Tess emerges from the bedroom, she finds that Lucy has returned with Emilia. They are playing on the floor beside the television.

"Wow!" Lucy says, laying eyes on Tess. "Wow, Mrs. Seager. What's the occasion?"

Tess blushes and smiles brightly. "Do you think I could talk you into putting Emma to bed tonight for me and sticking around a few hours longer?"

"Well, uh, I'd have to let my mother know."

"Give her a call, would you? I want to get out of the house tonight for a bit."

"Do you have a date or something?"

"Not yet," Tess replies coyly.

Lucy takes the phone and dials her mom. It isn't long before Lucy has her mother talked into the extra money, so Tess is free to go.

"Thank you, Lucy. I won't be very late. There is food for Emma in the fridge and half a pizza for you."

"No problem, Mrs. Seager. Have a good time."

With this, Tess empties her wallet, phone, and keys from her purse and places them in a much smaller, more appropriate bag for her outfit. Where she was going and to what end was as yet unknown.

Chapter Twelve
Friday, 6:30 pm

There are many bars and restaurants that Tess knows are good. The food and the wine selection are decent, and the costs are not unreasonable. Conversely, Tess also knows which bars are not so good. Tonight, she feels a self-destructive urge to find herself in one of those establishments, seated at the bar, ordering whisky shots and beer chasers. She wants to get noticed. She wants to stick out.

Driving through the bustling downtown, she veers north toward what realtors would describe as an 'undesirable' location. Where she lives now is one of the up-and-coming districts, so she and Sam had decided to put money into the apartment. She isn't unfamiliar with the neighborhood she is now entering; this is where she'd met Sam six years earlier. It's not up and coming and hasn't been since the forties.

Tess pulls in front of a building named 'Charlie's' and parks. The rest of the signage was faded. Tess supposes everyone in the area knew what 'Charlie's' was and that not many from outside the neighborhood would venture in.

She knew it once, too. She knew Charlie once. Whether he still owned the dump and sat at his corner table entertaining the local talent was anyone's guess, but the chances are he still owned it and occupied that corner table. Not many who grow up around here ever leave.

Tess feels reckless, but not so much so that she would go out of her way to hit a shitty bar she'd never supported. She checks her lipstick in the rearview mirror and reapplies. Her heart is pounding in anticipation of even stepping out of the car. Three young men walk past her, talking too loudly. "Just one drink," she tells herself into the mirror. "Just one drink, and if Charlie is there, just one more."

Tess mentally counts to three and opens the door. Her stilettos hit the cracked asphalt with a click. She pulls herself out of her seat and quietly closes the door. As she pushes through the worn art deco double doors, a gust of wind catches her short dress, pulling it up in front of her. She snaps a free hand down to avoid a peep show but manages one whistle from the mostly empty pub.

Tess doesn't let it throw her off. She expected as much. Nothing has changed inside. Billiard tables line the left side of the interior. The bar follows the south wall's length along the right, where the regulars hang off the bar rail. Round tables from another era fill the spaces in between.

The corner table sits just to the left and under the stage at the far end. Charlie is not there, not yet. Tess sneaks a look at her watch. 6:30. It's still early. If she remembers right, Charlie has to finish his shift at the steel mill before he can begin the night at his recreational job, managing the joint.

Tess strolls confidently to the bar and places her purse on the counter.

"Oh, I doubt you'll be need'n that tonight, lovely," the bartender tells her slowly.

"And why is that?"

"You've a line of men eyeball'n ya that would happily buy you a drink should you take them up on it." He eyes the line of men down the length of the bar. She does not yet feel brave enough to follow his gaze.

"Well, allow me to buy my first drink at least," she says, sliding onto the surprisingly comfortable bar stool.

"It will be my pleasure, lovely." The barkeep leans back and waves an arm out from his side, panning the available liquor on the back shelves and the taps on the bar. "What's your drink?"

Tess automatically orders what she always does. "Have you wine? Red wine?"

He smirks. "Nothing I'd imagine you would find appealing."

"I'm not asking you to *imagine* anything. I'm asking what you have."

He smiles wider, clearly appreciating how she carries herself, seemingly out of place. "I have white wine I put food colour'n in." He laughs.

Tess can't help but laugh at the absurdity of what he's said. All the same, her eyebrows raise.

The bartender laughs again and leans toward Tess. "No, but we do like to have our fun, don't we?" He admits and turns to the nearest patron seated four stools from Tess and winks. This man laughs under his breath, both hands gripping his pint.

"Well, just to be sure, why don't you pour me one of those light draughts over there?" The barkeep nods and turns. Still laughing, he pours Tess a pint of lager.

"I like you," he tells her in a loud voice. "Any man touches this one, and you'll be limp'n outta here!" He points down at her with a long, bony finger.

She doesn't remember him as the barkeep when she frequented this pub. He is tall, thin, bald, and shy of a tooth. A greying mustache covers his upper lip completely.

"I like you," Tess said, wagging a finger at the man behind the bar after taking a large mouthful of beer. "You've got a sense of humor."

"Look where I work!" he shouts, laughing again. Jeers from the regulars and a couple of balled-up napkins are fired his way.

"I'm Tess," she tells him.

"Tad." He offers a hand, and Tess shakes it. "It's my honor to meet a lady such as you." He bends and kisses her hand.

"The bartender always gets the girl!" A familiar voice calls out from behind Tess. Tad releases her hand and waves to the voice behind her.

"Charlie," he says. "This one's a keeper." He winks at Tess.

"You don't have to tell me," Tess spins in her stool to see an older version of the Charlie she remembers. He smiles at her and nods.

"Goddamn, if it ain't my Tess." He opens his arms.

Tess blushes and slips off her stool to greet Charlie. He's heavier than he was, thicker somehow, sporting his trademark 5 o'clock shadow. Pulling back, she peers into the eyes of the man she'd known years before to have an insatiable appetite for fine scotch and young women. His features are marked with lines now, and his dark hair is greying at the sides.

"How's my favorite girl?"

"Been better, Charlie."

Charlie looks about the place with his arms outstretched. "To have found your way back here, I don't doubt it! Come, sit with me." He invites her to his table in the corner. Tess feels the flush of youth invade her face, flattered he's asked her to sit at his table. She follows closely after turning to Tad and thanking him for his company.

"How did you know it was me?" Tess asks en route.

"Tess, you lovely thing, how could I forget? Please," he says, pulling a chair out for her.

"So, how's Sammy? Still traveling with work?" Sam and Charlie were acquainted through Charlie's younger brother. Sam had grown up in this neighborhood, where Tess and Sam had lived their first two years together.

"Oh, Charlie, I..."

"Don't tell me." Charlie read her expression perfectly.

"I – I don't know what's going on."

"Listen, Jorgie told me you two had a kid. He ran out on you and the kid?" Charlie's brother, Jorge, and Sam were still tight. A number she couldn't find when searching for contacts to call on his whereabouts.

Tess lowers her head and nods.

"Goddamn fool. Jesus, look at you! And this is *after* a kid?"

"Thank you, that's very kind."

"Fuck kind, you're a vision." Charlie is rough around the edges, and Tess remembers, never afraid to speak his mind.

"I have a lot of make-up on." Tess was never one for compliments, and with the image in the vanity mirror still haunting her, she couldn't accept one tonight.

"Don't be stupid; you're gorgeous." Charlie accepts his bottle of Johnny Walker from Tad and pours two shots. He slides one to Tess, and she picks it up. "Drink," he tells her and clinks her glass. They swallow the scotch, and he pours another.

"So, how long?"

"Just over a month now."

"Stupid sonofa, you know that kid never knew what he wanted. And when I saw him with you, I thought, *Hallelujah*. Turns out he's still a jackass."

Tess guiltily enjoys hearing someone talk like this about Sam. "He still doesn't know who he is."

"Jesus, what is he? He must be pushing thirty-eight. I knew who I was at eighteen: *nobody*. But maybe that makes it easier to do something with your life." He swallows his second shot and pours another. "I don't know, but damn, it's great to see you again. The place hasn't looked this good in years."

Tess places a hand on his and squeezes. "Thank you, Charlie. You were always so nice to us. I'm afraid I feel a little lost right now."

"Well, you've found yourself here, and you're talking to Uncle Charlie." He winks at her, and she smiles again, experiencing the girlish innocence she'd always felt in his presence.

"I don't want to monopolize your time. I'm sure you have plenty of women to fill this seat tonight."

Charlie laughs and places a hand over his heart. "Those days are few and far between now. But I'm flattered you would think so."

"What, you have that George Clooney thing going on now; more handsome than ever." She turns to her beer and takes a sip.

"Now look who's being kind. *Jesus*." He shakes his head and takes her hand. "Let me show you something."

They walk to a picture board hanging on the wall behind the bar. Tad moves a couple of bottles, and Charlie lifts it off its hook. He places it on the bar and points out a couple of photos.

Tess is on her tiptoes to see. Charlie points to a familiar photo. She smiles and looks at him. "I have a copy of that one."

"Look at you in this picture." The tape holding the corners are yellow with age and atmosphere. "What is this, six years ago?"

"I remember that top." She laughs, wondering how she ever got away with wearing so little.

"You're even prettier than you were then. That Sam's an idiot."

Tess frowns, looking back up at Charlie. She grabs his face and kisses his scruffy cheek. "Can I have another one of those Johnnys?" Charlie leads her back to his table, and they share another drink.

"You're good for me, Charlie," she tells him, nodding down at her beer.

"This old man?" he asks, pointing at himself and shrugging the comment off. "You'll be just fine. Baby or no baby, men will be tripping over themselves to get to you."

She leans toward him and rests her head on his shoulder. "I'm glad I came here tonight."

"No one more than me, sweetheart." He puts an arm around her and squeezes. Tess feels a familiarity that she realizes she's missed. Sam hadn't been more than a roommate the past year, and though she was okay with that, it wasn't really a marriage anymore. She wonders what changed and realizes Sam backed off once she started showing with Emma.

She watches Charlie's face as he acknowledges a patron and wonders what it would be like to sleep with him. Maybe she should.

"Are you still single?" she asks him.

"Me? Shit, yeah. But you know I was married once, right out of high school. It lasted about eight months. Seven too many if you ask me."

Tess sits up. "Really? I didn't know that."

"Oh, yes. Stupidest thing I ever did. It changes people. An unnatural union; marriage."

Tess drinks down the shot. "Would you say marriage deconstructs love?"

"I wouldn't say it so eloquently, but you nailed it."

"Something that had crossed my mind the other day." Tess puts her drink down and runs her fingernail over the dozens of names and phrases carved into the wooden table. "We were happy once. We were."

"And you will again, a girl like you, no question."

Charlie turns to the bar, where four men have begun harassing Tad. He places a hand on Tess's shoulder. "Go to the back, to my office. Stay there."

"Charlie?"

"Just do it, sweetheart. I know these guys. It's about to get ugly in here."

Chapter Thirteen
Friday, 10:15 pm

Tess gets up from the table and hurries into the office. There she waits. She's seen plenty of bar brawls break out in Charlie's, but something about how he reacted to seeing the four men with Tad makes her uneasy. First night out in months, and this is where I end up, she thinks. *What am I doing?*

Charlie waits for things to either escalate or settle down. Tad looks past the men to Charlie. Charlie nods at him. It's enough to spur Tad into action.

"Why don't you gentlemen have a seat? I'll bring a bottle to your table."

Tess has a perfect line of sight through Charlie's office door window, and that it has no glass allows her to hear what is transpiring. She watches as Tad delivers a bottle and four short glasses. He starts to pour, but a grim-looking man snatches the bottle and waves him away. Tess can read the look on Tad's face and feels anxious. Tad turns to Charlie's corner and nods.

"What am I watching here?" She whispers, pulling her cell phone out of her purse and punching in 9-1-1. She doesn't complete the call but feels better about having the number handy.

Tess watches the men take drink after drink from the bottle. Moments later, Charlie approaches them.

"Jessie," he says. The man looks up at Charlie and offers him a seat at their table. Charlie refuses and asks if he would sit with him apart from the group. The man agrees and rises. Charlie kicks out the man's leg at the knee, bending it at an unnatural angle, sending him collapsing to the floor. Tad pulls a shotgun from behind the bar and shouts at the other men.

Tess is terrified by the violence and shrinks behind the office door, keeping her eyes on the action. The other three men raise their hands and stand. Charlie thumps the one to his right on the side of the head so hard Tess hears the sickening sound and watches the man stagger sideways and then drop.

The other patrons have either left through the front door or stayed behind to back Charlie up. A much older man locks the front door and stands there, whiskey in hand.

The one Charlie kicked is yelping in pain, grabbing at his leg, and uttering threats. The other two are ordered to lay face down on the filthy, worn wooden floor as Tad hovers over them with the shotgun.

This is unlike anything Tess has ever witnessed here or anywhere, and she isn't sure how to process it. Then she looks at Charlie and sees that he is waving her to come out of the office.

Tess steps around the man Charlie had dropped first, writhing in pain and holding his mangled leg at the thigh.

"Can you drive?" Charlie asks.

Tess nods, expecting him to ask her to leave and forget what she's seen.

"Good. I'll explain later." He ushers her around the second body on the floor and leads her to the bar.

"What's going on?"

"Tess," Charlie leans in and whispers to her, "things are happening here that need doing. I hadn't expected them tonight, but here we are." He looks back at the men held hostage by Tad's shotgun.

"Do you want me to leave? I will leave."

"While I have you, I need to use you."

"What do you mean?" Tess realizes she's completely sober now and shaking.

Charlie notices Tess shudder and holds her by the shoulders. "I need you to be strong for me for a little longer. Can we borrow your car? You'll have to drive, but can we use it for a little while?"

Tess peers down at her watch. 10:30 pm. "I should be home soon; I- I have a babysitter." Her head is spinning with possibilities. *Why would he need my car? Why not just let me leave?*

"I promise I'll have you home by midnight. I need to slip out of here unnoticed. I can't do that in my car."

"Okay." Her heart is pounding in her throat.

"Listen, pull around the back alley and wait for me there. I won't be a minute."

The older man at the front doors unlocks them and peers outside. He looks back at Tess and Charlie and nods.

"Just round the corner and make a right at the alley. I'll be out in a second."

Tess nods and turns to leave. Charlie doesn't let go. "I'm counting on you." He smiles and nods, releasing her into the night.

She moves through the doors and walks to her car on shaky legs. Once inside, she wonders whether she will go to the alley or straight home.

Chapter Fourteen
Friday, 10:35 pm

Tess decides to pull into the alley and wait. The potential risks of this clandestine request have aroused Tess on multiple levels, preceded by the scene inside the pub and Charlie's abrasive tactics. She has known he had a reputation in the past for having a no-nonsense approach to people and a record to support it. But this was the first time she'd seen him act on it.

A heat envelopes her as she waits for Charlie to exit the back door. She feels dizzy with something akin to lust. She's never felt an attraction to violence before tonight and is confused by the stirrings taking hold of her.

Then, her passenger side door flies open, and Charlie slides into the seat. "Fucking fate," he says. "No fighting it."

Tess puts the car in gear and pulls away.

"Slowly," Charlie tells her. He looks over his shoulder and, smiling, looks Tess up and down. "Thank you for doing this."

"I still don't know what it is I'm doing," she tells him.

"Just follow my directions, and I'll explain. Head to the east end. Get on the valley parkway."

Tess nods and turns left. The next few seconds are filled with silence and feel like a lifetime. Tess thinks of Emma and grips the wheel a little tighter. Charlie has a scent about him, pheromones or something Tess finds difficult to ignore.

"It's not as bad as you may think."

"No?" Tess's imagination had taken her from one extreme to another.   "Why are we running?"

"We're not running. I have to see someone. Those guys were there for my brother, for Jorgie," Charlie tells her calmly. "I have to see him. Make sure he's alright before I decide what to do with them."

"What do you mean? What are your options?" Tess asks nervously.

"Never mind that just get me to him." He looks at her. "I'm sorry. I appreciate your doing this for me." His dark eyes find her breasts, which have been heaving ever so slightly since he entered the vehicle.

"Of course," Tess unconsciously places a hand on his thigh and lets it linger. Charlie looks down, puts his hand on hers, and maneuvers it to his erection.

"Turn here," he tells Tess breathlessly. It's a parking lot. "Stop over there." He points to a dark corner of the lot where an overhead lamp flickers out.

Tess pulls in and looks at Charlie with hungry eyes. There is an undeniable heat between them; she's felt it creeping in all night. As the levy breaks at the climax of their evening, the warmth of desire spills over her, flattening any misgivings she may have over rushing into Charlie's arms. Charlie turns to face her as she undoes her seatbelt, leaning in and kissing him on the mouth. Charlie returns her affection and runs his hand up the inside of her leg.

A satisfied groan comes from Tess as her lips break from Charlie's, and she watches as her dress lifts to reveal her lace panties. Charlie releases his seatbelt and moves closer to Tess, breathing heavily into her ear. He easily lifts her from her seat and places her on his lap. She gets to her knees and removes her underwear while Charlie undoes his jeans. Tess pulls his pants down around his thighs and mounts him. Charlie slides into her, and Tess's hips do all the work in the confined space.

Charlie climaxes quickly, but Tess doesn't feel cheated, having gotten exactly what she needed from the night: intensity.

Tess falls back into the driver's seat, hikes up her underwear, and pulls down her dress. Charlie wipes his face and zips his jeans.

He looks at her, panting. "*Jesus,* you're beautiful."

"Shhhhh," Tess whispers through a smile, eyes closed and head back.

Before closing the door, Charlie says, "You're one of the good ones, Tess." The door closes quietly, and Tess hits the automatic locks. She stays in place for some time, smiling. Her lips still tingling, she touches them softly. Her fingers linger there momentarily, and with her free hand, she finishes what Charlie had started.

* * * * *

Arriving home, Tess relieves Lucy and walks to the bathroom. There, she allows herself a moment to shake out the excitement that has followed her home. Next, she leans against the counter and looks intently into the mirror. She stares at herself until her face is all that remains in the reflection. All other objects in the mirror vanish, and she watches her features blink in and out of reality. She studies the characteristics of her face as it changes. Dozens of different identities reveal themselves to her. This bizarre hallucination startles Tess out of the trance. She runs the tap and splashes water on her face. Refocusing on the mirror, its reflection has returned to normal; the towel rack, tiled walls, and shower are all behind her. Tess closes her eyes and fixates on the string of violence she's witnessed in the past few days. The car accident, then the man crushed by the truck, and now Charlie's bar fight. She considers her timing and remembers something about things happening in threes.

But tonight, tonight was like a strange dream. Tess decides to take a shower and runs the water. Before slipping off her clothes, she checks on Emilia. She is sleeping soundly. Tess lightly places a hand on her daughter and smiles at the rise and fall of her tummy. Satisfied, Tess undresses and steps into the steamy shower.

Chapter Fifteen
Saturday

The following day, Tess prepares for her parents' arrival and all the good intentions and support that entails.

Thoughts of Charlie and what might have come from last night's bizarre events made sleeping difficult, but she managed between feedings. The night had offered Tess a new outlook on her life and a much-needed boost to her self-esteem. Tess massages her face where her cheeks feel sore from smiling. That it took going back to her beginnings with Sam to make her smile again seems fitting somehow. She finishes dressing the spare bed in the third bedroom while Emilia naps on the couch. Then the doorbell heralds the arrival of her parents, and Tess buzzes them up.

At the door, Tess is greeted with open arms and shining eyes. Her mother is glowing. She loves to help and is thrilled to have been invited to spend quality time with her daughter and granddaughter.

Tess lets her mother pass and receives her dad. He is frowning, and his eyebrows are turned up in the middle.

"I'm okay, Dad," Tess lies. He replaces the frown with a smile and hugs his little girl. He kisses her on the forehead and takes her face in his massive hands.

"You look good, baby," he says, kissing her again. "You cut your hair. Celeste," he alerts his wife. "Tess cut her hair!" They walk in together, his suitcase in hand.

Tess's mom already has Emilia in her arms, somehow not stirring the baby from her nap. Her dad sits on the couch beside them and gently kisses Emma's forehead. Looking up at Tess, he smiles.

"She's just so beautiful. So much like her mother."

"Oh, don't say that, Dad." Tess and compliments don't mix.

"Don't be silly!" her mother exclaims. "You're *both* beautiful. How you could ever think otherwise is beyond me. It's one thing to be modest, but don't cheat yourself out of the rest of your life thinking that you're anything but beautiful."

Tess cracks a smile and rolls her eyes.

"God gave you more than He did most. I'll bet you're the prettiest thing in the room anywhere you go."

Tess remembers Charlie's words on that very point the night before and blushes. Her dad rises from the couch with a grunt and moves through the apartment to the bathroom. "Long drive," he tells her and shuts the door.

"Would you like something to drink, Mom?"

"No, I'm fine, honey. I'll sit with Emma for right now, but your father may like something."

Tess busies herself in the kitchen and opens two beers. She pours a bowl of shelled peanuts and sets them on the coffee table. When her father rejoins them, they clink bottles and drink.

"The kitchen looks fantastic," her father remarks back from the bathroom.

"Oh, thanks. That was a project we'd started a couple of months ago. We, er, I just had it finished last week."

"It's very nice. And I love the counters," Tess's mother adds.

Small talk aside, Tess likes having her parents here. She misses them, especially now that she is alone. Her dad switches gears, noticing his daughter's need for more than pleasant conversation.

"So, what's the plan? How do you want to spend the next couple of weeks?"

"I had a thought," Tess begins with some trepidation. "I even stopped in to see the place."

"Oh?" her mother wonders aloud. "Like a retreat?"

"Yes, something like that, but with doctors and nurses," Tess stops herself. "Well, a hospital." She nearly chokes over the following four words, slipping a peanut in her mouth. "A mental health facility."

Her parents say nothing. Her father still wears an anticipatory smile, nodding, while her mother bows her head to study the baby.

"Listen, it's not like I'm crazy or anything." She stands and paces. This is a difficult position for their family to be in again. After what her little brother had done and the therapy they all endured after that. "It just seems right to me somehow, you know? I need to do this and understand where I am in life and what I can do to improve it for Emma and me."

"No judgment here," her dad says.

"Absolutely not." her mother agrees. "You do what you need to do to be well. We're here to support your decision."

Tess feels a weight lift. She was dreading this conversation. After her brother was declared dead all those years ago, Tess, her mom, and her dad were all entered into a counseling program in the hospital's opposite wing. They stayed there for the weekend and then were outpatients for years afterward. Each of them suffered from the same sense of helplessness. Each of them felt there must have been something else they could have done to prevent what had happened.

"You're a smart girl for taking action. This could be just the thing for you. I'm proud of you." Her father opens his arms, and moments later, Tess finds herself crying into his barrel chest.

* * * * *

Tess looks forward to crawling into bed tonight. Her mother has insisted on getting up with Emilia to handle the feedings and changes, and Tess couldn't be more grateful. She wonders why she hadn't asked for help weeks ago.

In bed, listening to her parents quietly chat over the TV in the next room sparks a warm glow in Tess. She hugs the sheets up to her chin, turns over, and brings her knees to her chest. She'd always loved when they'd had company over when she was young and could hear the glasses clinking, forks on plates, and the sounds of two or more conversations merging in a melee of gossip and conjecture. This memory of her childhood comforts Tess. It offers a sense of security and well-being tonight, making her feel safe in her parents' care.

Tonight, Tess falls asleep with a smile, color on her cheeks, and a hint of optimism in her heart.

Chapter Sixteen
Sunday

When she wakes, Tess can recall no dreams. Her sleep was heavy and uninterrupted. She woke once through the night when she heard Emma cry but listened as her mother sprang to action and settled her with a bottle.

Alarmed at the time, Tess slips out of bed and slides into her slippers. She opened her door and found her parents entertaining their granddaughter on the couch while bacon spit on the stovetop.

"Tess!" her mother shouts, getting up from the couch. "Breakfast is almost ready, dear."

Tess was groggy; she'd slept nearly thirteen hours. Her face felt like the skin of a peach as she rubbed her eyes and yawned.

"Hi, guys," she waves at her dad and Emma, smiling. Pulling her housecoat from its hook, she strolls to the kitchen island and sits on one of the four stools she'd purchased to complete the breakfast bar.

"Did you make coffee, Mom?" Tess pours a half glass of orange juice her mother had set out and swallows it in one gulp.

"Well, your father can't drink it anymore, you know; he has that ulcer now, and it's difficult for him to process acidic things like coffee, so I hate to torture him with the smell of it, but if you'd like a cup I could brew one for you."

"Please," Tess feels exhausted over her mother's explanation but thankful she is there to make it. "I don't think I'll ever wake up without one."

"You had a good sleep then?"

"Yes, thank you so much."

"Well, little Emma was a perfect angel; she only woke once in the night to eat and was up for good by seven-thirty. Your father has been keeping her busy with the TV and some books we brought."

Tess turns to watch her dad with Emma and rests her chin on her hand. She smiles again, enjoying the feelings the scene conjures.

"I love you guys," Tess tells them, tears balancing on the corners of her eyes.

Her mother places the bacon and eggs on the counter and sighs. "Oh, Tess, you're *our* baby, and we love you very much."

"Love you too, Bean," her father says from the couch, picking up Emma and carrying her to the highchair. Tess felt a tickle in her chest at the nickname he'd given her as a toddler: Bean. She decides she'll pass that on to Emma.

"So what are your plans today then?" he asks her. "Will you be going to the hospital to see about setting that up?"

"Yup," Tess nods, accepting a mug of coffee from her mom. She mixes in a packet of sweetener and a shot of milk and takes a sip. She leans back in her stool and allows the coffee's restorative powers to go to work.

Her father looks on in envy. "Well, at least I still have bacon!" He places a strip in his mouth and bites down. Emma, watching him, laughs at his exaggerated expression. The giggles spur him on, making more faces as he chews the bacon, Emma laughing harder and harder.

Tess reaches out, places a hand on her father's arm, and squeezes. He turns to face her with three pieces of bacon protruding from his mouth, and Tess laughs aloud. Emma is in hysterics. Her mother dishes out portions of egg and toast.

* * * * *

After a long shower and dressing for the weather, Tess says goodbye, heads to the parking garage, and is soon on the road. The hospital is a ten-minute drive up the hill. The new wing is hidden from this view, but the old building is still in use and completely renovated.

Tess approaches the front desk and requests a meeting with a counselor. She handed over the paperwork they'd given her earlier in the week, and the woman behind the desk asked her to have a seat.

Interestingly, Tess notices the same couple seated across from her who she'd spied with the teenage boy - the cutter. They nod pleasantly at her as she takes her seat. She thumbs through her phone, wondering where all her friends disappeared to once Sam had left. Had he really been the point of contact for so many?

"Will he be okay?" Tess overhears the boy's mother whispering to his father. She decides their conversation will be far more fascinating than her inner dialogue and abandons the question of her popularity.

"They managed to fix the damage he did to his wrist; now it's up to the shrinks to fix whatever damage was done in his head."

"But do you think they can?"

"Jesus, Liz, there's no alternative."

"Don't swear at me. This is not the time to take the Lord's name in vain."

"Oh, for fuck sake!" He springs from his seat and storms down the line of plastic chairs, exiting the hospital for what Tess imagines is a much-needed walk. Awkwardly, Liz addresses Tess.

"We've been here all morning," she says apologetically. "Our son, he hurt himself, and after the emergency room, they brought him here for an assessment." The mother looks shattered.

"I'm sorry," Tess offers.

"It'll be fine." Liz waves off the tension. "He's just a troubled teen; you know how that can be."

Tess keeps the conversation light. "I was young once."

"Are you waiting on someone?"

Tess freezes. She's not sure how to answer that question. Will this stranger think less of Tess if she tells her the truth? Should she tell her anything?

"Oh, I'm sorry," Liz says, picking up on the pause. "I shouldn't have asked you a question like that in a place like this. Forget I asked it."

"Tess," calls one of the women behind the desk. Tess looks over her shoulder and smiles back at Liz.

"It's nothing, don't worry about it. I hope everything works out for your family." Tess stands and follows the secretary to an office. She is greeted by a tall woman with glasses and red hair pulled up into a bun. She is older than Tess but not much, leaving Tess uncomfortable.

"Hi, Tess, my name is Christine. I'll be your counselor today."

"Hi," Tess says uneasily, looking about the small office. The counselor motions for her to take a seat, and she does.

"This is just part of the process, nothing to be nervous over. I will review your history with you and get to the heart of what has brought you here. Once we pin that down, we'll discuss what you expect from an in-patient program and what we can offer you."

"Okay." Tess rubs her hands together, already wet with nerves.

The counselor pulls a superficial history from Tess, never delving too deeply, gathering only what is required to allow the doctors an opinion. Her brother's untimely death came up. Tess's therapy and the question as to whether she feels she has recovered from the loss. Then, the remainder of her childhood and into adulthood, the choices she'd made, the man she'd married, and ultimately, her abandonment. Could this be a pattern developing? What was she feeling now? Was she happy?

"Alright, I have what I need. I will leave my report with the department head of psychiatry here, and we will contact you by the end of the day."

Tess is exhausted from the exercise, having all that history pulled out of her in such a short time. Walking to her car, she considers a drink. She thinks of Charlie's.

Chapter Seventeen
Sunday, 4:15 pm

No harm in just driving by Charlie's, Tess decides.

She feels pulled in two directions; even while her car takes the corner that will lead to Charlie's, she questions her intuition. "Just a quick look," she tells herself. "I won't even go in."

As she slowed down to get a good look at the bar, she noticed a sign that read 'closed' on the front doors. She can't remember Charlie's ever being closed, but perhaps he'd become a Mormon since Friday night and now observes the Sabbath. Then again, she thinks, maybe the four men Tad held at gunpoint had managed to overpower them.

An eerie feeling overcomes her, and she pushes on, careful not to look too suspicious. Arriving home, she collapses on the couch. Her parents are out with Emma. It's a foreign feeling for Tess to be alone in her apartment. It's distressing. Panic builds in her chest. She stands and shakes her arms.

"This is ridiculous," she tells herself, pacing the space between the television and her bedroom. "I should be able to enjoy this downtime."

She reaches for her phone and calls her mother. The phone rings and rings and never goes to a voice mail. *They still haven't set up their messages.* The phone call was a bad idea. They're probably fine, too deaf to hear the cell ringing in her mother's purse. Tess now suffers from the uncertainty of Emma's whereabouts and the claustrophobic feeling of being alone in her apartment.

She continues to talk herself down, remembering the list of symptoms from her internet search, mentally checking each of them off. The pains in her arm and chest subside, her breathing levels out, and she settles into one of the stools at the kitchen island.

"God, this is unfair," she mumbles, forehead resting on the cool granite countertop.

Chapter Eighteen
Sunday, 5:15 pm

An hour later, her parents resurface with Emma in tow, her father holding the door as her mother clumsily pushes the stroller over the threshold.

Hi guys," Tess says, turning away from the stovetop where she is preparing dinner. "I tried calling. Where were you?"

"Oh, sorry, Bean," her father says. "Your mother thought we should walk to the old neighborhood."

"It was a nice walk," her mom adds. "Have you seen what they've done to your old school? It looks brand new."

Tess dried her hands, picked Emma up from the stroller, hugged her, and gently kissed her rosy cheeks. She ignores her mother's observation and places her daughter on the floor with her toys, changing the television channel to an age-appropriate show.

"You guys need to up the volume on your cell phone. If I need to get a hold of you, it's important that I can."

"Message received." Her dad leans in and kisses Tess on the forehead. "No harm done."

Tess rolled her eyes, considering the panic attack she'd experienced over the empty house. Her father opens the fridge and pulls a beer bottle from the door.

Want one?" he asks her. Tess shakes her head, and he offers the bottle to his wife. She, too, turns him down. Her father shrugs and twists the top off, joining his granddaughter in the living room.

"So, how was the hospital? Did you like what they had to say?" Celeste hangs her daughter's jacket in the front closet and positions herself on the island.

"It was good, I think. They said they'd call by the end of the day to let me know."

"That's encouraging." Her mother joins Tess at the stove. "A pot roast," she observes. "Are you going to place potatoes and onions around it?"

The two are so similar in height and appearance that Tess sees her future in her mother's face. Though similar, she always wished she'd inherited those full lips and petite nose.

Celeste smiles brightly and rubs her daughter's arm. "Everything will work out just right, honey; you'll see."

"Thanks, Mom. Could you clean and cut the potatoes while I chop the onions?"

Celeste nods and places a cutting board on the island. The phone rings as Tess lands the bag of onions on the counter.

"Hello?" she answers with a hint of apprehension, hoping Sam has not decided to call now.

It's the hospital. They have agreed to enroll her in an intensive, custom-made in-patient program that would run for ten days. Tess takes the call into her bedroom.

"How much will it be?" she asks, considering her insurance will handle approximately eighty percent of the costs. The price seems reasonable, so she agrees to the terms, asking them to email her the schedule.

Sitting on her bed, Tess opens her laptop and finds the itinerary in her inbox. She brings the computer to the kitchen and sets it before her mother.

"Okay, it looks like I start tomorrow."

Celeste stopped what she was doing and looked over the email. "Ten days! That's wonderful, dear. This looks great. I like the idea of the workshops. You'll get a lot out of this."

* * * * *

That night, Tess decides Emma will sleep with her. She knows she'll miss her daughter terribly and wants to breathe her in while she sleeps, hold her close, and feel that connection only a mother can know.

Tess finds it challenging to sleep, the days ahead crafting a myriad of questions. She is excited by the possibilities, yet an underlying sense of unease plays an equal part in keeping her awake. A quick peek at Emma lying beside her settles these thoughts, and she snuggles in for the night.

Chapter Nineteen
Monday

It's late in the day when Tess is dropped at the entrance of the new wing. Her parents exaggerate the beauty of the building as they move to get out of the car. Tess asks them to stay seated, hoping for a clean break. She kisses Emilia a dozen times and slips out the back door, waving to her parents, both brimming with pride over her decision to take this step. She blows a final kiss to her daughter, turns on her heels, and, with the suitcase in one hand, pushes through the revolving door with the other.

* * * * *

As she is escorted from the front desk through security doors and then a long, bright, sterile hallway, she eyes a man approaching her from the opposite end; he's thin with dark, wild hair standing straight up and a chin that falls far below his mouth, his narrow face seems comically long.

"You're here," he says in passing as their eyes meet. His expression is warm, and his tone is inviting. "I'm so glad, I honestly wondered."His orderly holds him by the upper arm and does not stop.

Tess's caught off guard, turning to maintain their gaze. "What?" She doesn't recognize the man, but she is sure she is who he's targeted with his greeting.

"I'll see you in the common room," he shouts, stumbling over his slippers. The heavyset attendant at his side catches him, all without slowing. "I can't wait!"

Tess realizes she's stopped walking and is watching the man move down the long hallway, sharing an animated conversation with his orderly, nodding his head and chattering away.

Tess's head is slowly shaking. The boy pulling her luggage, a recent graduate of behavioral studies at a local college, he tells her, removes the amused smile from his face.

"Oh, I wouldn't pay him any mind," he begins, waving the incident off with his free hand. "He's a lifer."

She accepts his explanation, but for whatever reason, she feels a sudden sense of recognition in the wild man's eyes; it serves to scare her more than offer comfort in this new place.

"Well, come on," says the young man. "I'll show you your room, and then, if you like, we can go to the common room, and you can talk to Tebor."

"Tebor?"

"That's his name." He points down the hall after the man with the unkempt hair. "He goes by many names around here, but Tebor is his *actual* name."

"Oh." Tess turned to face the direction in which she was headed before Tebor interrupted. "I don't know if," she trails off, and her guide pushes forward, shaking his head, her suitcase rolling behind him.

Chapter Twenty
Monday, 7:30 pm

Tess's first night in her bedroom feels like the early days she'd spent in her college dorm, waiting on her roommate. Strangely, she feels she is waiting on someone here; perhaps that strange man who claimed he knew her? But the hospital room is a single, and the door locked.

Why she would liken the hospital room to her teenage dorm is an easy guess for Tess. The last time she'd slept in a single bed was at university. The third year, she'd met Sam, and once school ended, the two of them moved into a basement apartment together two blocks north of Charlie's bar.

She remembers how exciting it was; so new, so adult. Her parents were not big supporters of her moving in with a man ten years her senior but backed off once Tess had explained she was in love.

That same month, Tess was offered a job at a firm downtown and skipped out on the waitressing job she'd procured to get through the summer months. Things were looking promising, and Sam had never been happier. His friends would give him the gears, he'd told her, calling him a cradle robber and all that, but he was genuinely inspired by Tess and encouraged by her ambition. His career was also taking off, sending him all over the world setting up IT solutions for corporations. The two of them looked like a success story about to launch.

Tess smiles at the memory: they'd been so young and full of life and love. *But here I am*, she thinks to herself. *In a fucking mental ward.* She laughs at this, the twenty-one-year-old Tess laughing with her. Or is she laughing at her? No, Tess has never been malicious, at least not until the cutting, but even that was executed as a kindness.

Tess eventually works her body into the stiff mattress and kicks out the corners of the sheets. Sleep comes surprisingly quickly as memories fade to black.

Tuesday

Tuesday morning arrives with the sun shining brightly in the late October sky. Tess feels surprisingly rested, if a little confused by her surroundings. But once the initial disorientation of navigating a room that is not her own is overcome, she dresses, washes her face, combs her hair, and heads to the cafeteria, following the colored arrows on the floor.

Scrambled eggs and back bacon with toast and a choice of waffles or pancakes line the buffet. The smell is tempting, but Tess gravitates to a fruit bowl at the end of the long counter. Filling a cup, she sits at one of the dozen round tables set for six. Secretly, she hoped no one would ask to sit with her when she saw the *cutter.* He looks depressed, still dressed in pajamas his mother no doubt bought specially for him. His left sleeve is rolled up, exposing an elbow-to-wrist bandage, which he scratches. He walks past Tess, fixed on the buffet. An orderly, apparently sent to shadow him, sits at a table adjacent to her. Tess watches as the boy picks up a plate, and his wrist gives out. The plate slides from his hand, landing on the linoleum floor with a dull thud. The orderly moves to get up, but Tess acts first.

"Let me help you with that," she says, retrieving the plate. Her reaction surprises even her, while the cutter's is nonexistent. Tess walks to the buffet and points at the eggs.

"Would you like some of these?"

He nods, dead-eyed. Tess looks back at the orderly, sinking back into his chair.

She continued, asking and pointing until she had a pile of food on his plate. She then invites him to sit with her.

The boy, Paul, is tall, slim, and pale. "Thank you," he says in a whisper.

"Are you alright?" Tess asks, wishing she could take it back. Paul just looks at her and then back at the orderly as he pushes a forkful of eggs into his mouth.

"Just eat," she tells him, smiling awkwardly and returning to her fruit bowl. "My name's Tess, by the way."

"Paul," he answers, still chewing. "Nice bodyguard, huh? Worried I'll use the plastic knife on myself." Looking her up and down, Paul changes the subject and tells her she is pretty. Tess doesn't want this sort of attention and is immediately embarrassed by it.

"Are you seriously self-conscious over how you look? You're pretty. It must be nice to be pretty. Easier." He pauses to take another mouthful of the lukewarm eggs. "What are you doing here? Don't think you're pretty enough?"

Tess thought that was a cruel comment meant to hurt her. But she can tell that Paul is suffering and probably didn't mean to be an asshole.

"I tried that once," she admits, nodding at his bandage.

Paul looks down at his arm as if he'd forgotten the bandage was there. "What, this? I just went too deep."

"I got nothing from the experience myself."

"I like it." His focus returns to the plate of food, and he pokes at the bacon.

"Why?"

His mouth sags at the corners, and he places his fork down. "What are you, an undercover shrink or something?"

"I'm sorry." Tess wishes she could take that question back, too. "I was just curious. All it did was make me bleed."

Paul looks thoughtfully at Tess. "I don't do it for *nothing*. I think it's like, you know, the olden days where they used to *bleed* people to make them better." He turns back to his plate, head down. "It makes sense to me."

Tess thought this must be at odds with the popular reasons given by most kids that cut. It seems somehow more purposeful. It was misguided but purposeful.

"Where did you hear about that?"

"I just sort of came up with it, then I Googled it. It turns out doctors would cut people and drain some of their blood to cure diseases and stuff."

Tess remembers this from a show she'd watched on the Discovery channel years ago. Of course, the practice stopped as science realized *bleeding* was probably the worst thing they could do for the patient.

"But you know that was stopped because it didn't work, right?"

"Nobody does it anymore, I guess," he agrees. "Doesn't mean it doesn't work."

Tess thinks differently but doesn't want to get locked into a debate. She eats the remainder of the cut apples, oranges, and bananas in her bowl and considers another question.

"So, do you mind if I ask you something?"

Paul sips at his orange juice and shakes his head.

"What is it you think you have that you need to bleed yourself to be better?"

Paul sets his glass on the table and looks at her. His head slowly starts to shake back and forth. This reaction goes on longer than she feels comfortable and interrupts.

"You don't have to answer that, Paul. It's just a question. I'm nobody."

"Is that why you're here?" he asks, eyes fixed on hers. "Because you think you're nobody?"

Ouch. Tess thinks. This kid has no trouble asking the big questions. "No," she answers. "At least, I don't think that's it." She looks down at her bowl, picks it up, and turns it in her hands. "I guess I'm here to answer that question."

Paul returns to his breakfast. "Me too," he mumbles. Then his volume picks up, and his head turns enough that the orderly can hear him. "Just wish I wasn't separated from everyone else like I'm a *criminal* or something."

"Well, it was nice to meet you, Paul. I hope we can talk more again." She rises from her seat and fights the urge to extend a hand for Paul to shake. She nods at him, and he at her and heads back to her room to shower and dress for her morning meeting with Doctor Samuelsson.

Chapter Twenty-One
Tuesday, 9:30 am

Being buried alive has always been an irrational fear of Tess's. She knows this, always has, yet there it was, always in the back of her mind. Of course, she could never visualize a time when such an event would occur. What unlucky soul would be buried alive in this day and age? That question is answered today as she watches an entire mall collapse in on itself and over one thousand customers and employees in a distant part of the world as an earthquake ravages the once serene landscape. Was her fear still irrational? Yes, she thinks, wiping moist palms on her jeans and glancing at the ceiling, but she would think twice before entering another mall.

Tebor, the man who thought he knew Tess upon arriving - and now entering the common room - had overheard the news of her pending visit with Doctor Samuelsson and saw an opening.

"You know what I've heard of the good Doctor?" he asks Tess, sliding down the long couch towards her.

"Do I want to know?" she wonders politely, not making eye contact with him.

"I hear he'll hypnotize a woman and, you know, take advantage of the situation." He says it like it's nothing. Like he expects her to appreciate his wit. As if they'd shared a relationship and sense of humor for years.

"That's an *awful* thing to say."

"It's what I hear." He shrugs. Then their eyes meet, and he smiles a toothy grin. "It is nice to see you again."

"Listen about that. I'm pretty sure you don't know me, not like you think. I've never met *you* before."

He lets out a loud cackle. "No, not in this life, but here we are." His hand swings out in front of him as if inviting a hug.

"Yes, here we are." Tess feels uneasy around Tebor. Although he seems harmless, the familiar way he has approached her on both occasions is difficult to ignore.

"Why do you think you know me if you agree we've never met in *this life*?"

"That's for me to know," he starts.

"And for me to find out?" Tess finishes his sentence. "That's mature."

"But it is for you to discover. You're here, aren't you?"

"Yes." Tess puts down the magazine she had been leafing through, "And you're not helping by telling me terrible stories about the doctors here."

"Forget about what I said about the good Doctor. He's a quack. The nurses are the ones that can help you."

"Oh really? Then why aren't *they* the doctors?"

"Touché!" Tebor bows, and his age, hidden atop his shock of black hair, reveals itself. There, a collection of grey sits bordered by the tall, black, wiry hair surrounding it. She thinks it looks like a bad dye job where he'd missed the top.

"Well, anyway, I'm not here to find out whether you and I have met before."

"No? Then why *are* you here?"

"To get answers."

"Right, and who better to give you those answers than your teacher?" His right eyebrow rises toward his hairline, insinuating she should remember some long-forgotten memory.

Tess notices the time and stands to excuse herself. "Well, on that note, I'm off to be taken advantage of."

Tebor laughs. "Always a quick wit."

Tess stares at him and then walks to the nurses' station to ask about her appointment.

Chapter Twenty-Two
Tuesday, 10:30 am

"Hello, Tess," greets Dr. Samuelsson in a calm, gravelly voice behind his oversized antique desk. His office, though as new as the rest of the building, smells of worn leather and wood. Nowhere near as sterile as the front foyer and hallways. He sits before a large multi-paned window, which lets in the morning light, warming his desk's dark surfaces and animating the air around him.

"Hi," replies Tess, suddenly self-conscious.

"Please." The doctor waves his hand, encouraging Tess to sit opposite his desk in one of the two sizeable plush leather seats.

Tess sits. "I thought I was supposed to lie down," she smiles. The doctor smiles back as he studies her.

"You may find that things aren't quite as formal as you thought, Tess," he tells her as he removes his reading glasses. "In fact, you could stand through our sessions if you wished, but many of my guests find lying down to be most comfortable."

Tess smiles uneasily. She feels her cheeks redden as she follows his subtle nod toward the far end of the room, where a chaise lounge rests on an angle to the corner. "Sorry," she mumbles. "This is all pretty new to me."

"You've nothing to apologize for. You've done a brave thing coming to see us. That in itself is encouraging." He replaces his reading glasses and lifts a document to his face. Tess notices it's her submittal form, her distinct penmanship showing through as the window's light penetrates the thin paper.

"So, you don't take drugs, you don't smoke, you enjoy the occasional bottle of red wine, and who doesn't," he says with a wink and a grin. "You're a bit under your goal weight, no breakouts, rashes, acne, or otherwise; you have a baby, so there's your daily exercise."

Tess laughs uneasily, suddenly missing Emma.

"You've been to a therapist before." He shifts the paper to watch Tess's reaction. She bows her head and focuses on her hands as she rubs her palms into her knees.

"Yes," she tells him. "You'll see on the next page that there is a history of depression in my family, which led to my younger brother's suicide. At least that's what the doctors said after."

"Did therapy help you?"

"I think it did. It at least took the idea out of my head that I could have stopped it."

"Looking back, do you think you could have?"

"I didn't honestly know anything was wrong. I mean, my brother was so young, just a child."

"Were you able to heal then, or was your therapy more to convince you that you were not to blame?"

"Heal? I – I don't know, does anyone really heal from a thing like that?"

"Yes, Tess, people do," Samuelsson assures her.

"I guess I don't know then." Tess finds she's confused by the questions. *It's not your fault.* This was her mantra designed to get her through the pain, but had she genuinely gone through it? Had she only waded around the loss? Had she grieved for him at all?

"We'll revisit this later." Samuelsson clears his throat. "Your husband has left you."

"Yes." The shame in her voice is palpable.

"What he's done is a reflection on *him*, not you. Remember that, and we will build on it."

"I don't know how I feel about him anymore."

"You've been through a lot recently. In your own words, you're depressed, overwhelmed, lost focus, lonely, exhausted, gave cutting a shot." He peers over the paper for a moment to address her. "First time?"

Tess nods. "And the last."

"Good. Did nothing for you?"

"Just made me bleed."

"Not what you'd expected?"

"I had heard it released endorphins, that it could make a person happy for the moment."

"Does your daughter not do that for you? If you need a moment of happiness, I mean."

"Yes, of course, she does, but" Tess stops momentarily and realizes the wisdom in his statement. She laughs lightly and shakes her head, looking down at her hands folded and white-knuckled. "It was a dumb thing to have done. I'll be the first to admit it. I wasn't sure I was even going to write that down."

"I want you to be completely honest with me. That's the only way to approach this. Honest, blunt, fiercely so. I applaud your including this." He leans forward, and his chair squeaks to life. "If you can stay on that path of honest story-telling, I believe we will be able to assess and help you within the time you've allotted yourself here."

Tess feels a sense of well-being envelop her. It fills every inch of her with a warm shock of electricity. She's done the right thing coming here. She listened to herself and, by listening, found her way to this place, this safe house. She breathes a sigh of relief.

"Thank you, doctor," Tess says. "I just want to be well, for my daughter, for myself."

"It will be intensive, as you have not given us much time, but perhaps you can come back in an outpatient capacity for follow-up."

"I'm dedicated to doing this, whatever it takes."

"Okay, I'll see you for your first session at noon based on this interview. You have free run of the place, and if you want to leave the facility, we ask that you respect our curfews."

Tess considers this but decides to avoid the outside world while paying to be here. "I'll just keep to the interior, I think."

"Your decision, Tess. I look forward to working with you."

She decides this is her cue to get up, awkwardly nodding at Samuelson, almost bowing, and turning to walk out of the office.

"Tess," the doctor calls after her. She turns to meet his gaze. "Loosen up." He offers an encouraging smile. Her head tilts to the side, an amused grin creeping across her face. "It's a little like Wonderland here; watch the rabbit holes, and keep your head."

Chapter Twenty-Three
Tuesday, 11:00 am

Tess spends an hour wandering the facility, wondering what her session with the doctor will entail. Hypnosis is on the brochure, and though she has reservations about this sort of therapy, she refuses to let the pessimist emerge.

She observes that the majority of the patients freely milling about are withdrawn. Like her, they would be volunteers. Apparently, her breakfast companion, Paul, wasn't here by choice and so segregated from her and the others, save mealtime, and even then, he had an escort. After overhearing his parents twice concerning their son's cutting and now having met and spoken to him, she feels somehow responsible for him while she's here, a mother figure on the inside.

Tebor did not match her patient profiling. He is not withdrawn; he is animated, a live-wire, she thinks. Overall, it's much quieter here than she had imagined: people in straight jackets, troubled residents banging their heads against walls, and others writhing in pain from some unseen threat. But all of her preconditioned, media-driven predictions had proven untrue. Tess was glad, as she had reservations over that kind of environment, offering any chance at getting out of there with some sense of normalcy.

She feels the cell phone in her pocket vibrate and anxiously pulls it out.

"Hello?" she says, again forgetting to look at the number displayed.

"Oh, hi, honey," her mother's voice rings at the other end. "Are you busy?"

"No, what's wrong?" Tess pictures a myriad of potential disasters her mother might be calling about.

"Oh, nothing's wrong, dear. I just wanted to call and give you an update."

"Okay. Emma being good?"

"Oh yes, she and your father are at the park now. It's a beautiful day outside."

"How was it overnight?"

"Well, I'd be lying if I said she isn't missing you. But the feedings have gone well, and she's just a bundle of energy."

Tess frowned at the thought that Emma was missing her. She misses Emma too but has made peace with the idea that she was here for the good of both of them. She knows Emma doesn't share that capacity for understanding and briefly wonders whether she might feel abandoned by her mother.

"But she's not making too much of a fuss?"

"No, she just misses her mom, but we're doing everything we can to keep her busy."

"Okay, thanks for the update. I have a session with my psychiatrist in a couple of minutes, so I'd better let you go. Thanks again for doing this for me."

"You're very welcome; I wouldn't have it any other way, dear. You go on and see to yourself. We'll be fine. Love you."

"Love you, bye."

As Tess hangs up, she feels a pang of guilt. The line: 'You go on and see to yourself' plants itself in her head like an infection and, if left to fester, will ruin any chance at her feeling justified over being here.

Chapter Twenty-Four
Tuesday, 12:00 pm

Doctor Karl Samuelsson reached what he considers his profession's pinnacle at a young age due to his unique brand of hypnotherapy, what colleagues have termed *Quicknotherapy*. His approach to Tess's particular case will be no different. He has practiced psychiatry for more than thirty years, having hypnotized nearly one thousand people. His technique has been called abrupt yet effective by his peers once a patient is under.

* * * * *

Tess's first session with Doctor Samuelsson begins with her lying on the lounge, attempting to get comfortable on the worn leather. The idea that she is about to be hypnotized is foreign to her. Staring at the tiled ceiling, a sense of vertigo takes hold. Everything about it seems alien. She has never visualized herself giving up control so entirely like this. Her career as a marketing director with a top firm in the city taught her that giving up power meant letting go, and though she had always seen her life as a project, she knew it was no longer something she should direct alone.

Samuelsson moves from his desk to the corner, where Tess continues to shift around on the chaise's smooth fabric. "Are you comfortable?" He sits in a plush leather chair a few feet to her left.

Tess turns her head and nods, smiling uncomfortably. The doctor notices her apprehension and addresses it.

"Tess, this will be the easiest thing you do here. You will slip into an unconscious state and live the life you've known. Everything you reveal is what you already know."

"Then how does it help?"

"Just because you've lived it doesn't mean you've retained it in your conscious mind. But it *will* be in your unconscious, and I've found that hypnosis is the quickest and most effective way to bring that information to the forefront and deal with the memories."

"Okay," Tess says weakly. Her hands are clasped tightly on her stomach, and she feels her palms dampen as her nerves take hold.

"I need you to relax. Make yourself comfortable," Doctor Samuelsson's voice has become more profound, softer, and quieter, speaking very slowly. "Take a deep breath and hold it. As you slowly let it out, let your whole body relax." Tess follows the doctor's instructions, remembering the relaxing quality of her breathing exercises. "And now take another deep breath. This time, when you release it, release all the tension in your body." Her feet slump to the sides, and her tight grip on her jeans loosens. "Take another deep breath, and this time really let go. Allow your eyes, legs, hands, and head to become warm, loose, and heavy. Like a heavy sweater thrown across a comfortable chair." Her head falls gently to the side. "And as relaxed as you are now, you can become more relaxed, falling deeper and deeper into a tranquil state. Ten times more relaxed..." Tess's arms fall to her sides. She is under.

"Good. Now, let's begin. You are twelve; it's winter; your birthday is a month away. Your baby brother is playing with his toys. Where are you?"

"In the basement," Tess explains, eyes closed and voice a raised whisper. "There's Tommy," she says, smiling, and then she starts to cry.

"I want you to remove emotion from this memory."

She stops crying and obeys the doctor's command.

"Tess, what do you see in Tommy?"

"Sadness," Tess recites in a monotone. "He's withdrawn, pushing his trucks along the floor. His eyes hold no expression. He's only six, a baby, he should be smiling, he should be happy."

"Can you go back a month and tell me what you see in your brother?"

"Yes," she says. "Tommy's brushing his teeth. I pinch his side because he's taking too long. He giggles and pushes me playfully. He's smiling through the toothpaste in his mouth. He's happy."

"A month before your birthday, he was happy. Go one week into the future and tell me how he looks."

"He's quiet. Really, really quiet."

"Do you ask him what's wrong?"

Her head shakes slightly. "No."

"Do you want to ask him?"

"Something's not right. Tommy's sitting staring at his teddy bear; it's three feet in front of him. He always carries that bear around. The TV is on; we're watching a cartoon, but his back is to it."

"Where are your parents?"

"In the landing, they're talking to each other. Our parents are worried about Tommy."

"Block the sound coming from the TV, Tess. Mute it. Now concentrate on what your parents are saying."

Her eyelids close a little tighter. "Dad tells Mom that they should involve the police, that he should be questioned."

"Who should be?"

"Mom tells him no. That Tommy may be making it up. That Mr. Drummond is a good man. Dad disagrees but goes along with Mom. He tells her they're pulling Tommy from the school. Mom agrees, and..." A long pause prompts Dr. Samuelsson to ask another question.

"Is Mr. Drummond Tommy's teacher?"

"Yes," Tess supplies. "They are coming in the room now."

"That's good, Tess; this is a good start. We'll stop this session. When I count to three, you will awaken. Leave these memories with me for now; you won't remember the conversation you overheard your parents having. One, you're feeling lighter; two, you're starting to return to the present; three."

Tess opens her eyes and breathes deeply through her nose. She looks at the doctor and smiles. "I remember my brother. I remember Tommy. Why did you take me there?"

"I believe you still have unresolved questions over the circumstances in which your brother died, which may translate to your present trauma."

"Really?"

"Yes, you've made a great discovery, and we'll touch on that again tomorrow."

"Discovery?" Tess sits up.

"Yes, I've left that memory with me, though, for now, as we have more to learn through hypnosis before I want you to have it."

Tess feels uncomfortable with the doctor withholding *her* memories but reminds herself that she has decided to let this experience be what it needs to heal. She nods and slowly rises to her feet. The doctor is standing, too, and guides her to the door.

"It was an excellent session. You're going to make yourself proud."

Tess nods again, opens the heavy door, and turns to meet the doctor's gaze. "I'll see you at four then?"

He nods. "At four."

Chapter Twenty-Five
Tuesday, 2:00 pm

Tess spends the rest of the afternoon in the courtyard. Lying on the grass, she watches as birds pass overhead. The square has several saplings planted along its perimeter, with baskets of flowers hanging from the walls and picnic tables where residents can take lunch. It is a beautiful autumn day; the leaves are starting to turn, and the air smells of freshly mown grass.

Remembering her brother was a gift. She had so few memories to call upon when thinking about him. Before the hypnosis, she realizes that she remembered only the last day of his life, finding him hanging in his closet and the hospital and the funeral that followed.

Tess smiles at the sky now, able to recall his laugh. The hypnosis had opened up many more memories, and she meditates on those now.

She wonders, though, what secret information the doctor is keeping from her. Would it be a mistake for him to tell her about it, or would it help heal the pain she's harbored? Those memories haunt her. Something was wrong, and she didn't ask what, and she never gave him a chance to tell her why. She sits up abruptly and runs both hands through her short hair, scratching her scalp. Waiting for him to reveal the memory he was keeping from her would not be easy.

* * * * *

After a snack, Tess goes to Doctor Samuelsson's office for her four o'clock session.

"Hello again," the doctor greets her at the door. He waves her in. "So, have you had any memories of Tommy surface since our session?"

"Actually, a few more came rushing in afterward."

"Good, that's often the case." He takes his seat as Tess sits on the lounge.

"I'm a little stunned over it, to be honest. I haven't been able to remember much of my brother except for the tragedy. It's a real gift to have been given those memories today."

"I'm glad you think so. Anything you'd like to reveal to me?"

"No, I don't think so. Mostly just nice memories."

Samuelsson nods. "I'm going to put you under now and take you to the catalyst that brought you here."

Tess lays down, wishing he would take her back to happier times with her brother, but again resigns herself to the doctor's judgment. Her mind melts into the past as he brings her under and tugs at her unconscious mind to recall events leading up to the argument, which prompted Sam's departure.

"Go two weeks before the last time you saw your husband," he instructs.

"Construction," she tells him. "What a mess. My kitchen is a mess, and my baby is crying."

"Are you renovating?"

"Yes, bad timing. New baby, men everywhere, where is my husband?"

"Move forward a week and tell me where Sam is. Where is your husband?"

"Not here," she says. "And not that he'd answer his phone if I called, but he can't tonight. He's left it behind."

"What time is it?"

"It's two in the morning. I'm feeding Emilia and pacing the floors. His phone is on the kitchen counter. I pick it up, and then I put it down again. I'm not like that. I don't snoop."

"What sparks the fight between you two? Is there something on his phone that tips you off?"

"Yes, it's one week later, and dinnertime has come and gone. I text Sam to see where he is and hear his phone beep. I follow the beeps. I found it under a pillow on the couch and hit a button accidentally. A text comes up."

"What does it say?"

Tess swallows hard. "It says, 'I love you,' and it's from Sam. But it's not to me. I know that immediately because I hadn't heard him say it in months, never mind putting it in writing. I thumb up the thread and see a conversation. It's awful. It makes me nauseous. Emma watches me from her highchair." Tears roll down her face. "He's cheating on me."

"Tess, remember this already happened; this is a memory. You've lived this scene already,"

"I don't want to live it again," she whispers through a tightening throat. "I live it every day." Her head moves from side to side. "There is no point to anything." She tells him. "There's no point to my life." Now she is crying, as she had that night. She felt her life was a joke. Her love, her devotion, she felt utterly humiliated. "What do I do? How do I do this alone? Why would he do this to us?"

"I need you to remember this time without emotion." The doctor steps in.

She stops crying and sniffs a few times. The doctor places a tissue in her left hand. "I have to put the baby to bed."

Samuelsson allows the scene to continue.

"Emma is sleeping now," Tess explains.

"Good. Let's revisit your feelings over the text between your husband and another woman."

"Humiliation. I feel awful. I feel weak. I sit on the couch and cry. I am a weakling. I hate myself for not knowing. I hate him. I hate my life. I wish it away."

"This is a tough time, but you must know this is not about you. This is about him, about Sam. Everything he's doing is on him. His actions are not a reflection of you but of him. You know this to be true. You don't feel weak. You are the strong one. You rise above your pain, imagining a life in the near future, imagining yourself happy again."

Tess would have been smiling now if she hadn't been ordered emotionless. She envisions a future life where she and Emma sit in a park and have a puppy, and Tess has a boyfriend. He is attentive and caring. He loves her.

Moments later, Samuelsson eases Tess out of her trance and into the present.

Tess sighs and rises from the lounge. "That's a nice feeling."

"Good," he looks up at her and nods. "Take your time. You don't have to rush off."

Tess sits again and ponders the session. "You're good." She points a wagging finger at him. "I feel *good*."

"And that's how we want you to feel. With more one-on-one, we'll break down all your walls and rebuild."

Chapter Twenty-Six
Tuesday, 5:00 pm

Tebor is anxious to hear how Tess's first hypnosis sessions had gone and seeks her out in the common room. He finds her there and sits across from her, where she is playing a game of cards.

"Solitaire is a game for one," she tells him, not looking up from the cards.

"That's sad." Tebor rests his chin in his hands, looking forlorn. If it weren't for his ridiculous hair, Tess might have a chance at keeping a straight face, but since that is not the case, she cracks a smile, and Tebor finds his opening.

"I'm Tebor, by the way."

"Tess." She offers.

"Well?" he urges.

"So you want to know about the sessions?" she asks. Tebor nods, his head still resting on his tight fists. "Well, surprise, surprise, I wasn't molested!"

"So the rumors aren't true!" He pulls his chair closer to the table.

Tess decides to keep the conversation light. "It was interesting. He, what did he call it, *regressed* me to my married life."

"Well, that's no feat! You're still married!"

Tess tilts her head to the side and smiles sarcastically. "Ha, ha."

"Do you now understand why your husband left you?"

Tess is surprised. "Why do you know that?"

"Read your file," he jokes.

"No, really, *why* do you know that?"

"I can read you. Like I said, I know you. I know you from many lifetimes."

Tess can't tell if he is being sarcastic or has noticed the rings still adorning her finger. She leans back in her chair, studying his face. "Why do you say things like that? Stop saying that, please."

"Why? What is so frightening for you to believe we've met before?"

"I *haven't* met you before. That first day I walked in here is the first time I've ever laid eyes on you."

"In this life, I agree; it's the first time I've seen you too. I was beginning to wonder."

Tess stands. "This is what I'm talking about! I don't know why you *insist* on telling me these things."

Tebor raises his hands. "If you get loud, they give you pills in this place to make you silent. Please, sit. I'm sorry. We'll get to all of that."

Tess sits again. "I'm trying to get help here. I'm trying to learn to deal with the shit hand I've been dealt. Let me learn."

"Most of us learn how to live on the outside by living on the inside." He gestures to his head and then his heart.

"Riddles." She shakes her head hopelessly. "I'm going to call you *The Riddler* from now on."

"I wasn't kidding when I told you the nurses should be the doctors in this place. There is a woman here who can do more for you than Samuelsson and his peers can ever do."

"Why? Why would you say that?"

"You said the good doctor regressed you through hypnosis to a recent past."

"Yes, and it was *amazing*."

"You want amazing you come to see me at midnight tonight when Madhiva does the graveyard shift. Her whole religion is based on what I'm trying to impart to you, and she is a master at regression therapy where she comes from."

"Planet X?"

Tebor is caught off guard and laughs freely. "I have missed your quick wit in this life."

"I have a class at five-thirty on problem-solving or something." Tess gestures to the binder on the table.

Tebor nods. "Come see me in the courtyard after."

Chapter Twenty-Seven
Tuesday, 6:00 pm

Tess finds Tebor in the courtyard. He is seated cross-legged on the grass. His shoulders are pulled back, and his head down. Tess can't tell whether his eyes are closed, but the posture suggests they would be. She dabbles with sneaking up behind him and slapping him on the back but decides to curb the urge and instead sits atop a picnic table, waiting him out.

She studies Tebor as he meditates, and a moment of recognition suddenly and unexpectedly overwhelms her. The sensation frightens Tess, and she rubs at her arms to stay the goosebumps.

A question pops into her head: What had happened in his life to bring him here? Then Tebor lifts his head and opens his eyes.

"Hello."

"Hi." Tess waves at him. "Whatcha been doin'?"

"Calming my mind," he explains, brushing off the loose grass as he stands.

"I bet you have to do that constantly," she teases. "What, ten, twelve times a day?"

Tebor shakes his head as he walks a few feet to meet her. "You are too much." He joins her at the picnic table. "So, how was your class? What did you learn?"

Tess ignores the question; instead, she shifts to face him. "What are *you* doing here, Tebor?"

"Getting help, like you,"

"No," Tess shakes her head. "No, not like me, you're not. I go to the doctor twice a day for hypnotherapy or whatever it's called. I have homework and puzzles to do in my room. I have a goal to get out of here."

"Ah." He bites down on his lips and nods, turning to face the windowed wall of the courtyard. "You think I don't share that goal?"

"Are you doing *anything* to reach it?" she asks. "Is this a game to you? Did you just decide to take a walk one day, mess up your hair, and have yourself committed? I mean, I haven't heard one word from you about your own experiences here. What sort of treatments are you engaged in? Are you manic-depressive? Bi-polar? Schizophrenic?"

Tebor's head lowers, and he rests his elbows on his knees. Tess fears she's gone too far. *God, what if he has schizophrenia?*

"You're very perceptive," he admits. "You know me better than you think."

"What are you saying? Am I right about you? You just waltzed in here one day and left the world?"

"Sounds rather grim when you put it like that." Tebor sits up and crosses his legs. "But you're not actually wrong."

"Really?"

"Why so surprised? Didn't you do the same thing?"

Tess has to think about the question. She had essentially done the same thing. She laughs to herself and nods.

"Just because you have a departure date doesn't mean you're guaranteed to get out of here. If the good doctors decide you're mad, they'll keep you here indefinitely."

Tess feels her blood pressure rise.

Tebor can't maintain the straight face he's managed to hold and erupts in laughter. Shocked by his sudden outburst, Tess also begins to laugh, unsure whether Tebor is laughing because of the irony or because he is joking.

"I'm only kidding." He lays a hand on hers. "I'm sorry, but you should have seen your face!" He laughs again, wiping a tear away. "I owed you that. Trust me."

Tess blushed; a thousand scenarios ran through her head in those few seconds in which Tebor held his tongue, never seeing her daughter again, her parents' disappointment in their only surviving child, and Sam's surprise.

Tess lashes out with a shot in the arm. Tebor is in no way prepared for the sting of her punch.

"Ooowww!" he shouts in a whisper so as not to further disrupt the others trying to enjoy the evening in the courtyard. He rubs at the spot with his other hand, his fingers tingling and becoming numb. She'd dug a knuckle in a nerve. He stands and shakes it out. "You've got quite a punch."

"I've never hit anyone before," she confesses. Tebor turns to face her.

"Oh, you've done much worse than that, my dear. Much, much worse. You and I both. But we'll get to that."

"Oh? Were we Vikings in another life, raping and pillaging poor town's people?" Tess mocks.

"Something like that. But I think we've paid our karmic debt for that particular cruelty."

Tess stands and circles the table. "You still haven't answered my question."

"No, I answered it."

"So then that part was true? You left the world behind?"

"I did. It was becoming too difficult to navigate out there. I needed someplace to be alone with my thoughts, calculate my next life, understand my purpose."

"Are you married? Do you have a family?"

"My wife died of an aneurysm last year, and my children are grown and gone away. My world died with Lenore. I quit the university. I couldn't concentrate." He circles the table now, moving in the opposite direction Tess had been orbiting.

"So you just dropped everything and checked yourself into this place?"

"It wasn't as sudden as all that. I had a difficult time understanding why my life had taken such a devastating turn. I'm only fifty-three, after all, and Lenore, she was forty-seven. Too soon to take her, I thought, too soon." He stops walking and sits on the bench of the picnic table. Tess joins him.

"So, then, how long have you been here?" Tess asks.

"Six months. You see, I met Madhiva on the outside. She was performing past life regression out of her home, and I got caught up in it. I went to her daily, wrapped up in detailed remembrances of my past lives. My present life had lost all meaning for me. It was a miserable time, and slipping into my past lives gave me something to think about besides my sadness. Madhiva is the one who suggested I come here. She worried about me, so I did. I sold my houses and cars and all my material things."

"So Madhiva got you in here for regular therapy, and at the same time, you see her nights?"

"I gave up on the doctors a couple of months ago, but they let me stay because I pay them for the privilege."

"Why stay?"

"I like it here. I get three meals a day, and the people are interesting." He smiles, and Tess giggles.

"That's quite a story. I'm very sorry about your wife."

"Oh, that's alright. She's probably been born to some hapless woman by now who will have to deal with her stubbornness."

"You really *do* believe in this, don't you?"

"It's more real to me than anything. If you agree to see Madhiva tonight, you will understand why."

Chapter Twenty-Eight
Tuesday, 8:30 pm

That evening, Tess retires to her room after dinner to consider Tebor's proposal. The idea of it excites and frightens her. Who would she be after she remembered living other lives? Would she recognize herself anymore? She has no difficulty reaching a state of hypnosis, as proven through her sessions with Doctor Samuelsson. If she didn't like what her past lives showed her, she could stop and just chalk it up to a unique paranormal experience. But she'd always been interested in the afterlife. After Tommy's suicide, those questions became more and more pertinent. She'd settled on atheism, having only ever been exposed to the single god theory, where her baby brother was now experiencing eternal damnation.

"It couldn't hurt," she tells herself, changing into her pajamas.

A call to her parents and a quick nap later, Tess glances at the digital clock on her dresser. It reads 11:50 pm. Her internal pessimist tells her that seeing Madhiva is a waste of time and that she's progressing with the doctor. But Tebor has brought the unknown into the equation, and she is a curious creature. She thinks he seems to be sold on the idea, and Tess wants to trust him for whatever reason. She finds something about Tebor inexplicably familiar now.

Lying on her bed, Tess hears her phone ring. She'd never entered ring tones to distinguish one caller from the next and rarely remembered to check the number. Anxious for an outside voice, she picks up the phone from her bedside table and answers it.

"Hello."

The other end is silent. She waits a few seconds.

"You can say hello, Sam," she finally says.

"Where are you?" he asks.

"Why?"

"I had to hang up on your father at the house. They're watching Em?"

"What does it matter to you?"

"It matters. I miss her. I miss you."

She becomes silent for a few seconds, then says, "Why would you say that? Why do you miss us?"

"Don't be like that. You're my whole life; you and Emma."

Again, she goes silent; so much to process. This man who left her and their child for another woman is *missing them?*

"Do you want to come home?" She wishes she hadn't asked the question. She doesn't want to sound weak. She doesn't want to miss him, but she does.

"I – I don't know. I want to see you both, though. I miss you."

"Where are you?"

"Close by."

"I'm not at home. Don't go to the house. I'm not there."

"You moved our money from the joint account."

Tess had done this the day she had looked into the in-patient care program at the hospital and retrieved her doctor's referral for the stay. That money was to keep her baby and her from financial ruin. To keep them in the house they had called home.

"Yes."

"I'm in trouble, babe. I need to see you."

Tess struggles for breath at hearing this. Warmth ignites in her stomach, enveloping her. *He needs me.*

"Sam, I - I don't know what to say. *You* left us."

Sam sounds defeated on the other end. "I know what I did. I know I've been a bad husband and father. I - I need some *money.*"

Tess's blood runs cold, and she angrily fights the urge to throw her phone against the wall.

"So you want to see me so you can get some *money?* You don't miss Emma or me. You *need* us."

"It's not like that. I really need you."

"You go to hell." Tess pushes the phone icon and leaves her thumb on the button until the screen goes black, staring at the phone in disbelief. She drops it to the floor and curls up in the fetal position on her bed.

Through tears, she decides to visit Tebor and Madhiva tonight.

Chapter Twenty-Nine
Tuesday, 11:55 pm

Sam lights another cigarette as he slides the cell phone into his pocket three blocks from his former residence. *Fucked that up, royal,* he thinks, slamming a palm against a brick wall. His life wasn't getting any simpler. It had become increasingly complicated since his split from Tess.

The trench coat collar pulled up and wearing a hat low on his forehead, Sam looks like a man in hiding. A situation involving an old friend, a 'sure thing,' and a payday that would see them packing their bags for a comfortable life in the Caribbean had backfired, leaving him and Jorge very vulnerable.

Sam had heard that the people they'd double-crossed had already sent local toughs to Jorge's brother's bar in search of them. He'd also heard that Charlie gave them a beatdown. He thinks *That wouldn't be good for Charlie in the long run.*

Sam turns and cuts through the park, returning to Jorge's girlfriend's place, where they had been hiding out the past few days. They had no cash and knew not to use debit or credit for fear of the Molloys hearing about it. The Molloys, or The Molloy Group, as they are known in the business world, also managed a very aggressive hold on the black market, where Jorge's plan first took flight.

Sam and Jorge are virtually penniless now. He'd figured he would be hiding out on an island somewhere sipping Margaritas, not stealing around his old neighborhood, afraid to show his face.

Jesus, how had it all gone so wrong? It's a question he's been asking himself since the failed transaction: standing in an empty warehouse with his friend and a guy Jorge had just shot in the chest, shuddering on the polished concrete, laboring over his last breath.

Jorge was no sharpshooter, and the two of them followed the man as he slid slowly on his back in a futile attempt to escape his fate. Jorge was hesitant to fire again while Sam, trapped in a trance, stared into the desperate man's eyes. The dying man's lids fell heavier and heavier with each blink until they no longer opened, and his retreat ceased. Before they could grab the satchel filled with the supposed money from the dead man's grip, three of the Molloy men rushed into the warehouse, and the two friends fled.

Arriving at Jorge's girlfriend's, Sam stops short of rounding the sidewalk, stepping back behind a bush to see two men questioning the woman outside her home. He breaks into a cold sweat and crouches down, steadying himself, placing his palms on the cement.

Sam watches through the bushes as Donna nods at the men, a blank stare on her face. The men look at each other, direct her back into the house, and follow.

Sam wants to call out to her, yell for the police, and save her somehow. Was Jorge inside? He waits to hear gunshots or some sign of a struggle from within but hears nothing. He decides to approach the house, pulling a knife from his pocket.

Chapter Thirty
Wednesday, 12:01 am

In Tebor's room, Tess picks up the distinct scent of ginger and cinnamon. His room is no larger than hers but has an extra chair borrowed from the cafeteria.

"Tess, this is Madhiva." Tebor steps aside to reveal a small woman seated on his bed. She is East Indian and wearing the same purple linen uniform the nurses wore.

"Hello," Tess says apprehensively.

"Hello, Tess," Madhiva replies, her voice quiet, her accent hailing from northern India. The woman gets up and walks the short distance to shake Tess's hand.

"Please." Madhiva gestures for her to sit on the bed, and she does. The small woman takes the empty chair to the right of the bed. "You're new here."

"Yes."

"After Tebor mentioned you, I had a look through your files. I hope that's alright."

"I'm not here to hide anything from anyone."

"Good, you have an open mind then. You should take very easily to hypnosis."

"I've done it twice now with Doctor Samuelsson. Weird what I can remember from my childhood."

"Imagine how incredible it will be to remember things from another life." She gestures toward Tebor's direction, her actions slow and purposeful. "He recognizes you. I do not. You and I may be meeting for the first time where Tebor claims to have known you in virtually every life he has lived."

"Well, I'm game for anything if it will make me better, I mean, feel better."

"Do you know what it is to be human?" Madhiva looks from Tess to Tebor, standing at the end of the bed. He takes this as his cue to speak.

"We're here to learn, given the same opportunities today as we were in our past lives. Those who travel with us in each life are spirits we can learn from, either by wronging or offering kindness to one another. These actions create our next reality until we have understood our purpose and stop the cycle."

"I've never given it much thought," Tess admits. "It seems so off-center to believe in something like reincarnation."

Madhiva leans forward and rests a palm on Tess's knee. "I am offering you an opportunity to explore this possibility."

"But the doctor already performs hypnosis on me."

"He will never regress you far enough," Madhiva explains.

"How far are we talking here? A hundred years?"

"However many years it takes, hundreds, thousands."

"Thousands," Tess repeats shakily.

"Your spirit remembers everything," Tebor says, sitting on the corner of his bed. "Do you have a fear of anything? Spiders, or snakes, or flying, for example?"

"Being buried alive scares the shit out of me."

"Good, that's good. Then you have something we can work with." Tebor eyes Madhiva and urges her on.

"One of the great opportunities of past life regression is that we can locate the life that gave you this fear and, by understanding what happened to you in that lifetime, free you of the phobia." Madhiva removes her hand from Tess's knee.

"I wouldn't call it a phobia. I mean, it's not like I am actually afraid it will happen. It's just this eerie feeling that comes over me when I think about it."

"Do you think about it often?"

"Not particularly. I try not to get myself into tight spots where I might feel trapped or become stuck or anything."

"Has it ever taken hold of you and made you freeze in terror?"

"When I was ten," she nods. "I was touring these caves with my classmates on a school trip, and one of the caves became a narrow tunnel, and kids were approaching from both ends. I panicked. I tried to move forward, but the kids weren't deterred and kept coming; I turned back, and more were entering from that end. I was certain I would die there." Tess shudders. "It was horrifying."

"Would you like to understand why you have this fear and overcome it?"

"It's never interfered with my life."

"Let me put it another way," Tebor says, putting a hand up to stop Madhiva. "Would you like to know your purpose in this life?"

Purpose. This word sticks in Tess's throat like a fishbone. Purpose was everything to Tess up until a few weeks ago. She saw purpose in everything she did and every decision she made. She was here now because she had watched her whole life crumble around her and, with it, any purpose Tess thought she had in the world.

"Yes." Tess looks at Madhiva. "Purpose, I want to know my purpose."

Chapter Thirty-One
Wednesday, 12:05 am

Sam resigns to whatever fate awaits him as he approaches Donna's front door. The six-inch blade in his hand offers little comfort as he considers what hardware the men he's about to confront must be packing. All the same, Sam is stoic now, and if he waits, he may lose his nerve.

At the door, his cell phone rings in his pocket. Startled, Sam rolls over the railing and tumbles into the brush below. He scrambles for the phone and pushes the talk button. Before answering, he listens for the door to open. It doesn't.

"Hello?" he whispers.

"Sam?" It's Jorge's voice on the other end.

"Yeah."

"Buddy, they know we've been crashing at Donna's."

"I'm here now, and two guys just went into the house."

"What are you going to do?" His voice is cold and distant.

"What do you mean? I'm going to help her."

"Good, Sam. Help her. I'm dead already."

* * * * *

Jorge hangs up and addresses his brother seated across from him. "It's done."

Charlie rounds the beat-up gray metal desk and sits at its edge. "I did this for you, Jorgie," Charlie tells his baby brother. Jorge's head falls forward, a pang of terrible guilt settling in. Charlie had managed to make peace with The Molloys, blaming the violence on his brother's friend and offering him up as a gift. The Molloys paid no mind to his attack on the locals they'd sent to intimidate Charlie. What good were thugs if they were on the wrong side of a beating?

"Hey." Charlie lifts his brother's head with a hand under his chin. Jorge doesn't resist. "He ain't no saint, Jorgie."

"That don't make it right, Chuck. This is *my* fuck-up, and he's going to pay for it."

"Would you rather it were you at Donna's right now?" Jorge shakes his head.

"You told me the truth, right? Sam shot Molloy's man and not you, right?"

His little brother nods again, his head falling back to his chest. Charlie stands and lays a hand on his brother's shoulder.

"You're what matters to me, Jorgie. You get past the guilt, and thank God you have me as your big brother."

Charlie heads for his office, a bottle of scotch in his hand to put his conscience to bed.

"Stay here, sleep here, and don't you dare leave here until I tell you."

Chapter Thirty-Two
Wednesday, 12:15 am

Sam's not sure he should wait much longer. After just ten minutes, his legs are becoming numb.

He wonders briefly if he should flee the scene. But Donna had helped him; she'd housed and fed him and Jorge, and now her life is in danger. Sam couldn't just walk away. Jorge didn't sound very optimistic on the phone, and Sam hoped he could elude the Molloys after tonight.

He trusts his friend, and when Jorge introduced him to Sharon, the woman who seduced him into leaving his wife, he confided in his friend his feelings for her. Jorge backed him up, encouraging him to leave his family for a better and easier life, so the plan came to light.

The past week has been devastating for Sam. Having satisfied her morbid curiosity about whether she could break up a marriage, Sharon has left him. That was bad enough, he thought, but then for Jorge's plan to go south? Sam feels he has reached a crossroads.

With perhaps another ten minutes to live, Sam decides to make his move, help Donna, and die if that will make him a better man. He is full of regret and missing his wife and little girl. He feels like a failure on every level. Perhaps there is certain bravado going out like this, he thinks. Save the maiden, die in the act that may atone for his sins.

He gets to his feet slowly, climbs the railing, and silently opens the screen door. Inside, he hears Donna screaming in the basement. Sam wipes sweat with his shirt sleeve from his brow and starts down the stairs. As his foot settles on the top step, he is pushed the rest of the way. Sam tumbles down the wooden staircase, cracking this and snapping that along the way. When he lands on the cement floor, he sees Donna. She is seated in a folding chair, one of the men standing beside her.

"Donna," Sam manages, eyes flickering from the throbbing pain in his leg. The dim light of the basement mixes with tears, blurring everything together.

"I'm sorry, Sam," Donna tells him. "I'm so sorry."

Sam doesn't understand her apology at first, but as he watches her stand and head up the stairs, stepping over his broken body, the big picture takes form.

Realizing what was happening, Sam's expression makes the trip from sorrow to hate to defeat. His life is forfeit. Jorge had played him. He runs an internal diagnostic of his injuries from the fall, hoping he might have a fighting chance, but he can barely move his arms, and his left leg is undoubtedly broken. The smooth surface he's lying on slides under his head as he looks about the room. He is splayed out at the base of the wooden staircase on a large plastic tarp.

"I didn't," he pleads with the men as they close in on him. "I'm not the one."

Sam's body is carefully rolled into the tarp as though he were already dead. Helpless to escape, he fights to breathe in the plastic cocoon as the tape is liberally applied to the tarp, turning him over and over like a rotisserie.

What purpose have I served? He wonders. *What point was there in any of it?*

Heavy black bags are fitted over the wrapped plastic, leaving him in complete darkness. He asks for mercy but is offered none. He thinks about Tess and Emma. He sees them in his mind's eye, smiling back at him from their couch. Tess picks up his infant daughter's arm at the wrist and waves to him as he steps out of the apartment. He reads his wife's lips as she tells him: *we love you*. His heart soars at the memory and then falls heavy in his stomach at the realization that he would never again look into their eyes, touch their porcelain skin, or kiss their pretty faces.

This sadness is quickly overcome by a sense of well-being, enveloping Sam in the knowledge that he loves his family, a question he thought he'd answered in the arms of another woman, another life. He was so wrong, he thinks. But rather than embracing the sadness, Sam encourages the love as he reflects on his life with Tess: their first kiss, first date, first apartment, and then to Emma: her birth, feedings, his visits to her room to watch her sleep. The pain in his leg retreats, the anger in his heart falls away, and his regrets, though many, are forgotten.

Bats come down hard and in quick succession, breaking bones and crushing Sam's skull, ending this life in violence amidst his revelation of love.

Chapter Thirty-Three
Wednesday, 7:45 am

Leaning against her headboard, Tess feels anxious at the prospect of learning about her past lives. What if she hates the person she once was? What if she were a serial killer? It sounds like the stuff of horror movies. She has reservations. How can one soul inhabit more than one body or identity? Was this concept really more challenging to grasp than the idea of the one God she'd been raised with?

A knock at her door makes Tess snap out of her reverie. At the entrance stands Tebor with a package under his arm. Tess invites him in, leaving the door ajar.

"So," he begins. "Will you see Madi tonight?" Tess questions who *Madi* is with her expression and Tebor answers. "Madhiva, sorry. She'll go by Madi."

Tess nods. "I think so." She walks to her bed and sits, curious about what Tebor is holding. "What have you got there?"

"Oh, this?" he says, feigning forgetfulness. He pulls the package out from under his arm and sets it carefully on Tess's bed. "It's yours."

"What do you mean it's mine? Is this another riddle?"

"It may act more like an answer." Tebor looks thoughtfully at her, his wild hair still sticking straight up. She wonders if he'd let her cut it.

"Okay." Tess reaches for the package. Tebor bends to meet her hand and holds it a moment in his.

"I'm having a bit of a crisis of conscience about this gift, truth be told." He sits on the bed between Tess and the gift. "I'm not sure if I should tell you the story first, let you read it on your own, or just take it back."

"Well, you can't have it back," Tess insists light-heartedly. "You said it's for me; you said it's mine." She shakes her head. "Is it a book?"

Tebor hands it to Tess.

"Yes, it is a book of poetry written by a young man nearly two centuries ago. This is one of maybe twenty copies left from the original print. It was not a popular book in its time and was never reprinted. But I tell you, it's yours to read if you wish."

Tess carefully unties the twine, folding back the brittle paper. A shock of recognition strikes her as the cover is revealed. What looks like an engraving, a woodcut illustration adorns the front. The book's title, An Unfinished Life, is within the cover image.

"It's beautiful, Tebor. Why are you giving this to me?"

"We'll discuss that once you've read it. When you've completed the book, I wonder if *you* won't be able to tell me why I've given it to you." He smiles and leaves. Tess places the book gently on her bedside table and, noticing the time, showers and dresses for her session with Doctor Samuelsson.

Chapter Thirty-Four
Wednesday, 8:45 am

En route to her appointment, Tess calls to check up on Emma.

"Everything is fine, dear, nothing to report but a happy little girl." Her mother sounds tired today. Tess hopes she can hold out for the full ten days.

"That's great, Mom, just what I needed to hear. Thanks."

"We're taking Emma to the mall this afternoon. You know the big one they renovated a few years ago, on the west end? I have a flyer here that says they opened a new coffee shop in the food court, and I think we'll try it. Well, your father can't have any, but they have fruit smoothies, sandwiches, and so on, too."

"Okay, Mom." Tess chokes back a chuckle, never really ready for the detailed descriptions her mother presents. "Have fun, keep Emma safe."

"Of course. Be well, bye."

Tess hangs up as she knocks on the doctor's door. She hesitates a moment before knocking again. Looking at her watch, she confirms the time. As she's unrolling the itinerary from her jeans pocket, the door swings open in front of her.

"Sorry, Tess," the doctor apologizes. "Just finishing up a report." He waves her in, motioning to the corner lounge. He seems flustered, walking in quick, short steps, seemingly confused about what he should do first.

Tess sits on the leather couch. "Everything alright?"

"Perfectly fine," he assures her, sitting in his oversized chair. "Just a little out of sorts this morning."

"Should I come back?"

Michael Poeltl

"No, no, I'm fine." He waves away her concern. "Too much coffee, I think!" He laughs uncomfortably and reaches for his clipboard. "Now then, let's begin, shall we?"

Tess lays down, her neck resting on a stiff cylindrical pillow, allowing her head to tilt back, releasing any strain on her neck. She feels comfortable and ready to begin.

Once under the doctor's spell, she finds herself in her brother's room the night she'd overheard her parents talking about Tommy's teacher.

"He's crying into his teddy bear. What's wrong with him, anyway?"

"What *is* wrong with him? Do you ask him?"

"No, he's too sad. I don't recognize him like this. He's really different. Not himself. He'll get over whatever it is, and then it will be like before."

"Do you really believe that?"

"No," Tess replies. "Something is wrong. He's picking at his bear, pulling the stuffing out of it. He loves that bear."

"Where is the hole he's made located on the bear?"

"Between its legs, at the seam," Tess confirms the doctor's fears.

"Tess, I want you to go forward to when you overheard your parents talking again. It should have something to do with Tommy and Mr. Drummond."

"I'm not there. That doesn't happen again. I can't see that."

"Okay, go to the morning of your brother's suicide. I want you to tell me what's happening."

"Breakfast: poached eggs. Mom spreads butter over toast at the counter, and Dad works in the garage. It's Saturday. I'm excited about cartoons. Tommy should be, too, but he's not. He's not eating breakfast, and Mom is sitting with him now, kissing his head and lifting his fork to his lips. He isn't eating anything."

"Remember, you're only twelve years old, a child yourself. Whatever happens to Tommy is not something you could have prevented. No one is to blame for this but Mr. Drummond. Not you, not your parents, not Tommy. The decision was Mr. Drummond's alone."

Tess is nodding as tears run down her cheeks. "Not our fault," she says.

"Tess, I want you to remember how you feel now, that you blame no one for your brother's death; he was a baby, you were a child, and your parents did the best they could. Feel relief that you don't have to blame yourself or your parents anymore for Tommy's death. There was nothing you could have done. Remember only this."

Tess pulls out of the trance and sighs heavily. She wipes the tears from her face.

"How do you feel?"

"A little better," she tells him, rubbing her eyes. "I like coming here." She laughs and cries all at once. "Not sure why I'm crying! But oh well."

He smiles back at Tess with his kind eyes, shaking his head.

"We will do wonders with you in a few days. More was discovered today where your brother is concerned, and I promise you, I will reveal it all very soon."

"Thank you." Tess stands and walks to the door. "See you at four."

* * * * *

Samuelsson wrestled with whether he would allow Tess to remember her brother's desecration of the bear or wait until he had more to work from, proof and evidence of Drummond's criminal behavior. These cases, like others of their nature, become unprofessionally important to him. Call it vigilante justice, but Samuelsson would use every resource available to him to find Drummond and flush him out as the predator he was.

Left with an hour to himself between sessions, Samuelsson sits behind his desk and opens his laptop. On the screen, an image of Mr. Drummond flickers to life.

Chapter Thirty-Five
Wednesday, 10:00 am

Mr. Edward Christopher Drummond. His staff photo in an online PDF version of the grade school's 1998 yearbook comes to life on Dr. Samuelsson's computer screen.

The doctor continues the digging he had begun this morning. He had been excited to have found the man Tess identified as Tommy's predator and came off as a bit jumpy to his patient. With an hour to perform more detailed searches with the man's full name, the doctor's excitement escalates. Tracking down Drummond should prove simple now with Samuelsson's contacts at the police station, where he volunteers his time to shell-shocked cops.

Curiously, Drummond does not appear in any yearbooks after '98, nor has he popped up in other school-related searches. Then, a local article featuring missing persons surfaces. Drummond is named and briefly glazed over as 'currently missing.' This news article dates back to the winter of 1999.

This information prompts Samuelsson to pick up his phone and dial his contact at the station.

"It's Doctor Samuelsson," he tells the man on the other end. "I need information on an Edward Christopher Drummond, local man, missing since 1999."

"My pleasure, Karl." The familiar voice is as agreeable as ever. "Can I get back to you with that information? It may be a little while."

"That's fine, Donald, but I'd appreciate it by the end of the day if possible."

"Got a hot lead on your couch, do you?" Donald asks light-heartedly.

"Could be this man is a pedophile, Don, and I need to know if he's still available for questioning."

"So the usual then, Doc?"

"The usual."

"I'll get back to you ASAP with that information." The line goes dead, and Samuelsson hangs up. It's been a common request from the doctor to the station over his tenure practicing hypnosis on patients. The horrors he's discovered hidden in people's subconscious due to another's cruel intentions brought out the requiter in him. He's had twelve successful criminal convictions from his partnership with the department, bringing information to the police so they could gather the evidence.

Solving the case of Tommy Seager's suicide would be a great victory for Tess. What information he has kept from her already is enough to make her understand that her role in her brother's death was non-existent, but for her to truly heal, and perhaps her parents as well, he knows he needs to find Drummond, have him questioned, broken and thrown in jail. Once the man is in custody, he will fund an announcement asking for former students of Drummonds to come forward, canvasing the yearbook alums, and building an army of witnesses to tell their stories.

It is discouraging to Samuelsson that Drummond had disappeared, though. Without his confession, it would be much more difficult to prove what a monster he was, and people generally don't like to talk ill of the dead or missing. Perhaps the canvassing should start now, Karl thinks.

Chapter Thirty-Six
Wednesday, 2:00 pm

Tess wakes from a nap mid-afternoon with a start. Someone is knocking on her door. She clears her throat and rubs her eyes.

"Yes?" she calls out.

"It's Tebor. Can I come in?"

Tebor, she thinks, *of course, it's Tebor.* She doesn't have a lot of other people on the inside vying for her attention. She gets up and opens the door.

Tebor has - what could be described as a shit-eating grin on his face, which makes Tess smile.

"Hello again," she greets him with sleepy eyes.

"So? Did you read it? Did you like it?" Tebor looks past her at the book. Tess turns around to target his gaze.

"Oh, yes, well, I read a poem. It was beautiful. But then I fell asleep." Tess points at her unmade bed. Tebor looks past her at the book resting on the night table.

"I thought you would have devoured it all by now!"

"I'm not a speed reader, and it's poetry; you don't just power through poetry."

Tebor sits on the corner chair. "So, you liked it? The poem?"

"I loved it. So much thought goes into writing like that. It hits you in places you didn't know existed. It's like he lived it on purpose to put in prose what it's like to experience something like that and then relate it to the masses. A true artist, he agonized over that poem so we could understand suffering."

Tebor smiles. "Very astute."

She smiles shyly at the praise. "I'm no English major, but I have read a lot and appreciate writing like that. She peers down at the tattered volume. "There's something to this book, some reason you wanted me to have it."

Tebor is grinning again. "Well, I suspect you will make the connection once you've had more time with it." Tebor gets up and moves to leave. "Oh," he says, turning. "Were you still interested in working with Madi tonight in my room?"

"I'm still a little nervous over it, to be honest. I'm worried about what I might see."

Tebor steps back into the room and closes the door behind him. He sits at the end of the bed and leans in towards her.

"It's nothing to be afraid of, Tess. Knowing gives us power, and understanding offers us forgiveness and healing. It allows us to move forward in this life with renewed purpose."

Here it was again, that word which held such power over her: *purpose.* She has longed for it since Sam had left, her idea of a family no longer what it was, her view of her place in the world no longer clear.

"I love that idea, I do, but I'm much more guarded than I appear. I don't do things like this." She waves her hands. "I don't run off to find myself. I've never meditated, done yoga, or even sat quietly in a corner without a good book. Maybe it's the *idea* of knowing that is keeping me scared."

"Wonderful!" Tebor claps his hands. "You see, all you needed was someone to discuss your fears. You already know the answer." He taps his index finger against his temple. "We all know exactly what to do whenever there is a question of doubt. Now, you need to answer that doubt with action. Come, see Madhiva tonight, and let's get you back on the path that brought you here."

Tess nods.

He looks at his watch and points at the alarm clock. "Nearly time for your four o'clock with the doctor. Let Samuelsson take care of your marriage; Madi will offer you purpose."

Chapter Thirty-Seven
Wednesday, 4:00 pm

Karl has not heard back from the station on his inquiry and is becoming impatient. After his session with Tess this afternoon, he contemplates a drive to see his friend Donald.

Tess arrives on time and lies on Karl's couch, assuming the position. Once she is relaxed, the doctor puts her under. This time, Samuelsson takes her back to a few months after her brother's suicide.

"It's been one year since your brother's death. You've been going to a counselor all this time. Tell me what form the therapy takes; how does the counselor approach you?"

"She is very nice. I like her hair very much, and she has kind eyes."

"Okay, and what does she say to you?"

"She's telling me I've done well and should be proud of myself."

"Okay, let's go back a month. I would like to know the techniques she's using on you. Find yourself back -"

"Oh my God!" Tess yells, inching her way up the couch. Doctor Samuelsson almost jumps out of his chair.

"What's happening? Where are you?"

"I - I'm looking out the window. What are they doing?" Tess frowned and shook her head back and forth. "Why are they doing that?"

"What do you see?"

"A hole in the ground. There's a hole in the ground, a hole in the ground, there's a -"

Karl snaps his fingers, and Tess falls into a deep sleep. This is the default suggestion he plants in every patient should they suffer a distressing incident. He isn't sure how she's found her way here, but the event was traumatic enough to want to be remembered. He wonders whether this is something she can recall with her waking mind or something she's buried in her unconscious.

"Tess, you are floating through the atmosphere; you are light, happy, and calm."

She licks her lips, and Doctor Samuelsson watches as her eyebrows scrunch into the center of her forehead.

"Tess, you are happy. You are calm." He tries to relax her further. "I would like to discuss the hole in the ground with you."

He watches now as her chest rises and falls in rapid succession, her breathing bordering on hyperventilation. He decides he has to bring her back. "How do you feel?"

"The hole in the ground," she murmurs. The doctor waits to hear her out. "Why do I remember a hole in the ground?"

"That is something we will work towards understanding tomorrow. Until then, perhaps you will be able to shed some light on it as related memories trickle in."

"It feels like I don't want to remember that," Tess says, still looking fearful.

"That is for your unconscious to decide now. Though it may be a difficult event to experience again, I do not doubt it will free you of a demon that has lived within you more than half your life."

Tess is upset by the emotions this vision has produced. Why the hole in the ground? She was looking through her bedroom window at it. That meant the hole was in the backyard of her childhood home. Seated on the lounge, she looks abruptly up at Doctor Samuelsson.

"It's in my backyard."

"What is?"

"The hole."

Chapter Thirty-Eight
Wednesday, 5:00 pm

Tess moves slowly through the hall, the image of a hole in the ground flashing in her mind's eye each time she blinks. It's not the image that upsets her so much as the related sense of dread attached to it.

She feels a panic attack coming on and picks up her pace, hoping to exhaust the burst of adrenaline activated by the misfiring fight or flight response in her brain.

"Shit, shit, shit," she says as she speed walks past room after room until she reaches her own. Swinging the door open, she bends to her knees and lays flat on the floor. Push-ups, she decides, will assist in burning the useless adrenaline.

After over forty, Tess is exhausted, face flushed, and muscles aching. She practices her breathing next, sitting up with her legs crossed. She had learned this combination in a class at the hospital on coping with panic attacks or panic disorder.

Once her breathing levels out and her skin stops tingling, Tess stands and opens her door to allow air from the hallway to rush in.

"So unfair," she reminds herself. Then, the book Tebor had presented to her earlier this morning caught her eye. She has always been an avid reader but, since her separation, has lost interest in the practice. Something about this book, maybe its cover, title, or smell, sparked a hidden memory; she couldn't place it, making it all the more enticing.

Closing the door, she settles on her bed and picks the book up. Studying the illustration, she follows the lines of the woodcut print with her fingers. She brings the book to her face and breathes in its scent. How could she experience a connection to a book she's never known?

Opening it, Tess slowly turns one page after another, skimming the content, a book of cantos and poems from the mind of a young man nearly two hundred years earlier. Books amazed Tess. Their relevance to the present day was often not tainted by time; humans experienced the same emotions and opportunities for better or worse today just as they did a thousand years ago - or at least the significant ones.

Blindly choosing a page, excitement builds in Tess as she reads the first stanza in a poem of twenty. It is not obscure, for which she is thankful. It eloquently tells a story of a life lost in another's. A life unlived for its own sake - offered in sacrifice to another. Love can do that, but it is often an unrequited love that gives and gives with no thought of its own happiness. The question at the end is whether the life of servitude to love is enough. The poem strikes a chord in her. She wipes a tear from her cheek.

An illustration of the author and his name adorns the back page. Tess spends a considerable time looking at the man's face, getting lost in his features, unconsciously taking on the man's grim expression.

She lays the book on her lap as she revisits the poem. Closing her eyes, she lays flat on her bed. Within a few minutes, she is asleep.

Wednesday, 6:15 pm

After a long shower, Tess goes to the cafeteria. She picks a salad and a little baked ham and mashed potatoes there. She wonders if she could have snuck a bottle or two of wine in to enjoy with dinner and immediately dismisses the thought.

"Hi," says a young man behind her. She shifts to see whether the greeting is meant for her. It's Paul, the cutter, standing with a tray of food. "Is it okay if I sit with you?" He turns briefly to address his escort, and Tess watches as the large man nods for him to go ahead and sit.

"Please. How have you been?"

"Still here," he says, sitting down, leaving a chair between them. "So I guess I'm not cured!" A forced laugh from both Tess and Paul falls into an uncomfortable silence.

"Hey, are you doing any hypnosis?" Tess asks, taking a small mouthful of salad.

"No, that would be cool, though. Are you?"

Tess nods. "It's fascinating but can dredge up memories you didn't even know you had."

"That's cool. So, did you find out that you're like, Mr. Hyde or something?"

"I'd have to be a doctor first, wouldn't I?"

Paul smiles out of the corner of his mouth at her. Shaking his head, he goes back to poking at his food.

"You're really pretty, you know," he confesses. "You shouldn't think you're not."

"Well, we all have our obstacles, don't we?"

"There, like that's what I mean. You should be able to accept a compliment. You should say *thank you* and appreciate someone who thinks you're prettier than you do."

Tess straightens her back and pushes her head up high on her neck, chest out. She turns to Paul, who has returned to staring at his plate. Sucking in her cheeks, fluttering her eyelashes, and pushing out her chin, Tess assumes the posture of a beauty queen.

"I'm actually all for world peace. I love puppies and chocolate, and I believe women and men are *not* the same but equal. Everyone deserves the opportunity to be the *best* they can *be*. Blah, blah, blah, me, me, me..."

Paul watches, smiling widely. "You've been on the pageant circuit," he says.

Tess drops the façade and laughs with him. "No, I've watched a lot of TV lately, though, and there's no shortage of pageants."

"My mom has my little sister in those. It's messed up. I've been to a couple to help out."

"No kidding?" Tess remembers Paul's sister from the first time she had visited the hospital. While his parents looked on, She played with another little girl at the window.

"Yeah, some of those mothers are brutal. My mom does it because Lori, my sister, begged her to put her in them."

"Well, at least she's not forcing her into anything she doesn't enjoy."

"Is that why you're here? Because your parents forced you into something?"

"Who's the undercover shrink now?" she smiles. She likes Paul; she feels he's becoming good company. His being a teenager, she sympathizes with the difficult position he must be in. She wasn't exactly the class president in her teens, but Paul's disorder, acne, and tall, thin frame must make him an easy target.

Tess decides to pay him a compliment.

"You know, Paul, you're very handsome. If I were twelve years younger..."

Paul laughs nervously. His pimpled face burns a bright crimson.

"You should smile more, too. Your teeth are perfect!" Tess feels encouraged by the warmth building in her chest. "And are you more than six feet? You know women will be calling you tall, dark, and handsome the rest of your life with that thick head of black hair."

Paul can't stop smiling and giggling, shaking his head, his face contorting into an agonized grimace.

"What's the matter? Can't take a compliment? Who are you, *me*?"

He laughs louder now, tears building in the corners of his eyes. Tess smiles at him, but noticing the pained expression on his face growing increasingly intense, she leans in to place a reassuring hand on his shoulder. The orderly at the next table stands.

Suddenly, Paul reveals a small scalpel hidden in his bandage, still laughing uproariously. Tess's eyes widened at the sight of it, and before she could react, Paul acted.

Chapter Thirty-Nine
Wednesday, 6:30 pm

Charlie sits in darkness, his brother asleep on his couch after they'd drained a bottle of his special reserve. Jorge is having difficulty dealing with his betrayal of Sam, but Charlie knows his brother and expects a full recovery within a week.

What's keeping Charlie up are thoughts of Tess and how she might react to the untimely death of her husband and the father of her daughter and whether or not it was his place to tell her. The poor girl, he thinks, has been through so much already that this might kill her.

He struggles to stand, his head full of scotch. He's never been ruled by his conscience, but he finds he has one in light of his recent decisions.

Regardless, if he told Tess what he knew, she may go to the police. He couldn't put her in that kind of danger. No one was to know of this, he decides; the repercussions could be disastrous.

"Better left unsaid," he tells himself, holding the picture of Tess from six years earlier in his fingers. Charlie looks down at his brother, lit by a street light through the blinds of his back alley office, sleeping silently on the ragged couch. He bends down to stroke his brother's hair, remembering their childhood. It was always difficult remembering his past; both his mother and father were raging alcoholics. Charlie had always looked after Jorge and would look after him now. If he didn't, his whole life was for nothing. Jorge was his life, stupid, gullible, weak, Jorgie. Who was he if not his brother's keeper, he thinks?

Then, a sobering thought forces him to his feet. Sam would have had his identification on him. *What if the Molloys thought to investigate? What if they learned of Tess? What if they thought she was involved in Sam and Jorge's plan?* Charlie had not thought this through nearly enough and ground his teeth at the thought of a Molloy laying a hand on Tess or her daughter.

He moves to his desk and types: Tess Seager - phone number, into the search engine on his computer. He finds an S. and T. Seager in a neighborhood where he knows Sam had an apartment and dials the number.

Chapter Forty
Wednesday, 6:55 pm

At Tess's apartment, the phone rings while her mother, Celeste, cooks at the new gas range. Her hands are in heavy oven mitts, and she struggles with a pan holding an eight-pound chicken.

"Are you going to get that, Doug?" she yells to her husband, who has just emerged from the baby's room after rocking her to sleep. He likes to follow his daughter's scheduled nap times for Emilia and makes a point of not giving in even when Emma fusses.

"I'll get it," Doug replies, walking from the bedroom to the couch. Picking up the receiver, he says, "Hello?"

"Oh, uh, hi, is this Tess Seager's house?" The voice on the other end sounds surprised. Her father realizes Tess's friends may not know she is taking a hiatus at the hospital and is unsure how to explain that or if he should.

"This is her father, Doug. We're watching the house for a couple of weeks. Tess has gone on vacation."

Charlie is caught off guard.

"Um, hello, sir," he stutters. "Is there another way I could get a hold of her? It's very important I speak with her."

"I'm not sure there is. Can I take a message?"

Charlie considers this as perhaps his only recourse. He remembers Tess's parents from her wedding. Good people. It would be on his head now if anything happened to them. Then something else occurs to him; her daughter is probably with Tess's parents.

"Did she go alone? I mean, on vacation. You're looking after the baby?" Charlie couldn't remember her daughter's name if ever he knew it.

"Yes, she's gone away on her own. Her mother and I are here with Emma. Did you want to leave a message then?"

An audible groan leaves Charlie's lips. "If I leave you a message, will you be able to deliver it for me soon?"

"I think so."

"Thank you. Please have her call Charlie. I'll leave you my number. She can call me day or night. I must hear from her soon, sir."

Doug senses the urgency in the man's voice and agrees to take down the number. Charlie repeats the digits twice and asks her father to read them back. He hopes she will call as soon as she hears.

"Who was it, dear?" Celeste asks, removing her mitts and sitting at the island, sipping a Chardonnay.

Doug sits on the couch and shakes his head. "Charlie," he offers. "A friend with a message. Do you think we should call Tess and let her know?"

"What was the message?"

"Just to call him."

"Let's wait until she calls to check on Emilia again. Too many interruptions might upset her therapy."

Doug shrugs and picks up the TV remote. He tunes into the weather channel and watches as a hurricane threatens to terrorize the east coast.

Chapter Forty-One
Wednesday, 7:00 pm

They unwrap Sam's body at a site where his remains will be incinerated. Two men tasked with Sam's case removed his clothing and sniped off the tips of his fingers. They remove most of his teeth, cut out his eyes, and peel away any skin harboring a tattoo. This is all done meticulously and with the proficiency of a surgeon.

The act is ritualistic more than it is practical. They will cremate the body regardless at the funeral home, one of many owned by the Molloy Group.

As is customary, those assigned a task like this will destroy all identifying documents on the body. Contents of the wallet, rings, jewelry, glasses, phone, etc. But before they do all that, they will research the victim's personal life. Check each line of text on his phone, run through every contact, and investigate whomever this person may have spoken to recently.

In the basement of the O'Connor funeral home, one of the men, Seamus, shows the printout of Sam's address book to the younger man, Ryan, as the cardboard box containing Sam's mangled body rolls into the furnace.

"Well, we know about Jorgie; he gets a pass, and Sam's girlfriend who left him, I doubt she knows anything. He hasn't said boo to all these others in the last month, no siblings, no parents, no family. But this woman, Tess -"

"I like her name," Ryan admits, and Seamus offers a caustic smile, revealing yellow teeth. "I'll just bet she's a looker too."

"Well, whoever she is to him, he's called her more than once since things went bad for him."

"Look here," says Ryan, tapping at the printout. "There's her cell and a home phone. Easier to pay her a visit?"

"Reverse look up her number and get the address. Let us see if she's busy for supper tonight."

Seamus and Ryan laugh as the fires burn brightly through the small window of the oven beside them. The two men exit the basement with Sam's possessions placed in a separate oven and left to burn.

* * * * *

Charlie's frantic, pacing the bar. Jorge watches as the weight of responsibility overwhelms him.

"So, what can we do? Sam shouldn't have died for this, and Tess, Jesus, she's got a baby."

"Yeah, thanks, I know that. But Tess's on vacation, and all I can do is leave messages with her parents." He stops pacing, looks at his brother, and blames his choices on the blind love he feels for him. Why didn't he consider the repercussions? Why didn't he send them both away until this mess blew over? *Because it would never blow over.* Suddenly, a eureka moment appears on Charlie's face.

"You have a plan!" Jorge sits up and watches as the idea takes shape in his older brother's head.

"Come on," he tells Jorge, rushing past him.

"Where to?"

Charlie collects the shotgun from behind the bar and fills his pockets with shells. He throws his keys to Jorge. "Get my car. We've got a date with destiny."

Chapter Forty-Two
Wednesday, 8:00 pm

At Tess's apartment, her parents are blissfully unaware of the approaching danger. Celeste serves dinner, and Doug feeds his granddaughter a helping of mashed potatoes. The conversation revolves around the baby and Tess.

"Did you know your Mommy misses you? Do you miss Mommy?" Emma nods at both questions, smiling brightly up at him.

The buzzer sounds. Tess's parents look at one another quizzically. No one had rung the door since they'd been here.

"Well, might as well see who it is," her father says, moving from his chair to the door. Pushing the speaker button, he says, "Who's there?"

"It's Charlie, sir, we spoke earlier. Tess's friend with a message."

"Oh, yes, hello. Uh, we haven't heard from Tess since, but I'll tell her to call you as soon as I can." He looks back at Celeste and shrugs. "Determined fellow."

* * * * *

Outside, Charlie can't decide how he'll get across the imminent danger they're in without sounding crazy. Then he notices two men in the near distance moving towards Tess's apartment building. The streets are empty otherwise. Adrenaline floods his system. He taps Jorge on the arm and signals that they move off to the side.

"Light a cigarette or something, Jorgie, and hide your face."

Jorge obeys. As he lights the match, he turns away from the approaching men, escaping the wind. Charlie draws the weapon beneath his pea coat and aims it at the men.

"Your names!" Charlie demands in his most menacing voice, careful not to stutter.

"Oh, look at this, Seamus, we're being robbed," Ryan sneers. "Why don't you take that gun and shove it up your arse?"

"Names," Charlie repeats.

"Well, you know mine now." Seamus sends a thumb over his shoulder. "He's Ryan."

"What's your business here?"

"Meeting a friend."

"Uh-huh, and what's the friend's name?" Charlie is waiting for the moment they tell him what he needs to know, to know for sure these are the Molloy men.

"The fuck is it to you?" Ryan tires of the questions. "Are we being robbed or not? You wanna see what's in my pocket?"

"Relax, I feel these boys ain't here for our money." Seamus steps forward and is now within five feet of Charlie. Jorge puts out his cigarette and rounds his brother.

"Who's sent you?" Seamus asks, a glint of recognition washing over him as he lays eyes on Jorge. Charlie picks up on this quickly and tightens his grip on the firearm.

"You never mind about that. What you're doing here is what matters to me."

"Identifying us is what matters to you. Why's that? Jorge knows who we are." He nods at the younger brother standing behind Charlie, and Jorge realizes his mistake in not obeying his older brother's advice. "You know who we work for, and so you know that if you don't put that gun away and get on home, you'll be dead by morning."

"I figure that's a given either way," Charlie says as he pulls the trigger. Seamus is pushed back a few feet, the gory wound in his abdomen exposing his guts as he falls away. This startles the other man long enough for Charlie to turn the gun on him and fire.

Ryan squeals as the shot severs his right hand from his wrist, taking a chunk of the thigh with it. Scrambling for his pistol, Ryan is shot a second time, his face blown away from his head. Jorge reacts by pulling Seamus to the ditch beside the building. Charlie does the same with Ryan.

"Dig through their pockets," Charlie tells his brother, breathlessly. "They must have her address on something."

Seamus gasps and reaches for Charlie. Charlie pushes his weak attempt at retribution away and covers the man's mouth and nose. Seamus convulses, choking on the blood collecting in his windpipe. Once silenced, Charlie finds what he's looking for.

"I have it," he says. "Take the phones as well."

Slinking away from the gruesome scene, the brothers rush into the night, blending into the city they know so well. Sirens are just blocks away. They scored a victory, Charlie thinks. The evidence is destroyed; the Molloys will have no other trails to lead them back to Tess and her family.

* * * * *

Tess's parents look curiously out the floor-to-ceiling window facing the street in the apartment. Doug tracks the police lights to Tess's building. More than one cruiser and six policemen surround the exterior.

"Poor Tess," Celeste whispers, joining her husband at the window. "Living in a place like this."

Chapter Forty-Three
Wednesday, 6:30 pm

The scalpel digs into the top of Paul's forearm, and he drags it down towards his hand. The cut is deep, and Tess screams. She stands, and the orderly who had been shadowing Paul rushes over. The man pulls the scalpel from his grip and tosses it to the floor.

Paul is shouting at Tess now, calling her a liar. She stands stunned at the surreal scene that has transpired from their pleasant dinner conversation.

Another and then another joins the orderly as they struggle to lay Paul flat. A nurse rushes into the melee and jabs the troubled teen with a needle. Paul almost immediately settles, and the nurse ties off the self-inflicted wound. She shouts orders at the men still holding Paul's jerking limbs, and they take him to the emergency room, leaving a puddle of blood on the floor where Tess crouches.

Tebor finds her crying amongst the gore a moment later, alerted to the event by the shouting. He bends down and picks her up.

"Is any of this blood yours?" She shakes her head. "Come with me," he tells her. She is in shock. Tebor walks her to her room and takes her to the washroom. He places her hands in the sink and turns on the tap. He notices the sleeves of her top and the knees of her pants are soaked in the boy's blood and suggests she change. Tess remains at the sink, allowing the warm water to run over her hands as Tebor rummages through her dresser for a new outfit. She avoids the mirror, staring at the pink water collecting in the sink.

"Tess?" She hears Tebor's voice but does not respond. "Let's get you cleaned up. Come on. I want you to change out of those clothes and into these. He lays the fresh clothing on the toilet seat.

"What the hell just happened?" she asks in a shaky voice, rinsing blood off her hands.

"The kid cut himself."

"But it was going so well."

"Not everything is as it seems."

"Why did he do that?"

"It's what he does. It's who he is."

Tess is shaking now, and looking in the mirror, she sees blood all over her top. She unzips the hoody and tears it off. Looking down at her jeans, she pulls the button fly apart and yanks them to her ankles, kicking them off. Tebor steps out of the bathroom and allows her the privacy to take a shower. She does.

When she reappears a few minutes later, Tebor is seated on her bed. She is embarrassed to see him there.

"I can leave if you'd rather," he offers, reading the surprise on her face.

"No, don't leave," she pleads. "I- I just need a moment longer."

Tebor nods and remains. Tess moves to the clock radio and turns it on to a music station. "I'm so tired of being wrong," she tells him. "I want to understand what it is I'm doing here." She sits next to Tebor. "I'm ready to see Madi."

Chapter Forty-Four
Thursday, 12:00 am

Midnight is announced in Tebor's room by a knock at the door. He answers it and invites Madhiva in. Tess feels her heart pound in anticipation. She smiled, and Tess felt suddenly at ease. She is ready for this.

Madhiva's voice is soft and inviting. "Hello, Tess."

"Hello."

"I'm happy for you," she tells her. "This will be a good experience for you."

"I think so, too," Tess admits. The apprehension she'd felt before this meeting falls away. She feels a tingling in her chest, but it is nothing like the panic she's experienced. It tells her she is about to embark on a journey of knowledge. It is a good feeling, and she embraces it.

"Make yourself comfortable." Madi rounds the bed and sits on the wooden chair. Tebor excuses himself.

"No," Tess says. "Stay, please."

Tebor bows and takes his place in the corner.

"What do you believe, Madi?" Tess asks.

"I believe in Samsara, the cycle of reincarnation, a fundamental belief in my culture. Life is a lesson."

Tess finds comfort in this but questions the concept. She wants to believe life has a purpose, that it is purposeful.

"I don't pray to any God or subject myself to any rules as laid out in any book," Madi explains, "I live my life like each day could be my last: compassionately, lovingly. Knowing every life I encounter holds a purpose in my own, for better or worse. I may

135

not understand that purpose right away, but I embrace it with a knowledge that it is for the betterment of my soul."

Tess again finds a deep connection with Madi's ideals and finds peace there, which allows her to relax completely. Madhiva notices a calm envelop Tess and proceeds.

"Would you like to get under the covers?"

"I don't think so," Tess answers, her eyes closed.

"Then place your arms at your sides and uncross your legs. Your arms and legs will get heavy in the state of hypnosis."

Tess obeys. She listens as Madi directs her to a corridor with many doors. These doors represent her past lives. They have presented to her on either side of a long hallway. She must choose which to enter to help her understand the present by experiencing the past.

Tess is drawn to a door on her left. Each is different, and this one offers a view. She pushes it open and finds herself in a valley. Green hills surround her, fringed by forests. Brilliant green leaves frame her to the blue sky above. She is a young girl. She knows this by merely looking at her feet, as directed by Madi. She is dressed in strappy blue sandals and a blue skirt, a feeling of dread suddenly enveloping her.

Chapter Forty-Five
Thursday, 12:15 am

Charlie and Jorge sit at the bar. Charlie opens a bottle of bourbon and takes a long swallow. Jorge empties his pockets on the bar and realizes he's taken the men's wallets and three cell phones.

"Three?" he says, wondering whether one was his own.

Charlie turns abruptly and gently places the bottle on the bar's worn walnut finish.

"Three phones?" he asks, the phones in front of him. He looks at Jorge from across the bar.

"I don't know. I took everything I could pull from their jackets."

"Look at the phone number. Do you recognize one?"

Jorge's face tells the story. "This one's Sam's." He puts it in front of his older brother and picks up the bottle. Charlie reluctantly lifts the phone, thumbs through the texts, and then recent calls.

"Jesus, here's Tess's cell number." He wonders if he should call it.

"What do we do?" Jorge asks, then drinks, blowing the fumes from the bourbon through his nostrils.

"Smash the other two and toss them in the dumpster out back. I'll hang on to this one." His gaze is planted on the name Tess, staring back at him from the blue screen of her dead husband's phone. A man he sent to a violent end. A man whose wife he had fucked and child he had saved. He feels suddenly conflicted but thankful for having had the encounter with Tess. If he hadn't, he

137

might not have thought twice about the consequences saving his brother would have on Sam's family.

The back door slams shut, and Charlie jumps. Jorge walks back into the bar and sits on a stool.

"What do we do, Chuck?"

"We wait it out. The police have the bodies now. The Molloys will hear about it soon enough. They have no reason to suspect we had anything to do with this. They let you off the hook. We should be free and clear." He takes the bottle from his brother's grasp and pours another mouthful. He considers loose ends as he wipes the excess from his lips with his coat sleeve.

"No one saw us; if they did, they couldn't identify us. There were no cameras on the building's exterior. We were quick, careful."

"Were we?" Jorge asks. It had all happened so fast. Charlie had acted without hesitation; the shooting, the blood, dragging the bodies into the ditch. It was so surreal.

Charlie hands the bottle back to Jorge and gestures for him to drink. He does, and the burn tracks the trip to his stomach and comes up again in a puddle of vomit.

Chapter Forty-Six
Thursday, 12:15 am

Under hypnosis, which is similar to her experience with Doctor Samuelsson, yet different in that she feels very much in control of herself, Tess discovers a past she never knew existed.

As a young girl living in a small cottage in the French countryside, Tess wanders in her avatar through the cottage interior. Madi urges her to describe her surroundings.

"Is there a mother or father you can see?"

"No, no one."

Madi presses on. "If you look beside the door, are there shoes on the floor?"

"Yes. There is a pair of very large boots and then mine."

"Are they your father's?"

"Yes. Papa is a woodsman."

"Is he there with you?"

"No." Tess looks sad.

"Describe a time you last saw your father."

Tess goes on to explain as images rush in. She and her father lie on a heavy blanket on the cabin floor. A fire has been lit, and they are enjoying a snack of grapes while he reads a book aloud.

"Papa is reading to me," Tess recounts. "We're cozy by the fire. He has a hot drink at his side, and I'm lying on my stomach."

"And your mother, where is she?"

"I don't know my mother."

"Your father has raised you alone?"

"Yes, he's very patient with me, kind but strong. I love him. I feel safe with him." She smiles and continues to describe him in detail. "I am his princess, he tells me. He tells me one day, I will live in a castle, like the one that borders the woods. He promises me many things, and I know they may not all come true, but I love watching his face as he lists them."

"Where has he gone, your father?"

This question erases the warm comfort Tess has been experiencing.

"Men took him from me," she explains, her voice halting as though she were struggling for air. "Military men."

"Does your father come back?"

"No." Tess shakes her head, sounding grave. "He never comes back." A tear races down her cheek.

"I miss him so much," she manages. "I'm afraid." She explains that her father had hidden her in the floorboards when they heard a motor car approaching and told her she should stay there until he returned. She would never see her father again.

"Would your father have come back if he were able?"

"Yes." Her sadness amplifies in a sob that chills the room.

"Do you understand that your father was protecting you by going with them and leaving you there?"

Tess nods, overcome by grief.

"Let's practice forgiveness. Let's forgive your father for not returning. Let's forgive the men who took him from you for blindly following orders."

Tess nods. She feels everything: the girl's disappointment, fear, and anxiety. Lonely days and months followed. Her hope waned as she waited for her father to return and look after her. She feels herself as well, the tears on her cheeks, the shaking of her body as she relives a life of despair she couldn't have conceived on her own, a devastating end to innocence. The terrible loneliness that followed her father's disappearance is crushing, but in the end, she does forgive.

"What can you learn in this life from the cruelty that occurred in that life?" Madi asks in her muted tone.

Tess struggles with this question, as she sees no purpose in a life given no chance at happiness, no opportunity. But at that moment, reason presents itself.

"Indifference," she utters.

"In the men who took your father?"

"Yes. It's because of their indifference I died alone, always wondering, blaming my father for letting them take him away. *Where was he?* Why didn't he fight them off? Why did he just let them take him from me?" Tess sobs again, and Madi interjects.

"They were indifferent to his life and the lives he touched. They were indifferent to the consequences of their actions. You have learned that indifference is the opposite of compassion and is no way to live."

"Yes," she agrees.

"You've also discovered that you've lived a life of abandonment and resentment. But the resentment falls away in understanding. You understand now; your father wasn't to blame. He was protecting his daughter. He was protecting you."

"Yes," she whispers.

"Let's step back into the present. You have learned a wonderful lesson tonight and healed an ancient wound."

Madi brings her out of her trance, and Tess recalls every detail of her past life.

"Will there be more like this?" she wonders, looking at Madi.

"As many as you are willing to experience. Past lives are there for you to draw strength from. They are there for you to learn how to live a better life in the now."

"Then I want more."

Chapter Forty-Seven
Thursday, 1:00 am

Tebor walks Tess back to her room as Madi begins her rounds on the floor. She collapses on her bed and cries for the little girl. What an awful lesson to learn, she thinks. Had she learned compassion now? Had she been compassionate to Sam when he called in distress asking for money? Looking at the time, she decides to call him while the will to do so is strong. It is one in the morning, but knowing him, he will be up. She relives their conversations and thinks about how confused he must be, leaving his family for a woman who left him. *Now he was broke?* She still finds it hard to see him as the victim in this upheaval but resigns herself to reach out and meet him at a bank machine.

She opens her purse and pulls out her phone. Sam's number is on the calls received screen, and after a deep breath, she pushes send.

* * * * *

The brothers cringe at the sound of Sam's cell. They are exhausted now and bent over the bar. Charlie exchanges a look with Jorge, and they straighten in their stools.

"Should we get that?" Jorge wonders.

Charlie picks the phone up delicately in his fingertips, careful not to accidentally push one of the buttons. Turning it in his hand, he sees Tess's name on the screen.

"Jesus, fuck, it's Tess!" he exclaims, pushing off his stool and stumbling back a few feet. Regaining balance, he walks towards his brother, beckoning him to answer.

"Fuck, don't hand that thing to me," Jorge says, slurring his words as he backs away. Charlie turns the phone back on himself and watches as the name disappears. She has hung up.

"Okay, I really don't know what to do with that." Though swaying slightly, Charlie seems sober compared to his younger brother.

"Maybe we call it a night?"

"We'll regroup in the morning." Charlie shoves the phone into his pocket. Both men go to the office, where Jorge collapses on the couch, and Charlie sits at his desk chair, feet elevated, eyes closed.

* * * * *

Throughout the night, Charlie dreams. He's in a war zone. Aircraft push through the black smoke rising to meet them as they release bomb after bomb upon his devastated city. Charlie feels the broken pavement underfoot as he struggles to make his way home to his wife and children through the chaos.

A building explodes a block from his position, and debris rains down upon him. The sky is lit with searchlights as anti-aircraft fire peppers the black smoke with bursts of light.

How many are there? He wonders, stopping a moment to watch the winter sky fill with planes. It feels to Charlie like they'd been bombing the city for hours.

Disoriented by the trembling earth and ringing in his ears, Charlie pushes on. Though the streets are unrecognizable in their current condition, he manages to find his way.

A street sign twists in the breeze, hanging precariously from its post. Charlie approaches the sign and realizes this is his street. He pans the neighborhood. What he sees before him is a smoldering, flattened landscape. The only building left remotely intact is the church he and his family attend each Sunday.

Grief overwhelms him. Charging into the rubble, he stumbles several times en route to what he believes is his home. It's challenging to separate the street from the property as the destruction is so complete. Rubble is evenly spread out in a seemingly endless field of devastation. A chimney crumbles in the distance, and Charlie flinches in his armchair. Solemnly, he whispers the name he connects to his wife.

Chapter Forty-Eight
Thursday, 3:30 am

Tess wakes violently from a dream, thrashing and tearing her sheets off. The feeling she experiences as her eyes fly open can only be described as terror. The sort of fright that makes your heart race over the horror of knowing your greatest fear is about to be realized.

She stands and stumbles about her room, forgetting where she is, navigating the dark with her hands outstretched. Was she still in the dream, in that house, with bombs bursting all around?

She finds a light switch and returns to the waking world. Looking up at the ceiling, she ensures she is not trapped in a collapsing house, frantically searching for her children. Tess wipes sweat from her eyes and crawls back onto her bed, pulling the sheets up.

Before the dream fades, she writes down the horrifying event to understand its meaning. Once she reads through what she's written, a spark of memory takes her back a few days when she woke from the same dream. She recalls the anxiety that followed, despairing that she couldn't even escape into her dreams anymore.

Looking at the alarm clock, she sees it is three thirty-three in the morning.

"Good luck trying to get back to sleep now," she tells herself, falling flat on the mattress. As she rolled over on her back a moment later, she noticed the book Tebor had given her lying next to the clock radio.

She pulls the sheets over her naked legs and places the book against them. Moving through the volume's fifty pages of prose, reading them one after another, Tess finds herself captivated by the words and the staggering emotions the poet pulls from her. Arriving at the back of the book, Tess examines the author's headshot and a verse below the illustration.

As I leave you,
I would hope to have inspired and given pause to question.
Dedicated to:
My wife, my friend, my lover, my killer.

Tess is all at once inspired and disturbed by these words. She reads and rereads this passage, connecting with the boy poet. Studying his picture again, she puts him in his twenties.

Despite his youthful appearance on paper, this boy, she decides, knew more about life and the pursuit of truth and happiness than anyone she's ever known. He resonates with her on a level of familiarity, not unlike how she feels towards Tebor now. Like they'd met before. But of course, this is impossible until you consider past lives, in which she was fast becoming a believer.

Chapter Forty-Nine
Thursday, 8:55 am

That morning, Karl looks over what little evidence of Drummond's disappearance the police had gathered in '99. His friend Donald had come through for him, even pulling prior complaints against the teacher, but none of these complaints, he reads, ever resulted in an investigation.

Because children were often too afraid or too ashamed, abuse by a teacher or other authority figure rarely ended in a conviction. The defense would dismiss the child's accusations as a form of bullying the teacher, using the allegation as a threat to get better grades. And since the child's grades usually suffered because of the abuse, the defense had a textbook out.

Karl knows this all too well, himself being a victim of abuse at his stepfather's hands. He kept the secret from his mother for fear the man would kill them both and his sister. Karl allowed the abuse to continue for many years until his stepfather died after a long battle with cancer. That's when he finally told his mother.

He took a terrible beating from her after the fact for desecrating her husband's name. This is how he'd learned people do not take kindly to others speaking ill of the dead, and if Drummond were dead, so too is his case.

He decided to research the contact information for the people who had registered the three complaints against the teacher—one from 1991, another in 1996, and then again in 1998. The pattern was unmistakable; the predator decided to act on what had dominated his thoughts. He gets away with it but is cautious about trying again. Eventually, the urge is too powerful to ignore; he acts and again escapes notice. The attacks become more frequent, and soon, he is like an animal, hungry for the hunt.

"Why didn't anyone catch this?" he wonders aloud.

* * * * *

Tess knocks at his door. She sits in the lounge, looking a little uncomfortable. She's feeling a bit guilty over having gone behind his back to Madi for additional therapy, unsure whether she should tell him about it. She decides she'll keep this from him, as it may endanger Madi's employment.

"Good morning. How are you coping?"

"Do you know a boy staying here? Paul?"

"Paul, yes, I heard about his episode in the cafeteria. One of my colleagues is handling his case. You've met him?"

"Yes, well, twice now, once at breakfast and again at dinner, when he cut himself."

"You were there for that?" Samuelsson shakes his head. "I was against seeing anyone from his ward mixing with yours. Doctor Jacobs will keep him segregated going forward, I should think."

"I'm afraid I might have set him off somehow. We were talking, and I offered some compliments. You know how teenagers can be, so uncomfortable in their skin."

"I do, but Paul's way of dealing with his demons is an extreme case, and why he's here, at his parents' request."

"I know you can't really tell me anything about him, his situation or anything, what with the doctor-patient confidentiality and all that, but I feel a connection with him. I feel drawn to him somehow, like I'm supposed to help him."

"That's a noble thought, Tess, but you're here to manage your own life, and I'd discourage you from becoming caught up in anyone else's."

"Probably none of my business, I know. It's just, I don't know, I guess I'm just concerned for him."

"Leave it at that. Despite what you witnessed, Paul has excellent care here, and often, we can only help those who want to help themselves. Paul is a difficult case and one who requires constant supervision. You may not see him again during your stay, so let your focus fall on why *you're* here."

Tess can't leave it alone and wonders if some part of why she has ended up here is to help Paul.

"Do you believe in past lives, Doctor?"

Karl looks up from his clipboard and addresses her in a way she hasn't heard him speak, direct yet dismissive.

"Nonsense," he tells her. "Nothing in my experience leads me to believe in such things." Karl changes the subject by stopping short of discussing his outlook on religious practices in this session.

"Let's begin. Please lie down and close your eyes. We'll revisit your hole in the ground this morning. Have you had any other memories of the event since our last meeting?"

"No, nothing more."

Tess isn't impressed over how Doctor Samuelsson dismisses her question but understands he is a man of science and perhaps not open to spiritual thought. She decides to leave it alone.

She relaxes her mind and lets her limbs fall slack. The feeling of going into hypnosis is unlike anything she'd experienced before coming to the hospital. She has never known such a state of complete relaxation. Tess melts into the lounge, the atmosphere around her warming to body temperature. She feels as though she is floating. At one with her surroundings, Tess imagines this is a similar state to that of deep meditation. She is gently pulled through time, arriving when she first discovers the deep hole in her parent's backyard.

Chapter Fifty
Thursday, 9:10 am

Curious about the gunshots and police presence at his daughter's building the night before, Doug decides to put a call into an old friend. Frank, who still works in the evidence department at the station, had helped Doug in the past, and he hopes he can pull another favor out of him now.

Tess's father is a decorated ex-cop who had served his city for thirty years. After his retirement, he worked in the courthouse and remained in town for another ten years. He and his wife had children late in life; Celeste was nearly thirty-eight, and Doug was forty-five. At seventy-three, he counts himself lucky to be able to enjoy his grandchild.

"Frank here."

"Hey, Franky, you old dog, it's Doug."

"Doug? The same Doug that owes me fifty dollars from 1987?"

"With interest," Doug cackles.

"To what do I owe the honor of a phone call from retired detective Doug Armstrong?"

Doug relaxes against his daughter's couch, phone pressed firmly against his good ear, watching Celeste feed his granddaughter a fruit cup.

"I have a favor," he starts. Frank's trademark groan vibrates across the void. "Listen, you old coot, I'm staying at my daughter's for a couple of weeks, and there was a hell of a ruckus outside last night, and I'd just like to know what went on and if we can expect anything more like that."

"Where's your daughter living?"

Doug gives the address. Frank punches it into his computer.

"Boy, Doug, leave it to you to end up at ground zero."

"What do you mean?"

"Turns out two Molloy men were murdered there and left in a ditch. You remember the Molloys."

Doug doesn't like what he's hearing. The Molloys he remembers all too well. They'd been the ruling power in the city's underworld for more than forty years.

"The Molloys," he manages, letting the idea sink in. "*Jesus,* that's not good."

"Totally random, though. Seriously, nothing like that has happened in your neck of the woods since the neighborhood started to pick up."

"Do you have any leads?"

"No clue, Doug, sorry. It's pretty fresh. Molloys had already sent a couple of men to collect the bodies. If it's a rival organization looking to make a name or something, well, we're making arrangements for that possibility."

"Do you see it playing out here?"

"Nah, as I said, it's an isolated incident where your daughter lives. Nothing like this ever happens out there."

"Well, I may not sleep better knowing what I know, but thanks for filling me in." Before Doug can end the call, Frank hurriedly adds a new piece of information.

"It's weird you called. You remember the missing person's case: Drummond?" Doug remains silent. "Yeah, well, you might like to know that a psychiatrist, a guy that volunteers at the station for rehab and such, requested the file. He's a friend of the force and follows them up when he gets some interesting cases. He's looking at the Drummond file now." Frank waits for a response, but Doug offers none. "It's the one you and I worked on back in '99. Anyways, a weird coincidence."

"Thanks, Frank." Doug feels ambushed by the information but keeps his head. "Not much in that file, as I recall."

"Shouldn't be much of anything if memory serves."

"Well, thanks for telling me. You take good care and give my love to Betsy."

"You too; let me know if you need anything, Detective."

Doug hangs up and pulls himself to a seated position. Staring into space, he wonders what business anyone would have in wanting to reopen a case that had gone cold so many years ago.

Chapter Fifty-One
Thursday, 9:30 am

Tess recounts the night she first discovered the hole in the ground behind her parent's house during hypnosis.

"I'm in my room. I have Tommy's teddy bear. He sits on the beanbag chair in the corner. It's nine o'clock, and I kneel on my bed, my arms crossed on the window ledge and my head resting on top."

"And is anything abnormal happening this night? Is there something or someone in the backyard? Look down for me."

Tess becomes irritated, and Karl notices as her body becomes rigid. Her forehead creases in the middle as she struggles to understand what she's witnessing.

"There is a hole where before there wasn't."

"And how do you feel about this?"

"Afraid."

"Can you tell me why you feel afraid?"

"I see my father kneeling next to it. He's crying. I can hear him crying beside the hole." Tess becomes uncomfortable with the scene. "I've never heard my father cry before. It makes me feel like something terrible has happened."

"And has something terrible happened?"

Her head begins to shake back and forth, wishing the memory away, but she can't, and the doctor isn't going to snap his fingers this time. Karl has a sneaking suspicion about what or who this hole was meant for and needs Tess to face the memory, remember it, and heal.

"The light comes on over the back porch. Mom joins Daddy at the hole. The light shows me something at the bottom of the hole. It's my fault this happened. It's *my* fault."

Karl is surprised and pushes her for more.

"How is this *your* fault, Tess?"

"If I had talked to Tommy, none of this would have happened. I was his big sister. I was supposed to protect him. He was my baby brother."

Tears roll down her face once more, and Karl allows her to experience the emotions as they come. This time, he will let Tess complete the pain cycle to understand why she feels so trapped in this past.

"Who is in the hole?"

"Mr. Drummond." Her body trembles at uttering the name.

Karl sits back in his chair and nods slowly, chewing at the end of his pen. Drummond had done more than disappear; he was murdered. Aside from the apparent fact that Tess's father had killed the abuser, the lack of evidence he'd reviewed concerning the case gives him pause to question the police's interest in the disappearance.

"Tess, none of this is your fault. You were a child. You had no control. Drummond is responsible for his end."

Tess takes a deep breath, and her shaking subsides.

"This is *not* your fault. It would be best if you accepted that as *fact*. The man in the ground is the only person you need to blame. Understand this, Tess. You are innocent."

Karl asks what her father does for a living to answer his gnawing questions.

"A police detective," she offers, and Karl's suspicions are confirmed.

"You will remember everything we have discovered in our sessions when you awake. You will have questions and experience feelings associated with these memories that will confuse you. Know that I am here to help you work through these questions. This is a breakthrough for you. We will involve your parents if you wish. We will work towards a healthy resolution to your misplaced guilt and turn your life around." Karl explains carefully.

As she exits the trance, Tess places both hands over her mouth, "Oh, Daddy." She spends a long moment with the truth behind the hole in the ground and then purposely shakes off the stunning realization, managing a smile despite herself.

"Take your time as you process the information. It's quite a revelation you've experienced."

"I feel like I've been living a lie my whole life," she says, rising on one elbow. "I feel sad for my parents. I felt the desperation in my father's tears. It *wasn't* my fault."

Karl is glad for Tess's ability to put everything in perspective but is wary of whether it will stick without much more work. Just realizing the criminal nature of her father's actions and the potential repercussions could spark new trauma for her.

Tess sits up and examines the events that have made her who she is today. *Brother is abused, parents ignore it, brother kills himself, parents feel responsible, and father kills abuser. Tess witnesses the burial blames herself and hides memories where misplaced guilt slowly eats her alive. Tess marries Sam, has a baby, suffers a breakup, is nearly assaulted in the street, gets involved with a man from her past, and winds up in a mental hospital.*

"It all started going badly for me again once I had Emma," she concludes.

"Could that be because your unconscious was reliving the trauma of the last time you had someone you felt responsible for?"

Tess looks up at Karl, her lips parting and mouth falling open. "Could it be?"

"Something I want you to consider between sessions. I know we don't have another today, but give yourself the day and night, and perhaps you will come back to me tomorrow with an answer. If not, we have plenty to work from."

"Should I call my parents?"

"If you could keep this from them for the next few days, we'll make more progress. Involving them now would be disruptive."

"Are you going to report this to the police?" The question leaps out of her mouth as she realizes the implications.

"I have nothing to report. Anything you tell me under hypnosis is as protected by the doctor-patient statute as is this conversation. The only thing I could reveal is if you were to tell me you are planning on murdering someone, and even then, only to the intended victim."

155

Michael Poeltl

Tess relaxes. Her shoulders slump down. Unsure of how to proceed with her parents, she decides a phone call to check on her daughter is in order.

Karl stands as Tess walks to the door.

"You're doing a great job with this. You're very brave."

"Thank you," she replies solemnly and steps into the hall.

Chapter Fifty-Two
Thursday, 10:00 am

Doug decides not to upset his wife with the news of the Drummond case. She'd suffered enough through that time in their lives. It was a year of Doug blaming Celeste for talking him out of confronting Drummond over their son's accusations and Celeste resenting him for it.

Drummond had escaped all suspicion once their son had died, and so he and Celeste settled into a private hell while trying to raise a daughter who was suffering through the death of her brother.

He's been feeling anxious since the phone call and decides he might take a walk. Just as the thought occurs to him, the phone rings.

"Hi, Dad." It's Tess.

"Hi baby, how are you getting along?"

"Okay." She sounds a bit distant.

"Emma's fine; she's out with your mother, meeting an old friend for brunch. She likes to show off that daughter of yours."

"That's fine, Dad. I just wanted to call. So everything is okay?" She feels like she's testing her father now. *How could everything be okay? How has anything been okay since the day he buried a man in his backyard?*

Doug pauses a moment. There was the disturbance the night before; should he tell her about that? There was also that Charlie character asking her to call him; should he mention him? He decides to answer the question as he always has.

"Everything is fine."

"Alright, well, I'm free this evening if you want to call."

"Okay, honey. Be well," Doug says with a stab of guilt, wondering whether her current trauma was in any way linked to her brother's death. Then it hits him: Tess was pouring her history and heart out to a shrink, and Frank had mentioned that a psychiatrist had pulled the Drummond file. After he hangs up, he punches the air.

"Goddamn it," he curses. Doug had thought he'd kept everything from his daughter, but somehow the name Drummond had come up in her therapy, and this guy, this psychiatrist, was poking his nose around the dead file. What could Tess have given him? What could she know?

He pulls at his jacket on the wall hook, tearing a hole in the neck. He curses again and then gingerly lifts the coat free. The weather had turned over the past week, and entering late October, autumn's chill was making itself known. Doug investigates the rip in his jacket and replaces it on the hook. He takes a deep breath and holds it, exhaling after a few seconds. It helps center his thoughts, a trick he'd learned while on the force, a technique that got him through the worst two years of his life.

Rather than rushing out into the unknown, he decides to sit on the couch and make a list of why nothing would come of this.

The first thing he writes down is that no one knows where the body is.

Chapter Fifty-Three
Thursday, 1:00 pm

My wife, my friend, my lover, my killer.
This passage has been on Tess's mind since she'd read it. This afternoon, she decided to use one of the hospital's computer stations in the small library.

Sitting down, she punches the poet's full name into the search engine. To her surprise, not much more than a Wikipedia page appears. Tebor wasn't kidding when he told her the poet was not well received in his time. He had told her the copy he'd given her was one of the very few original volumes and that the work had never seen a second print.

Reading through the brief description of the poet's life, she learns that he had killed himself in 1833. The book now in her possession was his only venture. The wife he had referenced in the dedication had left him the year before it was complete. She reads that he had taken his own life with a pistol and died in his apartment, alone, at twenty-seven.

Tess becomes anxious at learning this, shifting uncomfortably in her seat. Without warning, she begins to shake and cry. Her hands move quickly to cover her face. Unable to control the overwhelming onslaught of emotions, she abruptly stands, her chair falling backward. Tess rushes out of the library, gasping and sobbing through the hallways to the privacy of her room.

Here, she shuts her door and sits on the corner chair for a moment, both hands covering her face while she rocks gently back and forth.

The emotions subside, and she removes her hands, wiping her eyes. As her sight clears, her gaze lands on the book. She stands, an uneasiness now enveloping her. She feels as though the book is beckoning to her. Its hold over her grows with each passing second as her gaze intensifies. Tess slowly approaches the nightstand, sucking in her bottom lip, remembering to breathe. She reaches down, collects the book in her arms, and hugs it tightly into her chest. Feeling weak, she settles on her bed and curls up with the volume.

"I'm so sorry for you," she tells the author. "I'm so sorry for what you suffered."

Poets are messengers, truth-tellers. They wear their heart on their sleeve. They allow themselves to experience the lows, exposed, naked to their emotions, to capture the essence of life in prose. Because of this, they can write equally eloquently of the highs. Beauty is found in both, through the eyes of one such as this. But to experience the depths of sadness a poet suffers, it must often be too much to bear, as it was for this artist.

Twenty-seven, Tess thinks. She will be twenty-eight in two months. Was it a coincidence that she should come to find herself here in her twenty-seventh year, meet Tebor, and be given this gift of poetry?

She considers what events had led her to this place. At the very least, she thinks it ironic that this book should be presented to her with her life in shambles. Tess shares heartbreak, desperation, rejection, and loss of purpose with the poet. Could that be enough to explain away her growing sense of familiarity with the man, she wonders?

"There's more to this." Tess sits up and opens the book again to a poem that recites the story of a life locked in conflict over its choices and the resulting consequences. Desperate to find the common thread intensifying the connection she's experiencing with the author, she skims over each line. Turning the pages, she again surface reads the poems, expecting to experience a 'eureka' moment.

Nothing comes of this reckless attempt to find herself in these aging pages, at least, nothing yet.

Thursday, 7:30 pm

As darkness settles over the city, Tess wonders what has become of Tebor. She hadn't seen him all day. After dinner, holed up in her room, thinking about her brother's suicide, her parent's response, and skimming through the book of poetry, she remembers she meant to call Sam again, just to check up on him, to make sure he hadn't done anything stupid. She looks at her clock: it reads ten-thirty. *Where has the time gone?*

She picks up her phone and places it to her ear in anticipation of Sam answering. Anxiously, she lets the phone ring until it's picked up by voice mail. She decides leaving a message is unnecessary, as he'll see she called on his history. She felt the same nervous angst at home at three in the morning when he wouldn't answer her.

Why is he the way he is, she wonders. But that question wasn't something she could answer, as Sam couldn't answer it for himself. It could have been such a good life, she contemplates. But it's what Tess makes of it now that counts. Even if he begged to come home, Tess doesn't think she can endure it all again. But the idea hadn't left her entirely because she feared she still loved him and wanted him in her life, bed, conversations, and pictures. What was wrong with her that she *needed* that? Shouldn't she be strong for herself, Emma, and women everywhere? It's too much to consider right now. Right now, she decides to take a walk and get some air.

En route to the courtyard, looking down at her phone, she wonders why her parents hadn't contacted her tonight. Maybe she should call them again; then, she remembers how awkward the conversation with her father had been earlier in the day.

Tebor bumps into Tess as he exits the courtyard.

"Getting cooler nights now." he relays, rubbing at his arms.

"Have you been *smoking?*" she wonders. The scent of tobacco is on his breath.

"Ah, you've caught me. It's my vice in this life, I'm afraid. Well, actually, in many of my lives. I imagine I won't reach nirvana until I've broken that particular cycle. Nothing enlightened about addiction!" He laughs it off and steps aside to let her pass. She remains in place.

"Huh, I would never have guessed."

"Yes, educated professor caught smoking; it's a pandemic in some countries, you know." He doesn't seem worried; his addiction is limited to three to five cigarettes a day, he explains. "But the smoking aside, are you coming tonight to see Madi?"

"Oh, yes, absolutely. I'm just trying to keep myself occupied until she arrives."

"Join me then. I was going to see what snacks might be available at the buffet."

Tess follows Tebor and slides her arm through his. Tebor looks down and smiles at her.

As they sit with their cupcakes and hot tea in hand, Tess shares a portion of her day.

"Doctor Samuelsson doesn't believe in past life regression."

"Well, he's got the head of a scientist, not a spiritualist."

"He really brushed it off, though, like he was insulted when I brought it up." Tess licks a finger full of icing.

"You didn't mention Madi's practices here, though?"

"Oh, no, I didn't want to get her in any trouble. I just wanted his opinion."

"Well, people can change, and often, as in my case, it's a tragedy, or what you perceive as a tragedy in your life, that makes you question what you know and gravitate towards what you don't."

"That's how I got here," she admits, chuckling to herself. "I still can't really believe I'm here. And the things I'm learning. It's all like a dream."

"Have you dreamt since you've been here?"

"Yeah, like crazy, vivid dreams. One is a recurring dream which started just before I came here."

"A recurring dream, that's interesting."

"Why's that interesting? It happens all the time."

"It does, but in my studies, I've come to accept that recurring dreams are a kind of past life regression in and of themselves. They haunt your unconscious, offering you information of a life lived but not complete."

Tess feels a chill rise up her spine, exciting the hairs on the back of her neck.

"That's ominous. You're so *ominous* half the time." She puts her cupcake down next to Tebor's. "The dream is about looking for my children in a war zone or something. Bombs are dropping, panic, anxiety, all negative feelings."

"In this dream series, have you found your children?"

"No, not yet, and it feels like I won't before it's too late." Tess stares at the painted brick wall across the room.

"It sounds like maybe you won't," he tells her. "Recurring dreams seem to be unfinished like that, an unfinished life. No proper ending." The title of the book of poetry pops into Tess's head.

"So what is to be done about them?"

"Relive it through hypnosis. Maybe we can pinpoint that life, understand what went wrong, get some resolution."

"I wouldn't know where to begin looking."

"Start with your surroundings; where are you? Which war is it? Can you guess a time frame?"

"If I had to, I'd say it was World War Two. That I was in England."

"Intuition! You see, you already know the answer! That's excellent! When we see Madi tonight, we will request she take you there."

Chapter Fifty-Four
Thursday, 10:00 pm

Charlie notices Jorge's growing discontent, trapped in the bar, like a rat in a cage, and can't shake the feeling they're just waiting out a potentially bad end. Although he's unhappy about all the delivery pizzas, wings, and limited television stations, Charlie knows how to lay low. He knows it's necessary.

Now, he plays with Sam's phone at one of the tables next to the bar. Its battery is half dead.

"So, what do you think? Should I call her? Tell her that her husband is dead. Tell her he was in over his head? What?"

"Just toss the fucking thing, Chuck," his little brother offers, but Charlie refuses. He feels too connected to Tess now. Too close to her. He waves his brother's opinion off and stands to pace the bar while Jorge watches a sports channel on the television.

"If she calls again, I'm going to answer it," he says.

Jorge faces him and drops his arms at his sides. "What good do you expect to do by answering her husband's phone? Seriously. Let's just ride this thing out, like you said, and let Tess just live her life. You really going to inform her Sam's dead? What else you going to tell her? It's your fault? Or mine? Or both?"

"I don't know. I, I feel bound to Tess."

"Because you *banged* her? How many women have you been with? Give me a break. What are you, *in love?*"

Charlie feels a strange warmth fill his chest at the mention. He hadn't likened his feelings to love for Tess, but considering the heat rising in his face and the butterflies fluttering against his ribcage, it's suddenly apparent that he *is* in love.

"Well, I don't know how a thing like that could happen," he lies, fingering the photo of Tess in his pocket. "But don't worry; I'm not going to implicate you. Once I'm satisfied we're clear with the Molloys, you're free to go. But I'm going to keep my eye on her. She's a good girl, and she doesn't deserve the shit that's happening to her."

"Who does?"

"Maybe *you* do, Jorge." Charlie turns toward him. The frustration of having to put out yet another fire his helpless baby brother had lit now burns in him. "Maybe if you're hair-brained scheme hadn't gone to shit, maybe innocents like Tess and her daughter wouldn't be in the danger they are. Maybe *I* wouldn't be. Maybe Sam would be alive. Ever think of that? It's called consequence."

Jorge stands up to meet Charlie. He's pissed and fragile and completely over-stressed.

"Listen, I told you to let me take the fall, Goddamn it! You think I like living with this shit on my head? I'm fucking *dying* here, man. This isn't how I saw it working out, *so you know*. Shit happens."

"Oh, shit happens, does it? Bad things happen to good people and all that, right?"

"Fuck yeah!"

"You should have come to me with your plan, and I could have made it work for you." Charlie points an accusing finger in his brother's face. "You're stupid, and I'm sick of having to clean up your messes."

"Fine!" Jorge's arms fly from his side. "You don't have to, *Big Brother*, consider me gone." He walks backward, kicking the front door open behind him. Charlie looks on, fuming. The door sticks open, and as Jorge exits the bar, Charlie hears a car's engine roar to life across the street, and a shot rings out. The car speeds away, and Jorge collapses on the sidewalk.

Chapter Fifty-Five
Friday, 12:00 am

Madhiva enters Tebor's room at midnight. Tess sits cross-legged in her pajamas on his bed while Tebor occupies the chair in the corner.

"Hello," Madi greets them, bowing slightly to both. Tebor bows back as Tess waves a hello. "You're back for more," she notices, smiling coyly.

"It's been a long day, but I'm very interested in a dream I've been having, which Tebor thinks could be an unresolved life." Tess points at her friend. Madi turns toward him.

"Is it not true, Madi, that recurring dreams could be images of a past life?"

"Let's find out." She turned back to Tess and moved to the seat beside the bed. Sitting, she removes her coat and toque and then her gloves. "The wind has picked up tonight. I think we're in for a storm."

Pleasantries out of the way, Madi begins putting Tess in a state of hypnotic meditation. This will better draw on her dream memories and allow Madi to confirm or deny Tebor's suggestion that Tess is dreaming of a past life.

Tess is getting used to the state and enjoys the calm that envelopes her each time. Once under Madi's spell, Tess is ready to begin.

They revisit her dream, and through detailed memory of the traumatic nightmare, Tess can regress further before the war and the scene she relives in sleep.

"We are happy," she tells them, smiling. "My husband is a good man. He works at a munitions manufacturing plant in the city. The war has started."

"Does your husband join the fight?" Madi asks.

"No, they need him to run the plant. We get together for lunch with the boys now that it is summer."

"The boys are your children?"

"Yes. They are three and seven."

"We're going to enter where your dream begins, and look at why you are reliving this life," Madi coaxes. "Take us there; tell us what you see."

Tess becomes agitated, her expression taking on a completely different appearance from a moment ago.

"The bombs, they're so loud. The power is out. I'm frantic." Her hands both ball up into fists. "I need to get us out of here. My home isn't safe anymore. Nothing is safe anymore. Where are my boys?"

"Can you remember where you saw them last?"

"In the yard. On the street. But then the sirens started. And people rushed down the road toward the church."

"Did they follow the crowd?"

"I don't know. I don't know where they are. Where are my children? Why don't they answer me?"

"Does it make sense that they are with the others that ran?"

"Yes," Tess is visibly shaken. Madi's suggestion has settled her down for the moment. "But how can I be sure? I can't leave if they are in the house. I can't go to the shelter without them."

Tess flinches as she recounts a bomb falling a short distance from her property. Her two-story ceiling gives out beside her, and she has to throw herself into a corner to avoid being crushed. She's yelling for her boys to answer, but there is no response to her desperate calls.

"Your boys are safe then; they have gone to the shelter. You must get out of your house."

Tess motions with her head to her foot and recounts what has happened. "It's too late," she tells them. "I'm trapped. My foot is caught under the rubble. I can't get out from under it."

Madi and Tebor share a look of concern. Tebor nods, and Madi turns her attention back to Tess, who shakes uncontrollably.

"Are the bombs silent now?"

"No. Oh my God, I'm going to die here. I'm going to die."

"Death is merely a rebirth, Tess."

"I'll never see my babies again. My husband." Tears flow freely now, searing red lines in Tess's soft white skin.

"You will see them again. You will see them in the eyes of those you know today. You will see your husband through the eyes of another in this life. They are with you always. They are your soul mates." Madhiva pauses a moment to collect her thoughts before she continues. "Remember the eyes of your children; remember your husband's eyes. Do you recognize him in anyone today?"

"Eyes?" Tess asks.

"Yes, they are the windows to the soul. You can identify those in your present with those who have come before."

"My husband." A long pause. "He's Charlie," she says, a look of profound understanding washing over her features.

"That's good, and your children?"

The bombs exploding around her jolt Tess back into the scene where she is trapped and helpless. "I feel so alone. I am going to die alone."

"You are not alone. Tebor and I are with you now. "

"Charlie," she whispers. "*Where are you?*"

Chapter Fifty-Six
Thursday, 10:30 pm

Charlie doesn't hear Sam's phone ring as he kneels over his brother lying in front of the bar, dying under the pale yellow light cast by the naked bulb under the sign that reads *Charlie's*. He has his hands pressed down over the chest wound and is screaming for help. Someone across the street calls 9-1-1, and within two minutes, an ambulance is screaming down the street.

Jorge is choking on his blood as it settles in his left lung. Charlie whispers into his brother's ear things like *it'll be fine, it's not that bad, I've seen worse.*

Jorge smiles at the last one and, though he is in terrible pain, manages to reach up with one arm and pull Charlie in close. He kisses him on the cheek and attempts to talk through the thick puddle of blood collecting on his tongue.

"I love you. I'm sorry." And then he is gone. In shock, Charlie remains kneeling, his hands firmly pushing down on his younger brother's chest, wishing away their argument, wishing away his angry words.

The ambulance screeches to a halt, and the paramedics jump out. Charlie barely notices. His attention is on his brother. They call for him to step away, and he snaps out of his trance after several requests. The men's voices in his ear, the twirling lights of the emergency vehicle, the breath as it escapes him. He stands and steps back, watching the men go to work.

"He was shot," Charlie supplies in a whisper. The paramedics don't respond. Looking down at his palms, Charlie studies the sticky red substance, pushing and pulling his fingers apart. The

Michael Poeltl

warm blood steams into the night air. Charlie perceives this as his brother's soul departing. He follows it with his gaze as it dances around the light bulb, moving ever higher, past the rooftop and disappearing into the darkness above. The very hands that had worked all these years to keep his brother safe now deliver him to what comes next.

"He's gone," he hears one of the men tell the other, shaking his head. Charlie knew this. The chest wound was the worst thing he'd ever seen. They'd used a shotgun. As the men stand and move away, Charlie stares at his brother's body as they wait for police support. A surreal moment, but not one he was unaccustomed to. His father had died of alcohol poisoning, and his mother of the same. He had found them both, one a year after the other. Lying silently on the floor, but instead of a pool of blood, they lay in their excrement and vomit.

Charlie wonders if he, too, would end up like this one day. Perhaps it was how his family died, as they lived, ignobly.

It is at this moment that Charlie takes back his life.

Chapter Fifty-Seven
Friday, 12:45 am

A bomb falls on a neighbor's house, toppling what is left of Tess's and burying her alive. Soon after that, she succumbs to multiple injuries, bleeding out, and is directed into the light by Madhiva.

Forgiveness is offered to those under orders to bomb her city. It is also given to her husband, who had not returned in time to save her; Tess's husband, whom she has identified as Charlie, in the present.

This interesting twist confuses her. Had she been married to Charlie in a past life? Is Charlie one of her *soul mates?* It all seems somehow wrong. It would never have occurred to her that Charlie might be a figurehead in her life. He had never done anything for her or she for him. They were acquaintances, and barely that. Sure, the random night they'd enjoyed at his bar was inspired, but certainly not life-altering, she thinks.

Sitting up in Tebor's bed, she looks at Madhiva and smiles weakly. "That was intense."

"You needed to live that life," Madi tells her. "I doubt you'll dream it again."

"Good." She runs her fingers through her hair. "So, what did I learn from this one?"

"Well, you were buried alive. I think we can safely say that life is where you get your fear from," Tebor pipes in.

Tess hadn't thought of that. "Oh yeah, right. Huh, that's interesting."

"And so, who is Charlie?"

"A friend," she offers. "He's someone who has been in and out of my life several times. I reconnected with him last week. It's so weird to think he and I are bound like that."

"We're more involved in some lives than others," Madi explains. "And sometimes it takes a few years to meet again or discover the purpose in the other."

"Should I pursue him then? Do I try to force a purpose from him?"

"No, dear. You live your life. Purpose will be revealed at a time of its choosing. You can experience multiple purposes in one life; most do."

Tess yawns and Tebor follows. "I'm so tired."

"Let me leave you with this, Tess. You have died alone in the two lives we've experienced. Please think about how it makes you feel to be alone, *really alone*. Not just for an hour or the day. But what does it do to you when you think about being alone?" Madi emphasizes the word to indicate the importance of what she's asking Tess to consider.

She nods in understanding. Madhiva leaves the room, and Tebor sits with Tess for a moment.

"I half expected you to see me in your husband's eyes back in WW Two." He smiles and laughs lightly.

"It's the strangest thing, Tebor. *Charlie*? I don't get it."

"You don't have to get it right away. These things take time. I'm sure there is some reason you've run into this, Charlie, recently. It just hasn't presented itself."

"I guess." She looks up at him apologetically. "I need sleep. Thanks again for this." She stands, and they hug briefly.

"You're doing wonderfully. Really."

She smiles and returns to her room, crawls into bed, and is immediately overcome by sleep.

Chapter Fifty-Eight
Friday, 7:00 am

The morning offers Tess time to consider the doctor's musings. That she may relate her child to the terrible things that happened to her baby brother and inadvertently be bringing this negative present upon herself.

She's read a thing or two on positive thinking and the effect of practicing it in your life. The same goes for negative thoughts. *Perhaps it's possible to have negative thoughts lingering in your subconscious, affecting your day-to-day.* A big question, she admits, as she pours a coffee at the breakfast buffet.

She also wonders how on earth she'll ever be able to bring up the Drummond murder with her parents but knows that she'll need to eventually. Also, the past life in which Charlie is her husband: he should hear about this. And Sam, she'd like to know why he's cut off communication. Then there is Paul; what have they done with him, she wonders?

"God, I'm getting my money's worth out of this."

The situation with her family holds her immediate interest. Her brother's death, though painful to remember, is at least a memory. That her father had anything to do with a murder and cover-up is what presently disrupts her thoughts.

Nervous over the amount of reflecting she has to do before entering the doctor's office this morning, Tess twists the precious metal on her ring finger with the thumb of the same hand. Looking down at the white gold bands and princess cut, half-carat diamond, she stops to reflect on never having taken the rings off.

She frowns at the sentimentality of it. Most women probably would have thrown the things across the room, flushed them down the toilet, or pawned them by now. Why hadn't she? What about Sam made her want to keep them on her finger, even now? Love, she supposes. She still loves him, and now that his girlfriend has left him, maybe they'll get back together. Perhaps they would never have parted if she hadn't found out. The girlfriend would have left him eventually, and Sam would have reintegrated into a life he'd never really left.

But Sam would never change, not now, she thinks. And she should never allow him the opportunity to hurt her again. What if she did let him come back? Then he got cabin fever another four years down the road and left? Then Emma would really feel the effects. No, she would keep him at a distance now. She would let him see his daughter but not be a part of her life anymore. That would be for the best.

The rings resist her attempts to pull them free. She is thin but not as slender as on her wedding day, and the knuckle on her ring finger seems swollen. Anger builds as she realizes her weakness in holding onto the romantic trinkets as if waiting for her Prince Charming to return. Such weakness she could no longer allow in her life. *The weak suffer, and the strong survive.*

Finally, the hurdle is overcome, and the rings slide off. Looking at her ring finger, she realizes it no longer holds the place it once had in her heart. It no longer houses a love or the fairytale life it promised. It is merely a finger, no more important than the others, no more magical than a forefinger, and less valuable than a thumb.

This act would usher in a new dawn, she decides. A tear escapes, and she quickly wipes it away. The phantom feelings would stay with her for a long time, wondering what had happened to all the rings supposedly represented, her heart wondering why bad things happened to good people.

If removing the rings could remove her memories, she thinks it a practical next step, but Tess has no misconceptions that her memories of Sam, the good and then the bad, would leave her anytime soon.

Her cup of coffee drained, Tess stood, slipped the rings into her pants pocket, and leisurely walked to her appointment with Doctor Samuelsson.

Tess examines her feelings over the idea her father had taken a life and her mother had become an accessory on her way to Samuelsson's office. If Drummond was guilty, and she's sure her father would have gotten a confession before he'd done anything rash, then the world is a better place for it. She could almost let it go altogether.

Entering Samuelsson's office, Tess sees the doctor behind his desk, holding a printout.

"Please, take a seat." The doctor says somberly.

Tess moves toward the lounge, but he waves her to one of the comfortable leather chairs adjacent to him.

"I have something I want you to look at." He hands her the printed copy of a headshot. She takes it and immediately recognizes the photo.

"That's him," she tells Karl, nodding. "That's Drummond."

"So you identify him from the hole?"

"No, he didn't look like this in the hole. I remember him from school."

Tess hands the picture back. Karl places it beside the laptop.

"Then we have a positive identification," he states.

Tess's heart sinks: will the doctor renege on his oath and turn her parents over to the police?

Noticing her worried expression, he smiles and raises his hands in a gesture of reassurance.

"It's just for me. I have my reasons for making the identification. It's nothing for you to worry about. Honestly, I'm sorry if you got the wrong idea."

Tess relaxes and exhales. "Do you have a side business locating missing persons or something?"

"Not missing persons; child abusers." He gets up from his desk and gestures for Tess to move to the lounge.

"Really? What do you do when you find them? Go all Batman on them?" She lies on the chaise and settles into a comfortable position.

"I'm not a vigilante in that sense," he laughs. "But I do have connections, and when I have names to follow up in cases such as your brother's, I do everything in my power."

"That's not against your oath?"

"It's not." He clears his throat. "It's a slippery slope, but when you have the right resources..." He trails off and shuffles through the papers on his clipboard.

His comment makes Tess like Karl all the more, showing that he cares enough to look into this in memory of her brother in defense of other innocent children who may fall victim to a man like Drummond.

"So, have you had an opportunity to consider what was remembered to you yesterday? Perhaps your current crisis with your husband may be due to unconscious guilt you're harboring over your brother's suicide?"

Tess can honestly tell him that she no longer entertains this thought - that she had a mini-breakthrough this morning. She tells him about her rings and the fantasy she'd bought into by agreeing to marriage and the fairytale sold with each dress, tiara, and ring. How she sees that Sam left her because he's Sam; not the marrying type, not the family man, not the guy that wants to see a thing through, grow old with someone, and fondly look back on shared experiences. He needs drama. He needs intensity, and that's just what he brought to the last month or two of their marriage, and he's to blame, not some repressed memory.

"Excellent, Tess, really, well done. You've found your footing."

"What are you saying? I'm cured?"

"You've certainly built a wonderful base to do just that." He pauses to write a note. "But I don't want your head getting too far ahead of your heart. I mean to say that you still need to accept your husband's infidelity and choice to leave you and your daughter. Removing your ring is a big step but one step in a long journey. There are no shortcuts, no going around your pain; you must go through it to heal. I don't want anger to replace sadness any more than I want you to rush into forgiveness. False forgiveness isn't forgiveness; it is a masked pain that can only hurt you further. We will get to all of that but in time."

Tess nods. Despite her revelation this morning, she still feels abandoned, humiliated, and discarded, and she understands that she is still in love with the person who has hurt her and that he will take a very long time to get over. Being alone has not been easy, but in retrospect, she's felt alone since she discovered she was pregnant.

"Let's revisit your unconscious and see what it says."

Under hypnosis, Tess can remember better times with her baby brother. Moments long before the tragic suicide, and there she can rebuild her relationship with Tommy and her parents. Good memories bring her out of her sadness and allow healing and forgiveness.

As she is brought out of the trance, Tess remembers everything and smiles at the doctor. Karl smiles back and stands, walking Tess to the door.

"I like the progress. You're coming into your own with everything."

"Thank you for bringing my brother back to me." She stops to catch a tear and fights an urge to hug him. "I'll see you tomorrow."

"Tomorrow."

* * * * *

As Karl sits behind his desk, he smiles. On-screen, he highlights the file he's compiled of Edward Drummond and drags it to the recycle bin. With two more clicks, he erases it permanently.

Chapter Fifty-Nine
Friday, 10:00 am

Tess calls her parents again. Her mother picks up this time.

"Oh, Tess, we've just been having the most wonderful time with Emilia. She is such a sweetheart. You know I took her out yesterday to see Carol. Do you remember our friends, Carol and Hans?" Tess wonders how anyone could forget a name like Hans.

"Yes, I remember."

"Well, Carol said hi and mentioned that if you need anything when your father and I return, just call her. I'm leaving her number on your fridge."

"Okay, Mom, thank you. So, Emma's fine? No problems?"

"No problems, dear. As I said, she's having a great time with her grandparents."

Tess wonders if she should bring up the Drummond disappearance at all. She would hate to upset the fragile peace they've developed over the years.

"That's great, Mom. How's Dad?"

"Oh, well, he had an episode with his stomach last night. Something's rattled him, and he won't tell me what. But you know your father, such a private man. I asked him whether it was the shooting the night before that had him all worked up."

"Shooting?" Now Tess is rattled. "Where?"

Celeste feels foolish for mentioning it but knows when she gets on a rant like this; she tends to forget who she's talking to. Doug will not be happy with her for letting the cat out of the bag.

"Oh, it's nothing, just some shots near here. The police came to the building, but they never came inside. It was probably nothing."

"Well, Jesus, Mom, if Dad's upset, it must be more than *nothing.*"

"Maybe it just reminds him of his time on the force. You know he was never really the same after..."

"Okay, Mom, kiss Em for me, please, and I'll try to call you again tonight. Bye."

"Bye, Tess. We love you."

Tess meanders through the halls. On her way to her room, she sees Paul being escorted by two orderlies. She stops to watch. She wants to go to him and talk to him but is afraid to upset him further. He looks broken. She feels terrible.

Paul turns his head and notices Tess. He mouths, 'I'm sorry,' and lets the orderlies guide him to his room. Tess follows. They move him down the east end through security doors, doors she cannot access with her code. This is the secure wing. She would have to use Madi's code to get to Paul now.

Leaning into the hall door's narrow window, she can identify Paul's room number.

Smiling, she concludes she will bring Madi to him.

Chapter Sixty
Friday, 11:00 am

Tess pulls the phone out of her pocket and sees Sam's number staring back at her. She wants to call it. She wants to hear his voice again. She wants to know once and for all what his choice will be.

Regardless of what it is, she is steadfast in her decision to keep him at a distance, but that's easy for her to tell herself in this place, removed from the world where he may want to pick Emma up every weekend or share a dinner with them once a week. What would the future hold?

She pushes the send button, and a choice comes up on the screen as to whether she would like to call her husband or text him. Tess decides she will text him, offering Sam a more comfortable response option.

Tess punches in a question: 'How are you?" Then she slides the phone back into her pocket and walks to the courtyard for some air.

* * * * *

After everything Charlie had been through in the past few days, he hadn't expected a text from Tess to be so alarming.

Seated at his desk, the bar still closed for 'renovations,' his brother's body at the morgue, and a police report behind him, Charlie wonders what he's to do about Tess Seager. How should he answer this text? Sam is dead, and if he knows the Molloys, no trace will ever be found.

Still, the urge to reply is powerful. Could he pretend to be Sam and tell her goodbye? That way, he could spare her the reality. But was that fair? What if she pines for him the rest of her life?

The moral questions force an ironic laugh. Charlie was the one who gave Sam up to protect his brother. Perhaps, he thinks, it is too late to ask moral questions.

The battery on Sam's phone is nearly dead. Charlie thinks it's now or never and types a line of text back to Tess.

* * * * *

When Tess's phone buzzes to life on the picnic table, her heart soars in anticipation. It bothers her that this is still her reaction, but she brushes it off as a force of habit. Surprisingly, it reads something entirely different than what she'd expected.

'It's Charlie, Tess, please call me.' Followed by his number.

"Charlie." Tess reads the name aloud. She's confounded. She checks the number and the contact name, both Sam's. She hadn't mistakenly dialed Charlie; she didn't even have Charlie's number. Maybe Sam was at the bar with Jorge, and she wondered if they were sharing a drink. Then, a tingling in her fingers quickly travels into her arms, meeting in the middle of her chest, squeezing the air out of her lungs. She goes flush and stands to shake the rush of adrenaline out of her system before it has the opportunity to overwhelm her.

She is dizzy now and cursing at her weakness. No one else is in the courtyard, so she can walk in circles, shaking her arms without anyone judging her bizarre reaction to this invisible attack.

Is the thought of Sam and Charlie being in the same room that causes her fight or flight mechanism to misfire? Maybe Charlie's told Sam about their fling. So what if he did? Sam should know that she is moving on with her life. Perhaps it would make him jealous.

"Oh my God." Tess stops and places a hand over her mouth. *Maybe Charlie had to fight him off, and Sam stormed out and left his phone.* Well, unlikely as that was, anything was possible if they were all sitting around Charlie's, drinking.

With a mischievous smile on her face and the adrenaline quickly disbanding from her system, Tess calls Charlie's phone.

* * * * *

At the other end of the city, Charlie stares at the incoming number and recognizes it as Tess's. This is it, he thinks. This is the moment he crushes the only woman that has ever mattered to him.

Chapter Sixty-One
Friday, 11:05 am

Doug wrestles with the idea that Tess may have somehow learned what happened to that filth, Drummond.

The night it all went down, still crystal clear in his mind, Doug poured tea and sat at the picture window in the living room, looking over the city he once swore to protect.

Celeste's soothing sounds, singing Emma to sleep in the back bedroom, afford him the luxury to relax and put the situation in perspective.

Fourteen years ago, nearly a year to the day his son had hung himself in his closet, Doug made a choice that would change him and his family forever.

The lump in his throat creates a dam, the tea becoming trapped in his mouth as he recalls that night and considers his actions.

* * * * *

It was late September and strangely warm in the city. School had just begun, and as was the tradition for him then, he drove by Thomas's old school before calling it a day. This was a silent memorial he had begun a month or so after the event and found difficult to give up. It was approaching seven, and the school was deserted except for a man in a trench coat bent over a small boy on a skateboard. They were on the sidewalk, and the man pointed at the track behind the school. Doug pulled in beside them.

"What's your name, son?" he asked the boy.

"Mark," the boy replied. Doug stared daggers at the man, still mostly bent over but slowly straightening out.

"Why don't you get along home, Mark? Your mother must wonder about you."

"Yes, sir." Mark ran off and jumped on his board, riding it to the end of the street. Once out of sight, Doug turned to the man in the trench coat. The man seemed nervous: he attempted to move away from the car, still bent over. Doug halted him with one word.

"Drummond," he called out, and the man stopped. He turned to reveal a toothy grin as he approached the car.

"Oh, hello, Detective, it's been a long time."

Doug's blood began to boil at the sight of him.

"Can I give you a lift home?" Doug offered through clenched teeth. Drummond declined. Doug got out of his vehicle. Drummond looked scared. Guilt, Doug surmised. Rounding the car, he quickly pushed Drummond up against his car, put his hands behind his back, and cuffed him. A moment later, Drummond was in the back seat, complaining bitterly.

Doug rolled up his windows, thankful for the tint job, and decided what, if anything, he would do with this man.

"Don't get your panties in a twist, Drummond; I'm just going to drive around and ask you a few questions."

"This is appalling," he announced from the back seat. "You have no right to pick me up out of the blue like this."

"You were talking to Mark, the little boy. Why?"

"Well, he's a student of mine."

"That's convenient." Doug watched the tall, thin man sweat it out in his rearview mirror.

"What are you insinuating?"

"Shut up, you piece of shit." This silences Drummond. "You think I don't know what you do to little boys? Huh! You think I don't know why my son killed himself?"

"Listen here, Detective, I'm very sorry for your loss."

"SHUT UP!" Doug's throat tightened. "I told you to shut your filthy mouth."

Drummond was frightened at that, Doug noticed. He pulled into an abandoned warehouse parking lot on the city's edge to continue his interrogation, one long overdue in his mind. He parked the car and shut off the engine, killing the lights.

"I'm going to ask you some questions. You're going to tell me everything I want to know. Why you do what you do, what sick thoughts play out in that messed up head of yours, what we're to do with you."

"What do you want to know?" he asked nervously.

"What punishment do you feel fits your crimes?"

"I've committed no crimes," he wiped snot from his lip with the shoulder of his coat.

Doug studied him through his rearview mirror as Drummond wiggled slightly, likely trying to find a comfortable position with his hands cuffed behind his back.

Doug turned around, his arm resting on the top of the bench seat, and slapped Drummond across the cheek. Drummond howled in pain and shrank away from him.

"If you don't tell me your thoughts on the punishment, you'll hear mine. You don't want to hear what I have to say on the subject, *Edward.*"

'I'm innocent! Please!"

This enraged Doug. He leaned over the seat and slammed a fist into his prisoner's eye.

"You're innocent!?" Doug exploded. "You, who prey on innocence, you fuck!" He came down hard with a left hook next, relieving the school teacher of two teeth. He did this three or four times, releasing all the anger, frustration, guilt, pain, and suffering the year had put on his family and himself.

Drummond collapsed in the seat, and Doug pulled him upright. The man was blubbering, blood and drool sliding over his broken bottom lip.

"I don't deserve this,"

Doug couldn't believe what he was hearing, but instead of hitting him again, he collected himself and waited to hear what else the molester had to say in his defense.

"It's not me. I don't want to -"

"Ah, but *you do* Edward, and you have before. If I'd found the complaints against you when it still mattered when my son was still alive,"

"Complaints?" The news sobered him up.

"Thought they'd gone away, didn't you? Well, it turns out nothing ever goes away, no matter how hard you try to bury it."

Doug slammed another fist into the man's waiting face, breaking his nose. The resulting nosebleed went on for many minutes as Doug watched Drummond slowly lose consciousness.

Not sure what to do with the man next, Doug contemplated his options. Drummond would likely make a complaint against him, Doug would lose his job, and the monster that killed his baby and ruined his family would have another victory over him. No, Doug knew that scenario couldn't play itself out. There was only one way to deal with this.

Thinking back on picking Drummond up, only the boy, Mark, saw him, and he'd left before Doug cuffed and threw him into his car. No one saw. If Drummond had had the wherewithal to have put up a fight outside the car and raised his voice, Doug would be rethinking his next move. Instead, he turned the car on and positioned it further into the abandoned industrial complex. Once inside the empty building, Doug exited his car, opened the trunk, and removed the tire iron. Then he pulled Drummond out of the back seat, letting him land hard on the broken concrete. He stirred.

Doug looked at the weapon in his hand, eager to finish the job. There would be blood in the car. There was already. He thinks he'd spend the next day cleaning it, then take it to the country and burn it. He couldn't do that with the body inside, though; he'd have to hide it. There could be no trace. His backyard would be the last place anyone would look, he decided.

"Jesus," Drummond spat as he looked up at the makeshift weapon in the detective's hand. *"I'm sick. Please, I need help."*

Doug reached into his jacket pocket, removed his wallet, flashed his badge at the desperate man, and tossed it through the open passenger window.

Drummond attempted a weak kick at Doug's leg, which spurred Doug on to slam the iron bar into the monster's head repeatedly until the body became still. A puddle of blood accumulated underfoot, and Doug dragged the corpse a safe distance away from his car, allowing it to bleed out. Once the monster was again in the back seat, wrapped in a canvas sheet Doug had found in the warehouse, he drove home. There, he would confront his wife and dig a hole.

Chapter Sixty-Two
Friday, 11:10 am

Though talking to Tess has occupied his thoughts since Sam's phone turned up in Jorge's pocket, Charlie is now at a loss as to what to say. He stares at the phone ringing in his hand.

Maybe a shot of courage would have made it easier, but it wasn't fair to Tess, he'd decided, to be anything but lucid while he explained the bizarre string of events that had once again brought them together.

"Hello, Tess," he answers quietly.

"Charlie?"

"Yes, from the bar."

"Well, I figured that much." A weak laugh follows. "What's up? Why am I calling your phone?" She paces the courtyard, still shaking the adrenaline out of her free arm.

"Sam's phone is nearly out of batteries."

"Okay, then maybe the better question is, why am I not talking to Sam? Why am I talking to you?"

"Listen, the thing is," a long pause interrupts his thought. "Sam's dead."

She has trouble understanding what she's just heard, suddenly feeling like she's floating through a fog. She hears Charlie's voice like an echo, calling her name.

"Say that again?" she manages in a soft, slow, deliberate tone as the fog lifts a moment.

"I'm sorry to have to be the one to tell you, Tess."

"Why *are you* telling me this? Shouldn't I hear this from the police, or my parents, or someone, anyone *but* you?" She is

187

suddenly angry. This replaces the anxiety Charlie has been experiencing.

"You won't be hearing this from the police. Sam's death; it won't be recorded."

Those last six words bounce around her head, and she scrambles them, trying to make sense of everything. The way Charlie has put them together tells her Sam's been involved in something illegal and been murdered. She attempts to ground herself, allowing a silly thought to occur to her like *perhaps dead, in this case, is slang for something else.*

"Charlie, tell me what's happening. What is happening?"

"I know this is the last thing you thought you'd hear today and to hear it from me, but I'm telling you, Sam is dead. He's dead. You need to accept that before I tell you the rest."

Tess nods blankly, leaves falling around her as the wind is caught up like a twister in the courtyard. She pulls the phone from her ear and looks at the screen. Her chin trembles, and she drops her phone, inching her way to the ground, hands covering her face.

Charlie listens as she sobs on the other end. He wants to be there, wherever *there* is, to console her, let her lash out at someone, and help her. He picks up a pint glass and throws it against the wall. He feels helpless as the harbinger of terrible news: *good luck having a future with this girl.*

After a few moments, Tess struggles to collect herself. *Sam's dead?* She still questions the truth of Charlie's statement but has no reason to mistrust him. She picks up her phone and places it against her ear, sucking in breath after breath to steady herself. In a voice that breaks Charlie's heart, she continues the conversation.

"He's really dead? *Really?*"

"Yes. I'm sorry."

"How?"

"Do you have some time to listen?"

Tess sits on a pile of leaves insulating her from the cold earth below and rests against the courtyard's brick wall. She nods as if Charlie can see her. In his mind's eye, he does and begins the explanation.

He tells her everything: Jorge's plan, Sam's buy-in, bailing out his brother while Sam took the hit, and their retaliation against the

Molloy men at her apartment. Finally, he tells her about his loss, his brother, shot to death in front of his bar the night before.

Tess has no words. The whole story seems made up, too surreal to be true. Again, she thinks Charlie has no reason to lie to her. Then, she considers his role in her past lives, as her husband in WW II.

She could blame him for Sam's murder, but how could she when he intended to save his brother? He'd saved her whole family from a similar fate. It's Sam who had almost gotten his daughter killed. Such a fool, she thinks.

"Jesus Christ," she says breathlessly, a hand supporting her forehead.

"I don't know what else I can tell you." Charlie is wiped out, short on sleep, and wondering whether he'll ever sleep again.

"I should, thank you."

"You don't have to *do* anything."

"Thank you," she tells him, nodding once and taking a deep breath. "Thank you for looking after my family."

"Tess, I -"

"Please, let me thank you. I can't imagine what I'd have come home to if it weren't for you. You've saved me this time." A shiver ran through her, and a fresh tear caught on her lip.

"What do you mean?"

"Can I tell you next time I see you?"

Charlie's becoming familiar with the warmth that fills his chest when thinking about Tess, and the feeling returns at her mention of seeing him again.

"Sweetheart," he answers in his candid, low tone that makes her feel like a teenager, "You just let me know when and where, and I'll be there."

"I know," she tells him and hangs up.

Chapter Sixty-Three
Friday, 11:20 am

From the courtyard, Tess immediately calls home after her conversation with Charlie.

"Mom?" she says as calmly as she can muster.

"Yes, Tess, hello!" her mother answers eagerly.

"How is everyone? How is Emma?" Tess places a finger in her mouth and chews at the nail.

"Oh, well, everyone is just fine. There's nothing to worry about, dear. How are you?"

"Can I speak to Emma?"

"Well, she's napping, honey. It's when you said to put her down; your father is just coming out of her room now. Would you like to speak to him?"

Tess pulls the phone from her ear and looks at the time. Sure enough, she's called precisely ten minutes into Emma's nap. She's anxious to hear her little girl's baby talk and considers having them wake her but allows her selfish impulse to take a back seat.

"No, it's okay. You guys have a rest, and I'll talk to you soon." A part of her wants to bring up Sam's death, but she has no proof to follow up the claim. Could she even mention it in her therapy sessions, she wonders? Hanging up, she notices that her hands are shaking, that she'd been shaking since she'd hung up on Charlie.

Tipping her head back and closing her eyes, a picture of Sam's face develops like a photograph in her mind: his eyes squinting, and crow's feet cutting into the sides of his face as they did whenever he smiled. She smiles, and then a wave of sadness overcomes her, forcing her knees up so she can wrap her arms around her legs and rest her head there as she sobs.

Tebor enters the courtyard a few minutes later to enjoy a cigarette when he notices Tess crying in the far corner.

He kneels beside her, placing the cigarettes on a neighboring picnic table. He touches her back and whispers in her ear.

"What's happened?"

Her head rises slowly from her knees; her eyes are red and swollen. She looks at Tebor, and he watches as her mouth pulls down into a terrible grimace.

"He's dead," she tells him, chin trembling. He picks the hair from her cheeks, matted down by tears.

"Who's died, Tess?"

"Sam. My husband; he's dead." she sniffles and wipes her face with the sleeve of her shirt. Her nose is bright red, and at this moment, Tebor feels connected to Tess in a very familiar way. He likens it to a déjà vu.

"I'm so sorry. Do you want to see the doctor?"

"No," she answers quickly. "It's all too bizarre to tell anyone. I *can't* tell anyone." She places her head on her knees again and weeps.

"You can tell me. You need to tell someone. You can't go through this alone. I'm here for you." He sits beside her, the brittle leaves crunching under his weight.

Tess looks up at her friend and manages a grateful smile with quivering lips. She mouths *thank you* to him, and he hugs her around her shoulders with one arm, drawing her into him.

"You've probably come out to have a smoke," she says, shuddering and then sniffles again. Tebor hands her a tissue, and she clears her nose.

"Never mind about that,"

"I'll take one if you are."

Tebor reaches for the cigarettes and lights two, handing one to Tess.

"I would never have guessed," he tells her, smiling sympathetically. She smiles back and slowly places the filter between her lips, pushing them together, completing the seal. Then she sucks the smoke into her mouth and lungs and blows it out a moment later.

191

Michael Poeltl

It's not a first for Tess. She had smoked occasionally during college and the first year she spent with Sam. The act was akin to a tribute, bringing her closer to her husband. Her head resting on Tebor's broad shoulders, she finishes the cigarette without another word.

"He'd been involved in some illegal mess with a friend's brother. They're both dead," she tells Tebor, removing all emotion from her voice.

"I'm so sorry to hear that. What a loss for your daughter to be without her father."

Tess nods, and again, her expression grows grim. She leans against Tebor and buries her head in his chest. Tebor hates to see her like this but doesn't want her to suppress her emotions. She still cares for her husband, even if he no longer cares for her. She should be aware of all the markers that this untimely death will negatively affect and grieve for them. For her daughter to have lost her father, for Tess to have lost a friend, lover, or husband, the fallout from this might set back a lesser person, but he knows Tess is strong; that is why she's here.

Chapter Sixty-Four
Friday, 12:30 pm

Doug wonders whether he should just come clean with his daughter over the fate of Tommy's abuser. Watching his wife feed Emilia a lunch of boiled carrots and other assorted mashed veggies, he tries to imagine her reaction to this idea.

He's managed some research on Tess's computer and discovered a Dr. Samuelsson works at the hospital where Tess is receiving treatment. With this news and another call to his friend at the station, he's put the picture together. The psychiatrist is one and the same.

This news unsettles Doug, but because nothing has come of it, he feels perhaps the information won't go any further than the doctor's office.

What benefit to Tess's treatment would showing her Drummond's file offer? Was it just a curiosity on his part? Was he building a new case for the disappearance? The questions began weighing on him, so he filed them away with the other unanswered questions a detective lives with when cases go cold.

Friday, 7:45 pm

That evening, after running through a multitude of scenarios in which Sam will no longer play a part in her life, Tess is all cried out. Tebor waits for her to shower while he leaves through the book of poetry he'd given her.

Tess reemerges from her bathroom, fully dressed but with a wet head. Seeing Tebor seated on her bed makes her smile. She has grown to really like this man, respect and admire him, eccentric as he is. He has been a great comfort and teacher to Tess, and she is grateful for him. Mindful of his unruly hair, she flattens it with one hand and kisses the top of his head.

Tebor looks thoughtfully up from the book.

"How are you?"

"I've got some bad nights ahead of me." She plops down beside him.

"I suppose you wouldn't be up for an evening with Madi tonight?"

"Are you kidding? Now more than ever, I need a night with Madi. When Sam left me, I lost purpose, and now he's gone forever. What does that tell me? There was never *any* purpose to us?"

"Well, you had a daughter together. Perhaps that is enough where the two of you are concerned."

"I guess it has to be." She stands to brush her hair in the mirror over her dresser.

"Alright then, can you eat something?"

"Oh, I don't think so. Not sure I'm going to have an appetite any time soon."

"Well, come to dinner with me, and we'll see if anything at the buffet looks appetizing to you."

The word buffet makes her stomach churn. She doesn't consider eating an option but wouldn't mind a cup of coffee. She agrees to join him, and they walk to the cafeteria.

Chapter Sixty-Five
Friday, 10:30 pm

Tess reflects on the phone call from Sam that sounded so desperate. He had wanted money. He was in trouble. She suddenly feels responsible for his death by denying him access to their money when he needed it. She shares this theory with Tebor as they walk the halls.

"Nothing happens randomly like that. You need to understand everything happens for a reason, and the reason is to learn. Suppose your husband died due to his poor choices, then no matter who or what intervened, he would still die by *his* choices. *We* choose how *we* live. If you want to take risks, you need to understand the consequences attached to those risks."

Tess believes in consequences. She remembers telling Sam that very thing amid the fight that sent him away. The memory stings and her heart sinks as she relives the scene.

"It's karma, Tess."

Again, another phrase she'd used in their fight. Perhaps she knew more about this stuff than she'd thought.

"Makes sense," she agrees.

It's eleven o'clock when they reach Tebor's room. One hour until Madi arrives.

"Would you like to come in and wait, or would you rather come back in an hour?" Tebor asks.

"I'll just pop into my room for a few minutes and be right back."

In her room, Tess paces, considering a call to her parents. She feels disconnected now, knowing they've kept such a massive secret from her all these years. She understands it is to protect her, but their closeness seems suddenly tainted.

Sam is also in her thoughts, as he has been since he left her and Emma. Her musings now turn from anger to sadness. How could she be angry with him now that he's dead? She so wanted another chance with him. At least to talk to him and get a clearer vision of why he'd left. Had she done something? Had she not done enough? Was it just about him? Questions she could never answer now. Answers lost in time. What was she learning from all of this?

At five minutes to twelve, she dresses in her pajamas and makes the short trip to Tebor's room, where Madi is waiting.

"Please." Madi directs her with a wave to Tebor's bed once more. She sits on the side of the bed and takes Tess's hand in hers.

"I'm so sorry to hear about your loss."

Tess looks from Madi to Tebor, standing in the corner behind her. She lands her gaze back on Madi and then averts her eyes.

"It's still difficult to process that when I get out of here, I'll never see..." She stops before her voice gives out.

"I understand. This is a shock. You should take some time for yourself and process this new reality. Let's wait until you feel ready to continue this therapy."

"What? No, no, I want to continue this tonight. I need to; it's good for me." Her eyes shift wildly from Tebor to Madi and back. She wonders briefly whether she is using this as an escape. "Honestly, I'm ready. I can do this."

"Oh, well, we can try. I'm just afraid it may be difficult, if not impossible, for you to reach the state necessary for regression with this new trauma entering your life."

"Can we? Can we try at least?" Tess pleads, both hands griping Madhiva's ringed fingers.

"Of course. Please, lay back."

After a time, Tess finds herself in the plain between here and there, where memories are far-reaching and knowledge eternal.

"I see myself in a thin leather shoe. Brown," she begins. "I am a man. My pants are tapered at the ankle, and I wear suspenders to keep them up."

"Good, Tess, where are you?"

"In a café, at a table seated high in a corner where I can work."

"And where is this café?"

"It's in London proper, a stone's throw from St. Paul's cathedral, where I always end up, the corner of Ludgate Hill and Creed. I love it here but do not enjoy the Jack Brag of a server I have today. Today of all days to have to put up with his ingratiating himself with the upper classes and ignoring me." Tess's voice noticeably changes as she describes herself and her surroundings. She is immediately comfortable with this life, fully immersed and enjoying the memory. She's beginning to assume the accent of a nineteenth-century Londoner of the middle class.

Tebor feels a shock of excitement rush through him as he recognizes the timeline and the café Tess is experiencing.

"Why is this day so important?"

"My publisher is coming to meet me today. I'd like very much to have a tea ready for him when he arrives."

"Let's move forward to when your publisher comes to meet you now," Madi tells her.

"It's Tebor." A whimsical smile slides up one side of her face. "Tebor is my publisher."

"What is Tebor's name in this life you're living?"

"Stephen," she offers. "He loves my poems. We met in a Taphouse months before. He'd ordered a draught, and I explained how I'd drunk the lot already. We shared a laugh and then a conversation. He read what I had and has encouraged me to write more ever since."

"What have you written about?"

"Pain, mostly. Life, as it's happening to me."

"Captured in poetry?" Madi asks.

"Stephen tells me the dark subject matter may not be popular right now, but it soon will. I don't care as I don't plan on seeing it in print."

"What do you mean? Why wouldn't you want to?"

"I could not bear to know, should nothing come of my work."

"What's happened in your life that makes you say that?"

Tess giggles ironically as she ponders the question. "I fear the chill of winter's approach in this summer of love."

"Has someone abandoned you? A lover?"

"A wife," she explains. "My friend, my muse, but ultimately, my undoing."

"Why do you say that?"

"I am nothing to her." She says matter-of-factly. "Why she stayed as long as she did is a mystery, though I am glad of it. She was not a good wife, but I reveled in the love I suffered for her, even if she never felt a whisper of it for me."

Tebor's face falls as Madi looks at him. He nods knowingly. He'd lived this life with her as the publisher and Tess, the troubled poet. This is why he'd gone to the trouble to find the book and spent so much money and resources to secure its safe delivery. He knew Tess would come, one day, into his life again and that the book would act as a guide for her.

"The book is published; let's move on to that event. Stephen has brought you the news."

"It comes by telegraph. The news heartens me; my purpose fulfilled."

"Explain your purpose, please."

"I've achieved immortality. My words will be forever, my experiences not in vain, my story heard through the ages."

"And what of your story; what is it you hope to have given the world?"

"I hope to offer understanding, a glimpse into an unfinished life."

"Did you choose to live this life in sadness to write a book on the subject?"

"It chose me. I'm afraid." A sense of foreboding fills the room. Tebor and Madi share a look of concern, and Tebor again nods. Madi nods back slowly, her eyes closing and then refocusing on Tess.

"And what choice have you made on this day?"

"To stop the sadness."

"There are many ways to change a life without ending it." Madi is acting in Tebor's stead. Where he failed in that life to stop his friend from killing himself, she hoped she could at least offer him a reason why, where none was forthcoming in the past.

"Yes, that may be true, but I am empty now. I have no muse, for better or worse; my inspiration has left me."

"Could you not confide in someone, in Stephen?"

"Stephen has given me purpose. I'll ask no more of him."

Tears well up in Tebor, and he blinks them away. The memory of this past life with his troubled friend is beginning to take a toll. He remembers it all very clearly: the suicide, the note.

He'd discovered Tess's recurring role in his past lives early on in his treatments with Madi: those same eyes coming back time and again either to play out a significant role in his life or he in hers. This particular life was unique to him. He lived a long time as Stephen, growing old and sick and dying at seventy-one, surrounded by family and friends. Tess's life ended at twenty-seven, with no one there to offer her a single prayer of safe passage. Tebor fought with the guilt over the suicide for many years until Madi appeared as a spiritual healer. She helped him in that life, and she is helping him overcome his grief in this life.

The book Tebor purchased in the present is meant for the author to meditate on for Tess. Once Madi brings her out of her trance, Tess will understand why he'd given her the book and wanted her to read it. It is his gift to the one who wrote it—the one he could not save.

Chapter Sixty-Six
Saturday, 3:00 am

Lying in her bed, hours after the regression with Madi and Tebor, Tess finds sleeping impossible. The realization that she was the poet whose words have so effortlessly moved her both frightened and amazed her.

Studying the man's face on the back page, Tess shivers. The idea that she was looking at the face of a life she'd lived nearly two hundred years earlier was not a concept she was prepared to encounter.

She shuts the bedside lamp off in an attempt to sleep once more. With so many things fighting for attention in her head, she somehow manages to silence them all: the questions, the grief, the excitement, all turning to white noise in the background. Exhausted, Tess sleeps.

* * * * *

Jorge's body sits alone on a metal shelf, awaiting a time to be reclaimed and put to rest. Charlie decides on cremation, recalling a conversation he'd had with his little brother more than once. Jorge always said he hated the idea of being buried. Jorge also said he'd like to be sent into orbit or allowed to crash-land his ashes on the moon, but that service has yet to be established. Perhaps, had he lived long enough, those options would have been available to him.

Charlie waits for news from the police in his hotel room, afraid to go home or stay at the bar. The Molloys will be upset with him for finger-pointing, but Charlie has had enough. He gave the full story of his brother's end to the authorities and left it with them to manage. He can't sleep tonight, thinking about what could have been. He wasn't one to deliberate over his own life, and he had always been proud of himself for having built what he had from nothing. It's his brother's life that keeps popping into his head; what could have been?

He handed Sam's phone over to the police as well. Evidence against the men he'd killed. Charlie didn't mention his involvement in any of it but did tell them that his brother's dying declaration was that they had killed Sam. He gave them Sam's full name and address. They could then connect that Jorgie had killed the Molloy men in front of Sam's building, and the hit on his brother was retaliation. The phone would be the best shot at getting a conviction against the Molloys. It wasn't much, Charlie thinks, but the Molloys had been untouchable for a very long time, and perhaps this was enough to give the authorities the opportunity they'd been waiting for.

Either way, he figures there must be a hit out on him now. He's removed what money he has from his bank account and his safe at the bar earlier in the day, preparing for the fallout. He's on the run now until the Molloy organization is brought down or the case goes cold.

With that thought, he feels a sense of peace come over him. Nothing he can do but what he's doing. No one they can use against him to bring him out of hiding. He is alone, with no one to care for any more or anyone who cares for him; whatever happens now, he has done the right thing in the end, which is enough.

Chapter Sixty-Seven
Saturday, 8:00 am

Overwhelmed is putting it lightly, Tess tells Tebor over breakfast.

"It's as though everything I thought I knew about myself was wrong. My whole life is changing. My parents have kept a secret from me for fifteen years; my husband is dead, my past goes much further than I had ever imagined, and a book I wrote nearly two hundred years ago has resurfaced. Now, does that *not* sound crazy to you?"

"Well, you couldn't be in a better place to make a declaration like that!" Tebor smiles, and despite the mental and emotional stress Tess is experiencing, she smiles back and sighs.

"Well, I don't know how people survive this kind of stress. I've been tempted to leave, go home, hug my little girl, and hide out for a few years."

"Isn't that why you came here?"

"Not for a few *years*, I didn't."

"Just give this place its due. I know I mock the good doctor, but I also know he's helping you, and Madi, well, you hit the jackpot last night."

"I won't say it hasn't been good for me. It's just been so much all at once."

"Imagine if you didn't have the infrastructure you have here to help you through it all. Everything happens for a reason. What's that saying: God will never give you more than you can handle? Well, maybe He knew this would be too much and arranged that you and I meet now."

"Is that a saying?"

"It's from the Bible. Corinthians, I think,"

"Does the Bible jive with your belief in past lives?" Without thinking, she stabs a strawberry with her fork and places it in her mouth, hungry for his answer.

"Depends on how you view the Bible. I could get into the Gnostic scriptures and tell you Jesus spoke of reincarnation and how the Church hid that piece of information to control the masses, offering just the one life to repent, but that's a conversation for another time."

Tess chews the berry slowly, allowing her stomach the opportunity to prepare for the gift. What Tebor has just said is another piece of information she was hearing for the first time. *He is a wealth of information.*

"Why do you know so much?"

"It's like Plato said; we all know everything already and only need to be reminded of what we know."

Tess's head jerks back as her fork stabs at a piece of pineapple. She swallows the strawberry and clears her throat.

"What do you mean by that?"

"Plato believed in past lives and figured we'd learned everything there was to know by living those lives and only need the information coxed out of us through education."

"Amazing."

"Well, he was Plato, after all,"

Tess's cheeks color, and she looks down at her plate, pushing the pineapple into her mouth. Tebor laughs and touches her arm.

"You must have thought you'd read those poems before."

"They certainly resonated with me right away. It was tough to pin down why until last night."

"How has it affected you? I mean, are you grasping it?"

"I think so, but I feel like there's a point I'm missing."

"Purpose will reveal itself." Tebor nods his head emphatically. "If one thing is for certain: you will pull purpose from what you're learning here. Perhaps more than one."

Tess's mood brightens. He's right, she thinks. She couldn't have done any of this alone, at least not without him.

"I have a session with the doctor in a few minutes," she says. "I'm not sure what to do about everything. Do I tell him my husband just died under questionable circumstances?"

"I think so. This is what he's good at, Tess. Let him help you through this."

Chapter Sixty-Eight
Saturday, 9:00 am

"So, how are you feeling today about everything? Have you had any more memories of your hole in the ground?"

"No, well, I've thought about the secret a lot and wonder how I'll ever bring it up in conversation, but no more memories."

"And of your brother? Have you managed to pull more from a happier time?"

"Nothing more there either, but as I told you, you've given me my brother back, and I'm so grateful for that." She becomes suddenly distant, and Karl picks up on it.

"Something else has happened."

Tess looks down at her hands, one pulling at the other's fingers, the joints separating and popping back in place. She looks up a moment later and decides to tell him the truth.

"I had a phone call yesterday," she starts, wondering if telling the doctor will make it more real. "It was a friend telling me that Sam, my husband, has died."

"Oh, Tess, I'm so sorry. Was he ill?"

"That's the thing; it's a total surprise; he was involved in something illegal with people he shouldn't have and was murdered. They say his body will never be found. They say it was payback." Her head shakes, and her eyebrows thread together, still grappling to comprehend the recent events in her life.

"Then, let me ask you again: how are you *feeling* today?"

"I don't know, honestly. Sam was my life for so long. I hadn't expected never to see him again. I never thought I couldn't be mad at him ever again."

"Okay, let's address that. You can still be mad at someone, whether they're with us or not because *you* need to heal, and now not just over his infidelity and abandonment, but also because Sam's never going to be able to make it up to you or hear you tell him you forgive him."

"He called me the other night. I hung up on him. My last words were cruel. I should have been nice. I should have said something nice."

"We'll work through your feelings, but you need to know that you had nothing to do with his life ending and that you are probably more angry with him now than you were yesterday because he's allowed this to happen."

"It's not my fault," she tells herself and the room.

"No, it isn't," Karl encourages. "But that doesn't change the fact that the man you loved, married, shared everything with, and had a child with is gone. That you'll never see him again and that your daughter will grow up without her father."

Tess throws her hands up to cup her face as she explodes into desperate sobs. Karl understands the healing power of release and lets Tess cry until she lives every possible scenario that will never happen for her or her daughter or Sam because of this profound loss.

"So *stupid*, Sam!" she cries out, pulling her hands away from her face.

"Good, Tess, pretend I'm Sam, and tell me what you think of me."

She looked up and honestly saw Sam in the doctor's place, her vision blurred by the tears; she lunged, fingers gripping the lip of the chaise lounge, keeping her from barreling forward onto the doctor's lap.

"How could you endanger yourself like that? You're a smart man, and you were a good father. You were good to me!" Karl listens as Tess fires off the words she'd never said to her husband, words she could now never express to him.

"What were you *thinking*? *Why* would you choose that life over me and our baby? How could you? How could you!"

She relaxes back onto the lounge to regroup.

"Was I such a bad wife? Was I so impossible to live with? Was Emma? How could you leave us like that and then leave us forever alone? I don't want to be *alone*. I don't want that..." Tess breaks down again and, feeling ashamed, rolls onto her side with her back to Karl, curling up into a fetal position.

Karl allows her to stay this way for a time, unwilling to free her from this self-imposed trance, allowing her the time to find her center again. He places a blanket over her shuddering frame.

"It's not fair," she mumbles, remembering that life is a lesson and that she should smarten up and see it for what it is. But the emotions have overwhelmed her now, and she cannot find her way back without first dealing with the trauma of Sam's death.

"Life is indifferent," Karl relays in a soft tone. "It does not understand fair or unfair. It has no concept of human emotion. It does not possess a conscience."

Tess rolls over, still convulsing from the deep pain of her sorrow. Karl handed her the tissue box, and she pulled a few free, wiping her face and blowing her nose.

"What do you believe, Doctor?"

"We're each here to make a difference. That's what I believe. Beyond that, I have no misconceptions about religion, but do not fault those who believe in something else."

"Don't you believe in a God?"

Karl questions whether he should become involved in this discussion with a patient searching for reason and purpose for her apparent run of bad luck. He decides to allow it to better understand Tess's belief system.

"I have seen things and learned of things that do not allow for a God to exist, not one that I would want to meet, anyway."

"I feel like that too sometimes. When Tommy died -"

"But you've had a change of heart," Karl presses.

"Yes, I have." Tess shifts herself back on the cushion. "I have experienced things here, a revelation of sorts."

"Would you like to share that with me?"

"It's all so contradictory." She shakes her head. "I don't know what to believe. All I know for sure is that my husband left me, was murdered, and now I'm supposed to raise a child on my own."

"Look at me," Karl asks, and Tess looks meekly at his bearded face. "Tell me, tell *Sam* how you feel about him. Tell him, use me."

"I love you," she laughs ironically. "That's pathetic. After everything, I still love him."

"What else would you like to tell your husband?"

"That I wish I could hold you again, that you would want to hold me, to look in your eyes and see you looking back. That I could kiss you." Tess breaks down again, but it is a silent lament this time. She jerks quietly on the lounge, bent over slightly. A moment later, she finds the resolve to continue.

"*You hurt me.* You don't understand what you've done. How leaving affected me. I feel like I could never be enough for anyone ever again."

"Can you forgive me, Tess?"

She sucks in her bottom lip and bites down, fighting off the lump forming in her throat. She swallows hard.

"I *want* to forgive you, I do, especially now. But I don't know if I say the words, they will carry any meaning."

"You don't have to forgive today; just knowing that you want to is enough for right now."

Tess shakes her head, hugging herself. Karl stands and lays a hand on her shoulder. Tess looks up and rises to meet him. She wants to hug him, hug someone but feels that would be inappropriate and unprofessional. Karl hesitates a moment and steps back.

"How did that interaction make you feel?"

"Better, strangely," she admits, wiping away the remaining wetness on her face. "What do I do with all of that?"

"Understand what you're feeling: the confusion, the anger, and sadness. They all come from the same place—a place of fear. You will know what to do when you truly understand their origin. We will investigate that more tomorrow, but meditate on it tonight."

"Thank you again," Tess turns to head for the door.

"Tess, you're remarkably strong," Karl calls after her. "You will find that place, and we will confront it."

Tess nods, the beginnings of a smile working its way across her lips.

Chapter Sixty-Nine
Saturday, 11:00 am

"It's a brave thing you've done," the detective reminds Charlie. "And I'm sorry about your brother."

"Thanks." Charlie accepts the officer's condolences but not his compliment. He'd been picked up by one of their marked cars a half-hour earlier and driven to the station, where he sat waiting for this detective.

"So, thanks to you, we've actually got something to work with against the Molloys." He opens a file folder on his desk, and a picture of Charlie's brother with a sucking chest wound sits atop the thin pile of papers. The detective quickly snaps the photo up and turns it face down.

"Sorry about that," he apologizes, licks his fingers, and rifles through the testimony Charlie had given not long before. Pulling one sheet free, he places it over the photograph.

"So, Sam Seager is missing, presumed dead. You say your brother told you the Molloys killed Sam."

Charlie nods, hoping they haven't found a way to implicate him in any of the killings.

"Good, we have Sam's phone, and the fingerprints on it match those of the two men your brother shot. We had those on file. Molloy men picked up the bodies, so we know they're connected."

"Okay, so what are you doing about bringing them down?"

"We've got men on the ground, Charlie. This would be much easier if they'd stop incinerating their victims, but we are checking every crematorium in the city that belongs to the Molloy Group."

"Have you tried to contact Sam's wife?"

"We had men stop by the apartment last night, but no one was answering. We also left a message on her home phone. I want to send a car today. She should know her husband is missing, presumed dead."

Charlie considers telling the detective that Tess is unavailable and that she's out of town. Still, he doesn't want to surrender any information that could cast suspicion over either of them.

"Okay, so why did you pull me out of hiding?"

"I wanted to update you in person and discuss your relationship with Sam's wife." Charlie's heart stops, but his poker face remains intact. "If there is one at all, I mean."

"Nope." Charlie decides to say nothing about their recent past. It would only give the police a new direction that would lead nowhere. "I knew her about seven years ago when she and Sam lived near my place and occasionally came in with my brother."

"Okay, well, that's something."

"Why is *that* something?"

"Oh, I just find when things like this happen, people are rarely strangers. There is always that degree of separation."

"Well, I guess, in this case, it's my brother. I'm just trying to do the right thing here and not let these deaths go unanswered."

"And we appreciate it. I'm just filling in the blanks. You're our star witness. You saw the car that sped away from your brother's shooting."

Charlie doesn't remember the car at all; it was black, but beyond that, he had no idea of the make or model. "I'll see whatever you tell me to see," Charlie insists. The detective ignores the statement and nods, his gaze fixed on the folder before him.

"Well, we do have another witness who saw the car. If you agree on seeing the same car, our case is all the stronger."

Charlie wonders who the witness might be, but before asking outright, he realizes the detective would keep that information secret until the trial.

"We need to get into Sam's apartment, though, pull some DNA from a hairbrush or something. Without it, the lab can't prove anything – that's another reason I asked about your relationship with his wife."

Charlie feels suddenly anxious; his story may fall apart if the police can talk to her parents or Tess. Her father knew a Charlie had called for their daughter, the police could check those phone records, and that he had buzzed them the night of the shootings. If he is caught in a lie, everything he's sacrificed will be in vain. Talk about a rock and a hard place. To keep their true relationship secret, he will have to call Tess again and fill her in on the details, and she would, in turn, have to tell her parents everything if she hadn't already.

Chapter Seventy
Saturday, 4:00 pm

Throughout the day, Tess wonders who she should call and who she should alert to Sam's death.

Realistically, she shouldn't even know about his murder. She might have lived the rest of her life believing that Sam had disappeared into his new life, never to be heard from again. This scenario does not appeal to her. She decides that would have been hell, worse than what happened.

"I won't tell anyone," she whispers, turning down the sheets on her bed. A gurgle in her stomach surprised her; she hadn't felt the urge to eat in some time. A promising sign, she thinks.

Moving through the halls, she enters the cafeteria and picks up a plate, piling it high with meats and portions of pasta. Sitting down, she shovels the food into her mouth. Starving, she thinks.

Finishing the plate, she believes she can eat again but pushes the thought away. Any more, and she is sure she would throw it all up.

Standing to leave, she sees Paul, again being escorted down the hall to the secure wing. He looks tired, drugged, maybe. She remembers her plan to bring Madi to him. Perhaps tonight would be the night, she contemplates.

Her phone rings, and she remembers to look at the call display before answering this time. It's a private number. She shrugs and answers it anyway.

"Tess, it's Charlie."

"Charlie, uh, hi, what's going on?"

"Listen, I've got the police working on Sam and my brother's case. I've made myself their star witness and need you to listen right now, okay?"

"Okay."

"They are close to nailing the guys that killed Sam. They need a hair sample, though, from a comb. Is there something like that at your place?"

"Sure, he used to use my brushes. I left one on my vanity. Why do they need his hair?"

"DNA. They're trying to put a case together from this. But you're not home. Are you somewhere now that you could get home and hand over the comb?"

"I-I could, but I shouldn't leave where I am. Not for another week."

"Have you told your parents any of this?"

"No."

"If it comes to that, where you do tell them or talk to the police, just forget about our hooking up the other night. You and I knew each other six to seven years ago, all that's true. I don't want the cops to lose focus on the people responsible for all of this."

Tess lets Charlie's words sink in. She examines them, running through scenarios in her mind. She is happy Charlie is helping the police but can't believe how complicated her life has become over the past week. Eventually, she verbalizes a plan that makes the most sense to her.

"If I let the police visit my parents, then I don't have to be the one to tell them. They'll explain where I've been and hand over the comb." She pauses a moment to consider their reaction. "At this point, it's just a missing person's case, right?"

"I told the police Jorge's dying declaration was that they'd killed Sam. So they're treating it as a murder."

"But what will they tell my parents?"

"Probably that he's missing and maybe presumed dead and that they need a hair sample to assist in tracking him down."

"Okay, thanks, I'll take care of it."

Tess hangs up and sits down again at the table, once again overwhelmed by the events. She wonders if she should place this type of stress on her elderly parents. Her dad would manage the police fine, but the initial shock may have them catastrophizing over her. She decides to call them.

* * * * *

Charlie hangs up the payphone and walks back to the police station across the street, where his ride back to the hotel awaits.

* * * * *

Doug picks up the phone at his daughter's apartment to make a call and hears the tell-tale beep of a message awaiting retrieval.

"Celeste," he calls to his wife. "What did Tess say the code was? She's got a message."

"Star -98," she calls back. Doug punches in the digits and listens to the message. To his surprise, the police are looking for Tess. They are asking to speak with her concerning her husband. Doug shakes his head, imagining what his fool son-in-law has managed to get himself into this time. He remembers twice getting a call on Sam's behalf after being picked up on DUI's. Just another reason to hate him, Doug decides and places the phone down.

Chapter Seventy-One
Saturday, 4:50 pm

"Hi, Dad," Tess announces as cheerfully as she can.

Wondering whether he should burden her with the message the police had left on her phone, Doug decides to handle them himself and moves on.

"What's new, Pussycat?"

"Just checking in; everything going well?" Tess thinks this should be enough that when the police arrive at the apartment door, her parents shouldn't worry that something has happened to her.

"Emma's great. Your mom and I are going to stick around the house today."

"Oh, perfect," Tess says a little too eagerly, hoping they'd stay close to home while the police were planning a visit. "Well, I'm still here," she laughs lightly. "I have a workshop in a few minutes, but I just wanted to know Em was okay."

"No problem. All is well." The call-waiting mutes his conversation a moment, and he quickly exits. "Talk to you soon. Love you." He pushes the button twice and raises the phone to his ear once more.

"Hello?"

"Yes, hello, sir; this is Detective Brice calling. I'm looking to speak with Tess Seager."

"She's not available for about a week, Detective, but this is her father, retired Detective Armstrong. How can I help?"

"Hello, sir. Would it be alright if I visited your daughter's residence and sat briefly with you? I have news of her husband's disappearance."

Disappearance, Doug thinks. This is much more than he was prepared to hear. Another DUI, sure, a hit and run, likely, but a disappearance? He feels a wall materialize between him and the detective now, wanting to protect his daughter from any accusations.

"What do you mean, *disappearance*?"

"I think you know what I mean, Detective," Brice appeals to Doug's former title.

"You believe he's *dead*?"

"Considering the company he's been keeping lately, yes. But I'd like to talk to your daughter more in-depth."

"They're separated," Doug offers. "She has been in the hospital the past few days. She's there for another week. What can I do for you?"

Brice explains his need for a sample of one of Sam's hair follicles but little else.

"This is my son-in-law you're talking about, Detective. I want to know everything there is to know. Tess is in a psychiatric care facility at the moment, and I don't want her upset by this news."

"Then allow me to stop in, and I'll collect the sample."

"Nothing more."

"Nothing more. Sir, your daughter isn't a suspect."

"Good. I'll remember you said that. Come by before too long. Buzz 404."

Chapter Seventy-Two
Saturday, 7:00 pm

Tebor stops in at Tess's room on his way to the cafeteria. He raps at the door until she appears.

"Dinner?"

Tess nods, enters the hall, and closes the door behind her.

"How have you been?"

"You wouldn't believe what's been happening. Charlie called me, and the police are working on my husband's case. They need DNA from my house. My parents are going to have to hear about Sam's disappearance. It's a nightmare!"

"Wow, I'm sorry. What a mess."

"I honestly feel like I should be home now, answering all these questions and asking some of my own."

"The best thing you can do is stay put. Keep out of it as much as possible for as long as possible. These things tend to work themselves out."

"Sure, at the expense of my parent's mental health." She fills a cup of coffee. "I feel so guilty."

"What on earth for?" Tebor sits at a table, and Tess follows. "None of this is your fault, not Sam's disappearance, not your family secret, none of it."

"I guess."

"It's true. You didn't kill your brother's abuser. You didn't kill your husband."

"But did I make Sam leave me?" Tess places the fork next to her plate, suddenly sad.

"Of course not."

"But what if he'd stayed with me? He wouldn't have done what he'd done."

"Don't put that on yourself. Sam's choices put him in the ground, not yours."

"And what of the poet? Was it his choice to have his wife leave him?"

"Is that what this is really about?" Tebor's mood brightens; he picks up his fork and stabs a piece of pasta. "I fear he may have been the architect of his demise."

"How so?"

"In such a person, sadness breeds purpose. They find inspiration in the darkness. Oftentimes, I believe, they will impress a hell onto their own lives in order to re-create it, that others might suffer the experience from the comfort of their armchairs."

"That's beautifully put, if not a little crazy."

"Well, that's another way of putting it!" He laughs into his napkin, coughing. Clearing his throat, he explains. "Clinically insane may be the most widely accepted description for such an artist."

"You're saying he – *I* was clinically insane in my past life?"

"Perhaps, yes."

Tess shakes her head, chewing slowly on a plain piece of bread. She doesn't appreciate this view of the man who wrote such profoundly moving prose. Did one also have to be clinically insane to value his works, she wonders?

"Don't trouble yourself with such things. The past is the past. What do they say? 'If you're depressed, you're living in the past. If you're anxious, you're living in the future. If you're at peace, you're living in the present.'"

"Know it all," she teases, her mood lightening.

"All I'm saying is remember the past, but don't live in it, learn from it, and never blame yourself for the choices of others."

This statement reminds Tess of her plan for Paul, the cutter. She wants to affect his life positively and mentions to Tebor her interest in bringing Madhiva to him tonight to understand why he does what he does.

"Likely, it's connected to a past life. Curious though, what do you suppose would encourage someone to cut themselves over and over again?"

"Paul has his own ideas about that, but I think past life regression could offer him so much more."

Chapter Seventy-Three
Saturday, 7:45 pm

Doug finds a comb on his daughter's dresser and gives it to the detective. The grey blonde hairs that were Sam's contrast heavily with the jet black hair that is Tess's.

"I hope this helps in your search."

"I know it will, sir. I appreciate your cooperation. Please ask your daughter to call us when she is home. Anything she can tell us."

"I'm sure she has no idea, Detective."

Brice nods and hands the comb to his partner, who places it in a plastic baggie. Extending his hand to the former detective, they shake, and Brice leaves.

"I'm sorry this has happened to your family, Detective Armstrong." Doug nods and watches the detectives move down the hall to the elevator.

* * * * *

That evening, Tess lies in bed, awake. Tebor has left her to read in the library, and she finds herself thinking about Sam. She thinks about the approaching holidays; he will be absent for: Thanksgiving and Christmas. She thinks about how different her life will be now that he is gone for good. Her eyes flood with tears once more, and she turns on her side, gathering her knees up to her chest.

When would this feeling end? She had felt alone since he'd left, but now its permanence was starting to take hold. She would never again lay eyes on him. He was gone, forever.

Why did she end up alone so often in the lives she lived, she questions? As the little girl, the poet, the mother, would she die alone again?

She sits up and dries her eyes with the sleeve of her pajama top. There is a lesson in the lives she's lived. She shivers and pulls the blankets over her shoulders.

Just then, a sense of purpose takes hold. A lesson revealed: to live alone, to die alone, to accept both, and to be comfortable with them. The fear, where her sadness, anger, and confusion originate, as the doctor had suggested, she concludes, comes from dying alone, from being alone.

She was abandoned by a father, a husband, a wife, and again a husband. Tess compares the three lives she's regressed to her present life. "I haven't learned the lesson."

Clearly, there is a theme to her lives; abandonment, followed by a crushing sense of loneliness. And perhaps because she hadn't learned how to forgive and let go of the resentment, as Madi has suggested she do, she died alone.

"I don't want that to be my life again." Tess takes a deep breath, drawing in the universal wisdom. She feels lighter somehow, clarity of purpose coursing through her veins. Her heart pumps the newly oxygenated blood through her body, exciting the nerves on her skin, her chest tingling with anticipation over this renewed sense of well-being.

With this revelation in hand, Tess is eager to see Madi again tonight, not for herself, but to offer the experience to Paul, who she believes could benefit significantly by looking into his past to better deal with his present.

Chapter Seventy-Four
Saturday, 11:00 pm

In his thirty-nine-dollar-a-night hotel room, Charlie prepares for bed. The room offers few amenities: no complimentary soaps, no bar fridge, and no coffee maker in the corner.

The sounds of mice in the walls and the three bugs he'd killed on his way from the bathroom to his bed do not deter him from sleep. Charlie is emotionally at his limit. He realizes he's never actually tested his limits in this regard since the passing of both parents. Even then, he hadn't feared for his life. He'd taken care of himself and Jorge for three years by then and was old enough to claim his brother as a dependent and stay in the rented apartment where both mother and father had died.

Charlie falls asleep, remembering those difficult times, explaining to his baby brother that Mom and Dad weren't coming home again. That they were in heaven. He pulls the thin sheets over his shoulders and faces the wall.

Charlie had decided long ago that heaven was a concept for desperate men. Heaven was a comfort the suffering embraced, a destination the weak, tired, and discontent eagerly awaited. He held no illusions from a very young age, watching his parents fight, drink, hit, and choke each other in front of him and his brother. Charlie saw no wisdom in a God that would allow this pathetic pair guardianship over children, and so he saw no place for God in his life. Instead, he grew stronger for his brother; he became someone Jorge could look up to, someone who put food on the table and worked an honest job. Everything he had ever done was for his brother.

And now his brother is dead.

As he plunges into sleep, Charlie revisits a dream. He crawls towards a burnt-out subdivision where he knows his house once stood. The sounds of anti-aircraft overhead are only trumped by the booming explosions as bombs slam into the ground all around him.

Once Charlie recognizes the ruins of his house, he sprints to the wreckage. He notices a hand poking out at the east wall and wrestles a portion of the neighbor's chimney from his path. Falling flat, he stumbles on a segment of roofing, his hand connecting with the hand resting limply over the wall.

The band on the ring finger is enough to send him into a frenzy. He knows this is his wife's hand. He knows she is dead. What he doesn't yet know is whether his children have been taken from him as well.

Before he can gather the courage to sift through the devastation, looking for his children's tiny, broken bodies, he peers over the leveled wall and confirms his wife's fate.

Her white skin is colored in brick dust. He gently brushes it from her face, her hair dry and covered in red soot. He closes the lids on her lifeless, staring eyes and leans in to kiss her cheek, shaking.

From his thin mattress, Charlie calls out to his wife, mourning the name he knows her by in this life.

He wakes to a soaked pillow, realizing he's been sobbing. Sitting up in bed, he remembers every detail of the nightmare. He remembers his wife and the overwhelming recognition he felt when he looked into the dead woman's eyes.

"Jesus, fuck," he says aloud, hands rubbing the back of his neck. "Tess?"

Chapter Seventy-Five
Saturday, 11:10 pm

Charlie's cell rings. He jumps at the unexpected noise, still trying to piece together his nightmare. A sense of loss equal to that which he's suffering over his brother's death hangs in the air. A sense of foreboding accompanies a wave of anxiety as he reflects on the dream. He picks up his phone and listens without answering. It's Detective Brice, the officer in charge of the Molloy case.

"Sorry to wake you, Charlie."

Charlie grunts, a lump still lodged in his throat.

"Listen, I'm playing a hunch. We've got you and the other witness to the shooting, and the lab is making some headway with hair fibers found at two of the Molly-owned funeral parlors. I'm curious: did your brother have any friends we could talk to? I mean, other than Sam, someone that could finger the Molloy men that supposedly killed Sam."

"*Supposedly*," Charlie says defensively, finding his voice. "What the fuck does that mean?"

"Relax, Charlie. I believe you, but everyone is innocent until proven otherwise. You know that. If Sam's phone had had any texts or call histories to view, it would have been easier, but someone erased them all. Even his provider hasn't any information they're willing to share with us."

Charlie was responsible for this, ensuring his texts to Tess would not be traced.

"So I'm asking you, is there anyone we could speak with that may have additional information or be an eye-witness to Sam's murder? I mean, how did Jorge come across this information? Did he witness it?"

"No," Charlie admits. "Jorgie didn't witness it." He considers whether to involve the one person who could break the case wide open, the one person who helped Sam's murder play out. The problem is, he considers, she could finger Charlie and his brother for organizing the whole thing, having the Molloy men go to her house and wait for Sam. The plan was for Jorgie to meet Sam at Donna's, but Sam was already there when he'd called. Then, all he needed was a push. Jorge gave him that.

"Let me get back to you on that, will you, Detective?" Charlie wants to buy some time to consider Donna's involvement. *Could she skew the story just enough to keep his involvement out of it? Just pick the story up where the Molloy men broke into her house, Sam happened by, and she watched them murder him in cold blood?*

"Sure. Remember, the more artillery we have to go at them with, the better chance we have at bringing them down."

Charlie hangs up and stares at his phone. Thumbing through addresses, he finds Donna's number. He wonders whether she's heard about Jorge's death. He quickly dials her number from his hotel room.

"Hello?"

"Donna, it's Charlie."

"Why are you calling me? Where's Jorgie?"

"Jorgie's dead, Donna." Silence follows. Since the incident with his friend, Donna has been frantically calling Jorge's phone, but Jorge hadn't picked up on Charlie's orders.

"Dead?" She swallows hard.

"Yes, Molloys shot him outside the bar the other night. I need you to let the police look through your house and get your statement. I need you to tell them what you saw."

"Jesus, Charlie. No, fuck that. I'm scared."

"I know you are, but you need to let the police know what you know: that they killed Sam in your house and show them where. We're close to taking them down."

"What do you mean? You *wanted* this to happen."

"Yes, but now they've killed my brother, they've killed Jorgie, and I'm a witness. I need you to witness against them, too."

"No, I – I'm not getting any more involved in this nightmare."

"They killed Jorgie in front of me, goddamn it. I *need* you."

"I'm *scared.*"

"Me too, but this is all going down pretty soon, and you should want to be on the winning side." Charlie wasn't sure which side he was on, but he needed to exaggerate their position to bring her on board.

"They'll kill us both before we ever get to trial. Where are you, in a witness protection program or something?"

Charlie can hear her exhale deeply and remembers her vice. "Jesus, you're not smoking that crack again, are you?"

"It's not *crack*, Charlie."

"You're no good to me if you're not straight. Clean up and do this for me. Do it for Jorgie."

"Fuck, okay, for Jorgie. What do you want me to do?"

"Come into the station with me and tell them what happened. Tell them the Molloys came to your house looking for Jorge and found Sam, Killed him and threatened you."

"Is that going to fly?"

"Well, there must be evidence they were there."

"They did it pretty clean. But there are a couple of blood marks on my basement stairs, where they pushed him."

"That will be enough. You need to identify the men who did it. They'll show you pictures. They're dead anyway."

"Dead?"

"Yes, Jorge shot them both. They can't hurt you."

"Well, where do we meet?"

"Meet me at the station tomorrow at noon, the big one, at William's and Bold."

"Okay." Her voice trembles.

"Donna, this is the only way either of us will ever feel safe again."

Safe, this word resonates with her. She hasn't felt safe since Sam's body was marched out her back door. She remembers the hitmen's accents and every pockmark and wrinkle on their cruel faces. She remembers the anxiety and fear that followed their introductions at her front door. She'd known bad men before, but there was something infinitely eviler in the hearts of the two who had visited her that night at her boyfriend's request.

"I'll be there for noon."

Chapter Seventy-Six
Sunday, 12:01 am

Madhiva and Tebor listen as Tess explains her plan to have Madi access Paul's room and ask if he'd like to be regressed to a past life.

"He had mentioned that he liked the idea of being hypnotized."

"Yes, but he hasn't been notified that we would be stopping in tonight. I don't want to ambush him with this."

"I'd go myself and warn him, but I can't access that wing. You would have to use your code to get us in."

Tebor looks to his friend, the nurse he has put so much faith in the past year, and tilts his head. Madi knows this look and what it means. She smiles, shaking her head at him.

"Alright, but if he flips on us and hits the panic button, you'll both be thrown out of the program, and I'll probably lose my job."

"I don't want anything bad to happen," Tess admits, and before she can put the brakes on the plan, Madhiva comes up with an idea of her own.

"I'll go in and see if he's awake. I'll tell him you've sent me and why. If he's responsive, I'll double back and get you. If not, then no harm done."

"Perfect," Tess agrees, nodding.

Tebor smiles brightly and bows out. "He doesn't know me. I'll keep watch at the hall door. Pretend I'm reading a book."

"What bird call will you make if an orderly comes our way?" Tess jokes and Tebor laughs abruptly on cue. He takes the cell phone from Tess's hand and pulls his own from his pajama pocket.

"How about I just text you an alert?" He copies Tess's number into his phone and puts hers on vibrate.

"You're sure you're up to this? You're taking your life in your hands," she kids, a giddy excitement building between them.

"Well, *if I live too long, I'm afraid I'll die* anyway," Tebor recites with a hint of irony, slipping his mobile back into his pocket.

Tess looks quizzically at him. She hadn't known him to quote anything other than philosophers or religious texts. She recognized this latest reference immediately from a band she happens to adore.

Tebor shrugs. "The Kinks," he winks at the girls, forcing a laugh from them.

"I love that song," Tess turns to Tebor, shakes off the unlikelihood of him quoting something she recognized, never mind a lyric that has stayed with her half her life. Slipping her purse over her shoulder, she eyes Tebor with a look of amazement as she opens his door and leads the group across the cafeteria and toward the secure wing.

The interior hallways and common areas are relatively dark; dim lighting ignites the dark corners and now empty steel buffet tables. Tebor stops just beyond the hallway door, and Tess hangs back with him as Madi approaches to enter her code.

Thunder booms overhead; rain falls hard and fast outside the picture windows that run the hall's length, and the courtyard accumulates puddles on its uneven patio. Tess raises her eyebrows at Tebor, a playful smile on her face.

"You're enjoying this, aren't you!"

The anticipation on her face is hard to ignore, and a sense of déjà vu washes over him. A life reveals itself where he and Tess had lived out a similar moment, brimming with adrenaline, uncertainty, and expectation. Tebor experiences lucid moments like this when a déjà vu is realized and can often pull from the past responsible for the feeling. After living so many lives, he has become a very sensitive intuitive. Tebor has learned to harness his intuitive powers, and in situations such as these, where he experiences a déjà vu, his intuition kicks in, and a past that uncannily resembles the present is revealed.

At this moment, Tebor sees Tess as a 12th-century warrior dressed in light armor and a sword at the ready. He is dressed likewise, positioned behind her as they crouch in the woods, eagerly awaiting their signal to charge into battle.

The moment passes, and Tebor returns to the land of the living.

"You okay?" Tess asks him.

"Fine, Tess." He leans forward to look past her and watch Madi enter the secure wing.

"We're halfway there," she squeaks. Tebor smiles at her fervor.

Chapter Seventy-Seven
Sunday, 12:30 am

Doug contemplates the missing person's case concerning his son-in-law. He doesn't see it as bad; Tess should be rid of him for good. If he's dead – which, in his experience, is pretty much what a missing person case is - then she won't have to worry about him showing up one day, trying to be a part of her and Emma's life.

However it turns out, he wants the best for his daughter and granddaughter. Sam was never going to be that in his eyes. How could he? How could any man?

Doug rolled off the couch and finished the last of the imported bottles Tess had left in her fridge. He turns off the TV and heads to the bathroom to wash up.

As he lets the tap run, waiting for the hot water, a memory of his son creeps in. He recalls how he and Tommy used to fill the plastic pool in the backyard. Tommy would always want to hold the hose. Doug always let him. That pool turned into a pond the summer they'd lost their baby. It sat untouched beside the shed, collecting algae and nesting mosquitos.

Doug leaves the tap running and grabs a towel from the rack, pushing it up against his face and muffling the sounds of his sobs.

Tommy would have been a man today. Twenty-one years old. Celeste has forgotten, he thinks. She will be upset she's missed her son's birthday. Their routine was to watch midnight roll in, spend time recounting their memories of their little boy, and cry each other to sleep. His wife was exhausted from the day with her granddaughter and had fallen asleep an hour earlier. Doug likes that Emma has offered this reprieve to Celeste and pushes back the *what-ifs* and basks in the memory of his son's innocent round face and careless hair as he sits at the tub's edge, composing himself.

* * * * *

At the hospital, Tess received a reminder on her phone. Looking at the screen, she is instantly sad.

"What's happened?" Tebor asks.

Tess lifts her phone, gesturing with it to her friend. "It's my baby brother's birthday today. Tommy's birthday." She focuses again on her screen and removes the reminder with a push of her thumb.

"You alright?"

"Oh, yes," she blushes, shaking her head, embarrassed over the overblown sentimentality. "He's been gone fifteen years. I shouldn't dwell on him like this."

"He's your brother. You take all the time you need." Tebor sets his kind eyes on Tess, and she smiles shyly back at him. "Oh, Madi is at his door."

Madhiva balances on the heels of her feet after lightly knocking at Paul's door.

Tess and Tebor watch as she uses a key card to access the room and explains why she's visiting Paul. Paul's head rounds the door frame, and Tess stands so he can see her. She waves. Paul turns back to Madi and tells her to bring Tess in. Madi nods and opens the hall door for Tess to slip in and follow her down the hall. Looking back at Tebor, she waves excitedly to him. He laughs louder than he would like, nervously looking about the place.

"Hi!" Tess says emphatically as she enters Paul's room.

"I didn't expect to see you," Paul sits on his bed, legs crossed. "Thanks for coming."

"Well, you'd said you thought hypnosis was cool when I mentioned it, and then I met Madi here, who's taken me to past lives through hypnosis." Paul's attention perks up at the mention of past lives. "Yeah, so I asked her if she would do you hypnotize you."

"Okay, cool," Tess and Madi share a smile. Tess is buzzing with electricity over the possibilities for Paul. "So, what do I do?"

"You'll need to relax. Do you know what the doctors have you on?" Madi asks in her soothing tone. Paul shakes his head.

"I take two pills a day now, one in the morning and one in the afternoon."

"How do they make you feel? Do you feel lethargic after you've taken them?" Paul looks to Tess, not understanding the word.

"Tired," Tess pipes in. "Do they make you feel slow and tired and not yourself?"

Paul nods.

"Okay, when did you take a pill last, Paul?" Madi continues.

"At three this afternoon. Why are they going to make hypnotizing me a problem?"

"I think you'll be fine. That was nine hours ago. I think we can go ahead if you're ready." Paul nods, and Madi asks him to lie on his bed, place his arms at his sides, and allow himself to relax every muscle, nerve and thought. She continues to relax him until he is very still. Madi counts to three and lightly snaps her fingers, and Paul begins.

"I'm a little older than I am now."

"And where are you?"

"I'm with my mother. We come from a town on the edge of the Sea of Galilee."

"Are others with you?"

"Yes." Paul's expression turns from flippant to grave. "They're all covered in scabs and bumps. Some of them are missing their fingers, toes, or ears."

Madi writes the word *leprosy* on a pad and shows it to Tess. Tess unconsciously makes a face and turns her attention back to Paul.

"Do you have the same marks on your body? Does your mother?" Madi continues.

"Yes, my legs are covered in them. My mother has lost both ears and is blind in one eye." Paul shifts uncomfortably in his bed and describes their surroundings as rocky, desolate, and lifeless.

"We've been exiled. Our group joined with another in the mountains to the south. The priests told us God was angry. That He brought this scourge upon us in retribution for our sins."

The scene is one of deep despair, and Tess has difficulty listening to the descriptions of the unfortunate left to die in this wilderness. It only proved to make Tess feel more maternal towards him.

"Can you go ahead five years in this life?" Madi asks. Paul shakes his head and mumbles no. Madi looks at Tess once more, and they share a knowing glance. Paul never made it five more years as a leper.

Madi runs through the forgiveness speech, asking him to release his anger about being discarded by societal fears and forgive those responsible. Paul is remarkably receptive to the process and forgives without a second thought.

"Would you like to live another life, Paul, or return to the present?"

"Another," he whispers. Madi sends him down the hallway of his subconscious, and Paul picks a door, or the door picks Paul; either way, he enters another life.

Paul experiences many lives after the first, each offering new and painful ways to die. It was as though he'd managed to experience the disease of the century in each life he relived through Madi. The Black Death, bubonic plague, cancer, pneumonia, you name it. In the six additional lives he experienced tonight, he had died in agony.

Tess questions Madi with a look: how could anyone deserve such cruel ends?

Madhiva explains that during hypnosis, lives are chosen by the subconscious to assist in the person's present. - that these lives are coming through now for a reason. She suggests Paul's masochistic approach to this life is directly connected with the sicknesses he had contracted in those past lives.

As Paul is released from his trance, Madi offers the same explanation she had just given Tess.

"I can't believe it," he says, saddened by the lack of gladiator and gunslinger references to his past, no doubt. "I can't believe I died like that so many times."

"Your past is speaking to us. I believe you know why you died the way you did, and I believe once you come to understand it, you won't feel the need to hurt yourself any longer." Madi explains. Paul straightens out of the defeatist position, hunched over himself, sitting cross-legged on his bed.

"Me?" he wonders. Tess is nodding, her eyes locked on his. Paul gathers strength from her conviction.

"It is a lesson in this life that you must learn to break the cycle. You have not learned it yet." Madi points to his bandaged arm. "You won't need to do *that* anymore when you have."

Paul pulls his arms into his thin frame, embarrassed. Rubbing his eyes, he tells them it's late and that he should sleep. Madi and Tess share a look of concern, and Madi speaks up.

"Think about the lives you've lived tonight. Relate them to this life. Dream. Write your dreams down. We can discuss them Monday night."

Tess and Madi leave Paul's room silently. Scooting along the hall, they move through the security doors. Mission accomplished.

Chapter Seventy-Eight
Sunday, 9:00 am

The following morning, Tess wakes from a dream that can only be described as horrific. She considers the nightmarish lives Paul recounted while under Madi's spell but can't blame those for the disturbing scene from which she'd just woken.

Sitting cross-legged, her sheets on the floor, Tess holds her head in her hands. The dream was a vivid recreation of the death of a poet. She whimpers as she recalls the feelings of despair and sadness that brought him to his end. An emptiness as vast as any ocean guided his hand as the pistol rose to meet his temple.

Most disturbing, perhaps, is the fact that she could see herself as he raised the gun to his head, watching herself pull the trigger, reflected in his darkened window as a storm raged outside.

Tess felt every thought and emotion that assaulted the dark poet's heart. She understood what it is to hate yourself, criticize yourself, and plunge yourself into depression. Though she'd connected with the words in his book so profoundly, there are no words formidable enough to describe the devastating turn his life had taken after his wife, the woman he professed to be his muse, deserted him.

Tess recalls Tebor's statement: *'In such a person, sadness breeds purpose. Often they will impress a hell onto their own lives to create their art.'*

Tess thinks this sentiment seems to ring true when put in the poet's context. Her eyes danced around the room, not focusing on anything in particular but scanning her memory. She lives the poet's final thoughts, his last words to himself, speaking to his reflection: *Make me more than I am, that I might be remembered for all that I wasn't.*

Tess shivers and pulls up the blankets, making herself as small as possible on the bed. She had been given a message from the grave, a message from herself to herself.

The words repeat in her head; they repeat and repeat and repeat. She fears she isn't grasping their meaning while she wishes the verse away in the same breath.

Make me more than I am that I might be remembered for all that I wasn't.

Tess decides she'll write the verse down, silencing the repetition. She's weeping now, half because of her tremendous emotional burden, having lived in the poet's head even a short time, and the other because she is afraid. Afraid of the vision. That she could pull the trigger, the idea that she could end her own life, no matter the pain.

The book is still at her bedside table; she reaches for it and scribbles the verse on the back inside cover. A rush of electricity moves through her, and an idea is born.

Make me more than I am, that I might be remembered for all that I wasn't.

Tess clambers out of bed and slides into her slippers. She charges out of her room and to the library, where she sits in front of a computer station. Here, Tess punches in the name of the book and its author. Scrolling down the page, she finds no reference to the two coexisting except in the Wiki article she'd read earlier.

Next, she tries online book retailers and enters the same query - nothing. He doesn't exist - his work is forgotten. She looks up publishing houses, wondering whether one may own the rights, but again, nothing.

Tess is beginning to feel flush as the excitement builds, her nimble fingers repeatedly asking for the search to appear but finding nothing again and again. Then something catches her eye: the Millennium Copywrite Act. She skims its content and discovers the book is so old it is considered public domain, meaning no one owns the work. On the right side of her screen, an ad appears for the opportunity to self-publish. This is it, she thinks.

She clicks on the ad, taking her to an online retailer where adding a formatted version of any book is 'quick and easy.' She read the instructions on going about the process and considered what she would need to do next.

"I could scan the pages!" She stands, anxious to get started. She notices a scanner that happens to be built into the library's printer and flips the top gently. It buzzes to life.

Without a thought for her appearance, she jogs past a few residents milling about the buffet table in the cafeteria and, once in her room, snaps up the ancient volume.

Chapter Seventy-Nine
Sunday, 11:45 am

Charlie's escort pulls up to the station; the officer chauffeuring him turns and waves his hand at the building.

"Well," he says. "Getting out?"

Charlie places a hand on the cage, separating the front of the cruiser from the back. "Just give me a minute, will you?" He watches as Donna crosses the street a block ahead. Excitement builds in his chest. She's come. She's going to cooperate, he thinks.

But Charlie's moment is ripped away in a blur of violence as he watches a car from nowhere accelerate from behind a truck as Donna makes the mid-point of the crosswalk.

"Jesus," he says, and the cop turns at the sound of the screeching tires. They both watch helplessly as Donna is struck down by the car, thrown over it, landing hard on the asphalt. The vehicle races towards them now, and as Charlie hopes to catch the license plate, a barrage of bullets pepper the cruiser, killing Charlie's driver.

Charlie is on the floor, brushing glass off his bare neck, the tiny fragments indiscernible from the bits of skull that had burst from the officer's head. Covered in the gore of blood and brain, Charlie listens as the car skids to a halt behind him. He goes for the door, knowing he has no chance if they find him lying there. Charlie pulls at the handle, but the door doesn't budge. He's locked in.

As the men approach the cruiser, Charlie kicks out the remaining glass of the shot-up window. Shots are fired from the station and returned from behind him. The Molloy men have taken up a defensive position behind his cruiser!

The tip of a rifle passes over the kicked-out window, and the man attached to it stands to take a shot at the cops now gathering at the front of the station. Charlie decides it's now or never and kicks the man in the chest through the open window. The man falls backward, stumbling into the suppressing fire from the officers, numbering more than twenty now. The man is hit several times in the torso, pushing him further and further into the street until he drops.

The other man scrambles back to his car and, on his hands and knees, opens the driver's side door and crawls inside. The car roars to life, but before he can get two feet, he is gunned down.

As the gunfight ends, Charlie can only hear the scattered screams of on-lookers and the officer's voices as they approach his cruiser.

He is in a state of shock. As an officer peers through the broken glass, Charlie cannot understand what the man is telling him. His ears ring from his proximity to the gunfire. The officer opens the door slowly and reaches in a hand for Charlie to take. He does and cautiously steps out of the vehicle.

A moment later, paramedics are on the scene, tending to the woman on the street and the expired policeman. Donna is placed in a black body bag, and with her, any chance Charlie had at bringing down the Molloys. Or so he thinks.

Chapter Eighty
Sunday, 1:45 pm

"It's not a total loss," Detective Brice explains to Charlie, seated at the officer's desk. He doesn't appear shaken from the earlier violence in front of the station, but the look on his face is intense. "Our main witness is dead, yes, but the men who attacked you have been identified as Molloy men."

Charlie sits up in his chair. "That's a good thing."

"Well, not for Donna or Officer Bergeron, but it does open up a whole new case against the group, and believe me, killing a cop is going to be their downfall. This is it for them. We'll be methodically taking them apart piece by piece. It's already begun."

Charlie can't believe his luck. This is more than he could have dreamed. With the police on a vendetta against his enemy, he may live to see another day.

"We're going to keep you in protective custody as they clearly know who you are and what you're up to. I doubt we'll need your statement, but let's keep you safe until this thing goes to trial. I'd say we have a month at best. The Molloy's top people are all accounted for; we've seized Molloy assets, and with the bosses in custody, their lieutenants will be leaderless, and we suspect some infighting. In fact, we already have undercover op's set up to ensure that."

"You knew who the bosses were all along?"

"Of course, it's hardly a secret. They've just managed to keep clean while their fall guys take turns in the pen. That's not how it's going to go this time." He shuffles through the documents in front of him. "This time, we have enough to bury them once and for all.

We've been waiting for a mistake like this. That it came at the cost of an officer's life wasn't part of the plan, but it's got the whole station up in arms. We can expect other districts to volunteer their time to this as well. It will move very quickly from here on in."

"So, what will you do with me?"

"You'll be processed through witness protection in a few minutes," he lifts the paperwork and nods at Charlie. "That's what I'm holding in my hand. You'll be placed in a safe house for the month and released after the trials. Probably it won't take that long. The trials will be expedited for sure."

Charlie thinks about Tess. Wonders where she is and whether she's safe. He imagines the anticipation playing out in their embrace the next time he sees her.

Chapter Eighty-One
Sunday, 2:00 pm

Tess hovers over the scanner as she carefully bends the book flat, placing page after page of her past life's work on the glass plate. She clicks the mouse, and another page of prose is saved forever. Once the entire work has been captured, she saves the electronic version to a USB drive. Reviewing the document, she feels a warmth envelope her. The phrase set on repeat in her head fades away as purpose finds its footing again.

She spends much of the afternoon researching the best opportunities concerning whom she should publish the book. Tess concludes Amazon to be her best bet and creates an account, building her marketing platform and profile. She does not shy away from admitting the artist's work is, in fact, a book she had authored in a past life. She also includes a history of the author as pulled from the Wikipedia page.

By seven o'clock, Tess is exhausted, and her eyes heavy. She stands, stepping back to distance herself from the computer station.

At dinner, she sits with Tebor and excitedly announces what she's done with the book of poetry.

"That's brilliant!" he tells her. "Whatever gave you an idea like that?"

Tess explains the nightmare she'd woken from this morning, living the poet's last moments and his final words.

Tebor places his cutlery beside his plate. "I think you have experienced something with this past that will stay with you the rest of your life."

"Or lives," she adds spryly, leaning back from the table. "I mean, isn't that the point? To learn your lessons and grow into your next life."

"Exactly."

"Well, I have another session with Doctor Samuelsson early tomorrow, so I'm going to hit the sheets. Will I see you for lunch?"

Tebor nods.

Tess heads back to her room and takes a long shower. The time spent at the computer today has produced a stiff neck and shoulders. She rubs her neck as the hot water penetrates her muscles, loosening the tension and offering her a better chance at sleep. She feels good. She feels accomplished. She thinks that purpose was served today.

Chapter Eighty-Two
Monday, 3:30 am

After finding his wife in the rubble of their family home, mourning her loss, and delicately placing her free hand upon her broken chest, Charlie moves through his dream world, floating over the devastation in search of his children.

The dream has him digging through the debris, frantically calling out the names of his sons. With no luck locating them at his home, he moves down the street, shouting their names as the planes retreat into the night and the anti-aircraft artillery falls silent.

The quiet was noticeable, but only because the bombs and guns were a touch louder than the air-raid sirens and roaring fires spewing out of the wreckage all around him. Focused on finding his children, Charlie beats a path to the one place he thinks someone might survive an attack like this: the church basement, reinforced to withstand aerial bombings.

In the distance, the church still stands, and so long as the basement ceiling held out, those underground would be unharmed. As he reaches the building, he sees only three walls, with a collapsed roof between them. He pulls rubbish from the staircase entering the basement, stone and wood, and clay shingles. He calls out the further down he digs, stopping when he hears a distant voice beneath the debris.

"I'm coming!" he yells to them. Encouraged by the voices below, he throws rubble ten feet in every direction, his pace accelerating. A finger slips through the space between two heavy stones that once made up the gothic pillars that stood row on row down the aisle - the same aisle he watched his adoring wife float up to meet him on their wedding day. The same aisle they walked their children down when they were baptized. Grief aside, the possibility his sons were in this basement injects another rush of adrenaline, affording him super-human strength for a short period.

"Get back; I will kick the rest down towards you!" Charlie yells to those within. He can see very little through the narrow space he's cleared but hears those below shuffle out of the way. The remaining debris funnels into the basement as he braces himself and kicks to dislodge the stone.

The rubble gives way, and he listens as the stones smash upon the basement floor. Cheers rise through the new passageway, and people pour out of the darkness.

Charlie steps aside, anxious to see his boys emerge. Daniel is first; his face is scratched but otherwise unharmed. Charlie's heart sores. Nathaniel is next. Charlie gazes at Nathan and recognizes Jorgie, his little brother, in his youngest son's eyes.

He then experiences the sensation of floating upward, both boys securely tucked under one arm. They rise together and, from this vantage point, witness the extent of the damage the enemy has unleashed. It is total. It is terrifying.

Chapter Eighty-Three
Monday, 8:30 am

"I think it's time you call your father. Tell him what you know. If you want to bring them in to discuss it, that's up to you. You should clear the air. Let them know you know, and rebuild from that point. You've all lived a lie far too long." Karl tells Tess during her morning session. "There is little left for us to do through hypnosis. Now, it's got to be something the three of you openly discuss. I can help facilitate this if you want to include me."

Tess considers his recommendation. He's right, she thinks. Of course, he's right; he's the professional. She decides she'll approach them on her own. She believes her parents would be mortified to know anyone else knew what had happened to her brother's abuser, never mind meeting him. She tells the doctor that she will broach this with her parents alone.

"Whatever you feel most comfortable doing. My advice is not to let it go for much longer. Your parents will feel a weight lifted, too; you will be doing them a favor. They don't want to live a lie; they want to be honest with you. They just don't want to come off as the bad guys."

"How could they ever be the bad guys?"

"Your father killed a man and hid it from the world. He knew what he'd done was wrong but managed to live with himself all these years. Your mother knew it was wrong, but she, too, has lived with it half your life. They need to talk about it. They need to relive it with someone who understands your father's choice and to what end."

"If Mr. Drummond did this thing to Tommy if he abused him, I'm glad for what my father did."

"Then tell him that. He needs to hear that. Your mother kept this secret, too. She needs to hear that as well from you."

Tess stares at her feet, cross-legged, seated on the lounge. She fans her face with both hands and jerks as tears well up. She cries for Tommy once more but also for the terrible burden her parents have withheld for so long. For her father, such a good man, to have been put in the position he was. And for the terrible grief their family endured over her brother's suicide.

"I will call him," she tells Karl. "I will let him know what I know."

"It's good therapy for the family. Let them know if they want to discuss this in a closed forum. I will see you all in a place of your choosing at no cost."

"Thank you, doctor. That's very kind."

"Would you like to talk further about your husband?"

"No," Tess says without skipping a beat. "What we've done has been very helpful, but I need to get back to life before I can think of him again."

Karl nods and scribbles down some notes, then closes his folder. Standing, he signals the end of the session and walks Tess to the door.

"Revisit the five stages of grief. Write in your journal, and share your thoughts in your next class. Understand each stage and allow yourself to experience each in its turn. They exist to help you through this difficult time."

He places an encouraging hand on her shoulder and opens the door. This affectionate gesture motivates Tess to hug him, regardless of the moment's awkwardness. She hugs him tightly, pulling at his collared shirt. When she steps away, he looks down at her; the resolve he knew she was capable of has returned to her eyes.

They nod at one another, and Tess moves out into the hall. She walks with a confidence she hasn't experienced in over a year.

Chapter Eighty-Four
Monday, 12:30 pm

After lunch, on a whim, Tess walks the short distance from the cafeteria to the windowed security door leading to the hallway where Paul's room is located. Peering through the caged glass of the door, she notices a gurney across the hall from one of the rooms, and her heart sinks. She frantically counts the doors and realizes the gurney is outside Paul's room. She places her palms against the cool glass and watches two paramedics exit the room, a crash cart trailing behind. Behind them, a doctor moves slowly, directing the men to push the gurney into the room and down the hall. Tess waits in terrible anticipation for the men to reemerge.

"Oh God, oh my God, no, please," Tess whispers as the gurney is removed and a white sheet is on it. Beneath the sheet is the long silhouette of her troubled friend. He is still. Tess finds standing difficult and allows her knees to bend as she reaches for the ground. Once on the floor, she folds her legs into her chest and tucks her head into her knees, struggling for breath with no regard for the other residents milling about.

Tebor finds her before the orderlies are alerted. He bends to one knee and gently touches her trembling back. She allows him to lift her to her feet and guide her to a bench along the windowed wall overlooking the courtyard.

"Whatever it is, we can work through it."

This time, Tebor's wisdom is misplaced; Tess thinks and tears herself away from him. "You're *wrong*," she tells him. A trembling behind her eyes alarms Tebor, and he backs off.

"Let's get you to your room at least." He offers his hand, but she refuses it. Instead, she stands abruptly and races through the cafeteria and into her room, slamming the door behind her.

Tess picks up anything that hasn't been screwed down in her room and throws them against the walls smashing an mp3 player, exploding a ceramic coffee cup, and breaking her clock radio. She wants to scream but finds the lump in her throat has restricted her windpipe, and so all she can manage is a strained cry. She collapses on her bed and pulls at the covers, digging herself in, with a mind never to resurface.

She is sure he has died. The doctor's slow retreat from his room, the paramedic's gradual handling of the gurney and cart. They looked like they'd all had the fight sucked out of them. They must have been in there for a while trying to revive him, she thinks through the tears. Biting the sheet in anger, Tess pounds her fists into the mattress, disillusioned by this new setback.

After two hours of reflecting on her friend's loss, there is a knock at the door. Tess is hesitant to answer it but then hears her doctor's voice softly call her name. At this, she untangles herself from the thin sheets and opens the door.

Karl looks down at her and sighs with a frown. Tess is red-eyed. Her hair is messy, and looking up at the doctor's kind face, she sulks. Karl asks if he can come in, and she closes the door behind him.

Samuelsson takes a seat on the edge of her bed. "I'm sorry this has happened."

Tess sits next to him. "He has sisters, you know. And a mother and a father." She manages through a small, hoarse voice. "I've been thinking about them. How difficult this will be on them."

"Are you relating to Paul's sisters?"

Tess nods her head and cries again.

"Don't put yourself in their place, Tess. You've been there. It's an ugly place to be. We will offer his family help. I don't want you to hurt your recovery by questioning your impact on Paul. If anything, you were good for him; I'm certain he would have seen that. What he's done is of his own volition. No one else can be held responsible for Paul but Paul."

"Why couldn't you help him?" She demands. Karl isn't prepared for this sort of backlash. He knows the parents will undoubtedly have their share of what-ifs, and he has a booklet of answers and explanations tailor-made for this sort of thing, but for Tess to ask, he is unsure how to answer.

"I can tell you things like he was a difficult patient, a stubborn boy, a hopeless case, but I have seen excellent results from similar studies. I can only tell you that we are all responsible for ourselves at a certain point in our lives, and our decisions are our own."

"It's *not* fair."

"What did I tell you about life? It's indifferent. It is what you make it."

"But did Paul even have a chance?"

"Yes. Aside from the cutting, Paul was a bright boy with interesting ideas and honest questions. He didn't have to resort to cutting."

"Didn't he respond to any drugs?" Tess slides away from Karl so she can look at him. "I mean, lots of people are on drugs here. I see them every day at the medication station."

"We were working towards finding the right combination. We weren't getting the results we'd hoped for, and so I was about to recommend alternative treatments."

"You mean hypnosis?"

"Yes."

Tess feels sick. She had tempted Paul with hypnotic regression, and he had welcomed it with open arms. His past lives were horror stories. Could he have killed himself over what he'd experienced in hypnosis, she wonders?

Karl sees Tess struggling with an idea and touches her shoulder.

"Whatever it is, *whatever it is*, Paul's decision is his. Nothing you said or did is to blame for this."

Tess stares up into his sympathetic smile and knows this must be true on some level. That Paul's choice to end his life was his own, but had she nudged him with his sad line of past lives?

"Whatever it is, Tess," Karl reiterates, looking her deep in the eye. "This is *not* your fault." He stands to leave. "I'll see you tomorrow, and we'll talk more about this if you wish. Tess nods, and Karl exits her room, leaving the door slightly ajar.

Chapter Eighty-Five
Monday, 8:30 pm

Tess finds no peace in her head or heart over Paul's decision. She questions the point of everything: all that she knew and all that she's learned in her short time at the hospital. Paul was offered every chance through regression therapy to understand his past and change his present. But he chose to end this life, possibly to attach himself to a new, better life, but has he only regulated himself to another life in which he will suffer?

* * * * *

Charlie sits in his safe house with a plain-clothed police officer in the kitchen, making coffee. He's finding it difficult to get comfortable with so many unknowns floating around his head. The first of which is Tess. He feels he needs to speak with her. To know she's alright and to explain his dream. Stepping out of earshot of Richard, the officer assigned to him, he dials Tess.

* * * * *

It takes Tess a moment to register the ringing of her phone. After several rings, she absently reaches for it.

"Yes?" she says softly, her thoughts still with Paul.

"Hi," Charlie says with a sigh. A silence follows on both ends.

"Charlie," she manages, pulling the phone from her ear and looking at the contact name on her screen.

"Yes," he tells her. "Are you alright?"

"No," she answers dreamily. "Something's happened. Something I don't understand, and I *can't* understand."

"What's happened? Where are you?"

"At the hospital," she says pragmatically. "Where are you?"

"The *hospital?*" Charlie's tone rises enough that Tess has to move the phone an inch from her ear.

"I have a few more days here before I come home. Where are you?"

Charlie searches for the right thing to say but can't fight the need to know what Tess is doing in a hospital.

"Why are you in the hospital?"

"On vacation. I've been here a week already."

"In the city?"

"Yes."

"I just wanted to talk to you. Is this not a good time?"

"It's fine. What would you like to talk about?"

"Jesus, you sound like you're full of Valium." Silence follows. "Are you still there?"

"Yes, I'm here." A brief pause. "You know I had a dream about you." Charlie goes silent now, Tess trumping his reason for calling. "You were my husband. We were at war or something. We had children. You were my husband..." she trails off.

Charlie is momentarily stunned, and it comes across in his response. "I – Tess, that's why *I'm* calling *you!* I had the same dream. You died, and our children –"

"Did you find them? Did you? Did you find my babies?" Tess trades her dreamy state for one, suddenly alert.

"Yes. They were in the church, Tess. They were safe."

Tears well up and release on both ends of the conversation. Tess feels her heart leap and stands to meet it.

"Oh, Charlie, thank you." Her voice is shaky but enthusiastic now.

"Was it - just a dream?"

"It's much more than that. Another life, another *lifetime*. Thank you for finding my children."

"Our children."

"Yes, our children. Thank you for telling me. Thank you."

"Tess, I -" He stops, having never heard himself say the words aloud; he feels anxious over her response.

"Charlie, I know. I know."

Chapter Eighty-Six
Tuesday, 7:00 am

Tess has slept nearly eleven hours and wakes to darkness. The autumn ushers in later mornings, and in the dark, she feels rejuvenated. Since Charlie shared her dream that he found her children and single-handedly proved the existence of past lives, she can't stop smiling. Perhaps Paul hadn't died in vain, she considers. Maybe he did learn something from his experience with Madi and then decided to move onto a new life, one he would be better prepared to meet. Tess holds onto this notion as she gets into the shower.

At breakfast, she sees Tebor seated at a table. He sends a benevolent smile to her, and she returns it. Tess pours a coffee and sits with him.

"You look well." Tebor offers.

"I think I am," she tells him, still smiling and sipping the hot coffee. "I spoke with Charlie last night." She turned to meet his gaze, and Tebor put his fork down to listen. "Remember the life I'd lived through a dream and then through Madi? The one where I recognized Charlie as my husband? The one where there was a war going on?"

"You've discussed it with him," Tebor says knowingly.

Tess nods back enthusiastically. "Yes, but Tebor," she leans in and takes his hand. "He recounted the same dream. He told me I died. He told me he found my children."

"The boys." He squeezes her hand, and she squeezes back. A tear traces her sharp features, and Tebor wipes it away with his thumb.

"Happy tears," she says, running a napkin over her cheek. "It changed everything for me."

"It would." He cocks his head to the side. "An epiphany."

"Yes, exactly, my *epiphany*; I've had an epiphany!" She leans back in her chair and, still holding Tebor's hand, places her free hand on her chest. "And he *loves* me," she continues, eyes staring at the ceiling.

"Loves you?"

"I think I love him too, if that's even possible. He's so much older than me, and we're from two very different worlds."

"Don't discount your feelings. Don't do that. You deserve to be happy." Tebor squeezes her hand again, and she leans in.

"I *do* love him." she nods, a smile building on her face as the sun breaks the horizon.

Tebor watches on as her smile eclipses the sun's brilliance.

"Hold onto that feeling. Keep it safe, keep it close. I'm very happy for you. You've no idea how this news completes me."

Tess takes Tebor's face in her hands and kisses his cheek. "You have been a friend like no one I have ever known. I cherish you."

"You see?" he responds, clearly moved by her touching assertion. "I *told you* we knew each other."

Chapter Eighty-Seven
Tuesday, 9:00 am

Detective Brice reviews the forensic evidence from one of the Molloy Group's funeral parlors about Sam Seager's hair samples pulled from his wife's brush. They have managed to match the DNA to the blood on Donna's basement staircase as well, confirming the story Charlie relayed to them in Donna's stead.

"Got you," he whispers emphatically. Spinning in his chair, he jumps up and rushes to see his Captain. There, they discuss the building evidence against the group. Brice walks back to his desk and puts a call into the man who has become his star witness.

"Charlie, we have the evidence we need. The blood at Donna's matches the DNA we've secured from Sam's hair follicles and the funeral home."

* * * * *

Charlie is speechless. He sits on the couch of the safe house and weeps. The detective continues to tell Charlie what would happen next: that there would be several separate trials involving the Kingpins where many of their own would testify against them for lesser sentences. His case would be first. It would begin in two days, and then he would be free to go. "This is incredible." Charlie sees the light at the end of the tunnel, and standing there is Tess. The possibility of seeing her again soon stirs the familiar tingling in his chest. Then the feeling sinks to his stomach as he considers any contact with her will put Tess and her family at risk. He can't be sure who has his picture in their pocket and whether the hit on him will follow him all his days. This leaves Charlie at a loss as to how to proceed. The thought of never seeing her again feels like a knife pressing into his chest. The sensation was so real he placed a hand on his heart to remove the invisible blade.

"Just tell me when and where, detective. I need to do this quickly."

"An attorney will be at the house tonight to talk you through the process, and then the officer will be given the information to deliver you to the courthouse when it's time. Charlie, I don't have to tell you how important this is. You'll need all your wits about you."

"I understand. What happens after? I mean, they obviously want me dead. Will I be safe when it's all said and done?"

"We're working on a witness relocation plan for you. Don't worry; we won't leave you hanging."

"Thanks." Charlie hangs up the phone and stands. He's never felt so helpless in his life. He thinks the relocation plan is a good thing, but where does that leave him and Tess? Could he walk away from her, just disappear? The thought of it stirs up emotions he has never experienced. He is unsure how to deal with them. They come in waves, anxiety overwhelming his senses. He paces the floors, trying to stay ahead of the feelings, trying to think of a plan that would place him and Tess together, but none is forthcoming. He stops suddenly and wills his heart to stone.

She was never mine to leave.

Chapter Eighty-Eight
Tuesday, 10:00 am

Tess wants to call her parents to know how everything is going with Emma but fears she'll break into the speech about Drummond. En route to see Dr. Samuelsson, she nearly makes the call but decides to save it for later in the day. As she arrives at the office, Karl opens the door.

"Always right on time," he greets her with a sympathetic smile. Tess sits at the lounge, and Karl notices she is grinning.

"Well, you look like the cat that swallowed the canary. If I didn't know better, I'd say you were happy."

Tess explains her revelation the night before, not about the dream or the past lives, but of her love for a man who had come into her life the week before enrolling herself in treatment.

"An interesting turn of events."

"Yes, after speaking with him again last night, I felt this overwhelming goodwill. My heart filled up, and the feeling hadn't left me. I slept better than I have since I've been here. I just, I don't know, I feel *good*. Is that bad? I mean, after what's happened with Sam and Paul?"

"Feeling good is good, Tess. Paul wouldn't want you to feel bad. He was your friend, right? He didn't do this to hurt you. Suicide is a selfish pursuit. When people enter that mindset, they no longer see the world for what it is, filled with people who love you and will miss you. They see only pain, only darkness, and seek only an escape. What they don't see is that suicide is a permanent solution to a temporary problem."

"What do you think my brother saw when he -" She stops herself, the good feeling fading in place of the memory.

"Your brother was a child. My experience with this sort of thing tells me he was ashamed, frightened, and confused. He might have read or watched something on TV that put the idea in his head. I don't want to tell you your brother was selfish for doing what he did. I mean to say that the act is selfish because people no longer see the good. They can't get past the pain and shame. When someone has reached that point, they no longer recognize their loved ones. You saw this in how disconnected Tommy was in those last days. What I'm saying is he didn't do what he did to hurt you or your parents; he did it to flee a present that he couldn't understand."

"Yes, I see that now."

"If those that were suicidal could only put their problems in perspective, see them for what they are," he clears his throat and puts down the clipboard. "Well, life is a work in progress."

"Will I be alright?" Tess asks.

"You're *in love*." he reminds her. "If I could tell everyone to go out and fall in love, I'd be out of a job." He chuckles to himself. Tess smiles again and quickly looks down at her feet.

"I'm in love," she repeats. A deep breath follows, and she stands, waving her hands in her face. Karl stands and walks her to the door.

"You keep that good feeling. You're in a good place. You've accomplished so much in these nine days. Will you call your parents today?"

"Yes, I will do that today."

Karl watches Tess walk down the hall, both hands on her chest, breathing in love and life.

Chapter Eighty-Nine
Tuesday, 12:30 pm

Tebor steps beyond the walls of the hospital. His trepidation over this action falls away when his feet hit the pavement. He hadn't ventured out of the facility in months. Today, he's decided, will be a day of rebirth for him. He takes a stroll along the sidewalk, framing the parking lot. The air is cool, but he's dressed appropriately. A smile grows across his face the further he travels from the hospital. Here, he is reacquainted with a confidence he had lost once his wife had passed. On this short walk, he reclaims his life. He calls his kids from his cell phone. They are delighted to hear from him. They want to see him, and he is ready to see them. He enjoys a cigarette before returning to his room and packing his things.

* * * * *

"Hi, Dad," Tess says breathlessly.

"Hi, Bean, how's everything going?"

"Lots of ups and downs, but I'm up right now, so there's that."

"Glad to hear it, sweetheart. Stay in the moment." A nervous chuckle follows the fatherly advice.

Tess takes a deep breath and launches into the conversation that has haunted her the past few days. "Listen, I discovered something here I'd forgotten or blocked. I'm okay with it, but you should know I know."

Doug's heart sinks, and palms begin to sweat. This is it, he thinks; she knows about Drummond, she knows. What will she think of him?

"What is it you think you know?" He asks, adopting the cop façade he'd retired so many years ago. Tess is immediately intimidated by this and tries a different strategy.

"Well, it's nothing bad; I mean, I understand why it happened, it just, I guess what I saw was so upsetting at the time – I'm not upset anymore though, you should know that - I think what you did, I mean what happened, was in everyone's best interest." She feels her mouth go dry.

"I'm sorry, I'm not sure I -," but Doug stops himself short of denying his daughter what she's learned from her time at the hospital and yields. "Tess, I – I'm sorry if what I did somehow hurt you. I was only trying to protect you. After Tommy -" He stops again. The reality of the conversation is beginning to get the better of him.

"Oh, Daddy, please don't cry. I understand why you did what you did. I get it. I do. I guess I don't understand why -" Tess stops, not wanting to hurt her father further.

"Why did I wait," Doug finishes her thought. "Why we didn't listen to our little boy." He pauses to breathe. His daughter hears a shaky breath through the receiver, and she feels awful for her father.

"Daddy, please, I don't need to hear any more; stop now. I understand." She is shaking as tears collect on the phone, pressed tightly to her face.

"No, Tess, you *do* need to hear. We had nothing on the man at the station, no history or records. They didn't surface for another six months after." He breathes deeply. "And after that, I knew I couldn't *not* act. I was so full of hate, baby; I was so full of anger and self-loathing, and I just couldn't let Tommy's death go unanswered any longer."

"Okay, Daddy, please, I understand. I'm so sorry I said anything." Tess is crying into the phone now.

"I couldn't live with myself for a long time after; I couldn't stand who I'd become; I couldn't look at myself in the mirror."

"Oh, Daddy, please stop," but he can't.

"And it's not because I killed that bastard. It's because it brought me no peace. Tommy was gone, Drummond was dead, but none of it meant anything."

"It *did* mean something. It meant it wouldn't happen again."

"What must Tommy think of me?" Doug is sobbing now into Tess's ear, and she in response.

"Tommy forgives you; you and Mom believe that. *Please.*"

"I can't believe what I did. That's not who I am. Please don't hate me."

"Oh, Jesus, *Daddy*, I *love* you. Please know that. You're everything you ever were to me before I knew, please know that. I love you." Tess sits hard on her bedside, collapsing on her back. They cry into each other's ear, consoling one other with words of love and affection. Their conversation effortlessly shifts as Tess justifies her stay with the memories the doctor returned to her of Tommy. This transitions to Tommy's recent birthday and Tess's release from the hospital, making arrangements to pick her up on Thursday.

* * * * *

Doug tells his daughter he will see her soon and, hanging up the phone, welcomes his wife as she walks through the door with his granddaughter. He hugs Celeste, kisses her forehead tenderly, and cries into her hair, explaining what has happened.

* * * * *

Tess hasn't seen Tebor even once today. She is intrigued more than upset by this and considers where he might have gotten. The remainder of the day is spent in group activity sessions, and after dinner alone, emotionally drained, she falls asleep before eight and dreams of Charlie.

Chapter Ninety
Wednesday, 6:20 am

Tess wakes feeling better about the open back and forth she'd had with her father, relieved of the thing's weight. She considers calling him again, discussing the weather or Emma or anything *normal.* But she decides to give him time to collect himself and discuss it with her mother.

As she thumbs through contacts on her phone, she lands on Charlie's. A stirring in her stomach motivates her to call him. She pushes the phone icon and feels a warm tingling enter her chest in anticipation of connecting with him. What she'll say is uncertain; what she wants to tell him is undeniable.

"Tess, hi," Charlie answers enthusiastically after just one ring.

Emotions battle nerves for control over her senses after hearing his voice again. "Hi, I'm sorry it's so early; I just wanted to say hi and see how you're holding up."

"I'm okay. I was prepped by the lawyer who will be questioning me at trial last night."

"Oh, interesting, how does that work?" Thankful for their easy conversation, Tess's nerves settled, and she sat on her bed.

"Oh, well, you know, shave your face, wear a suit, comb your hair, speak up, and then he ran me through some questions he wanted to ask to lead me in the direction they wanted to go and came up with answers for potential questions the defense will likely ask."

"Are you nervous?"

"Only for my life!" A light-hearted laugh follows.

"I would be nervous, oh, but you probably don't want to hear that."

"Hey, Tess, what I wanted to tell you last night, well, I don't know how you're going to react to this, but I told myself I would say it. I'm a damn coward if I don't. I know we only had one night, and I know it's a little crazy to hear this, but -"

"*I love you, Charlie.*" The words feel right coming out of her mouth. Silence follows, pressing Tess to fill the empty airwaves. "I love you. I know I love you. I love you, and it's felt like forever I've wanted to tell you."

"Tess, I - I love you too," he manages.

"I wish I could hold you right now," Tess admits.

"I've been thinking hard on you lately. I can't get you out of my head, you know? You're just; I love you." So much for his heart of stone, he thinks.

Butterflies flutter from her stomach up into her chest, and Tess reacts to the sensation with a giggle.

"I'm sorry, I'm probably doing this all wrong," he says.

"Don't be silly. N*othing* could be wrong with this. I'm so happy right now." The muscles in her cheekbones begin to ache from her exaggerated smile. She envisions Charlie suffering the same trauma to his face as they both stop talking and listen to each other breathe.

"I hope I can see you very soon," he tells her.

"Friday." She proclaims. Charlie goes silent once more. "Can you see me on Friday? I'll be home then."

"I want to, you've no idea how badly I want to, but the trial, and then after -"

"What happens after?"

"It's complicated. I'll call you once my part in the trial is over: It could be as early as Thursday. Until then, know I'm thinking about you and us."

Tess melts at his mention of 'us' and tells him she loves him once more before telling him goodbye.

Chapter Ninety-One
Wednesday, 6:30 am

Charlie watches from the breakfast table as Officer Richard O'Boyle, the man put in place to protect him, answers the front door. It's still very dark, but he witnesses a handshake and a large duffle bag passed from the stranger to the cop. O'Boyle looks on as the man disappears into the street, and Charlie notices the grip O'Boyle has on the bag, white-knuckled. This sets off a peculiar sensation in Charlie's gut. He knows this feeling; it's the same one he felt when the Molloy men wandered into his bar looking for Jorgie.

Charlie stands and positions himself just out of the officer's sight, this dread now occupying his entire being. The officer turns and walks back into the kitchen. Charlie watches as the bag is placed with a weighted thud on the countertop, and O'Boyle is heard lightly rounding the corner into the living room. Charlie is one step ahead of him and is now back in the kitchen. His head is spinning with what might be in the bag. O'Boyle moves down the hall toward the bedrooms, and Charlie sneaks towards the black bag on the kitchen counter. Unzipping it, he stares in amazement at stacks of cash. His intuition over the morning transaction is now confirmed, and Charlie considers his next move.

"Charlie," O'Boyle shouts. "Where'd ya go?" The thundering echo of the big man's voice carries throughout the house. He decides he must answer and unsheathes one of the larger knives from its block on the counter. Slipping it up into his shirt sleeve, he picks up the unfinished bowl of cereal and greets the officer.

"What's up?"

The kettle signals that the boiled water is ready to make instant coffee. Charlie walks to the stove and turns the element off.

"I wanna show you something out back," O'Boyle tells him with a jerk of his meaty head. This is it, Charlie decides. This is the moment.

"Aren't I supposed to remain inside at all times?"

"I figured you'd be getting cabin fever by now. It's cool. I want to show you this one thing."

Charlie is confident now of the big man's intentions. He's bigger than anyone he's put down before, a cop, and armed.

"Sure, why not." Charlie's free hand grabs hold of the boiled kettle and, moving to meet the cop, swings it at O'Boyle's face. The weight of the heavy cast iron weapon would have knocked most out, and the combination of the hot water releasing over the cop's face would have sent most others screaming for cover. But O'Boyle yelps and goes down on one knee. Charlie kicks him in the chest with the sole of his foot, and the officer falls flat on his back. The knife slides out of Charlie's sleeve, and he puts a knee into the cop's neck, the knife hovering over the man's right eye.

"What the fuck!" O'Boyle manages, both hands floating over his face, one side bruised and the other burnt.

"The fuck you think I am? *Stupid?* What's out back, big man? A shallow grave?" Charlie presses the blade into O'Boyle's cheek, drawing blood.

"Are you *shit crazy,* you asshole?! I'm trying to be friendly here!"

"Oh yeah? What's the bag of money for? You sell a lot of tickets to the Policeman's Ball?"

O'Boyle's face turns suddenly cold, his hands stop shaking, and he stares at Charlie. Wham! He lands a haymaker on the side of Charlie's head, and Charlie goes down. The knife, though, drags across the cop's face, leaving a deep cut that bleeds profusely. As the man stands and Charlie staggers to his feet, the house phone rings. It's enough of a distraction that Charlie can tackle the big man and slam him down hard on the dining room table. But O'Boyle gets him in a headlock, twists him over, and hammers a heavy fist into Charlie's sternum. Charlie is winded, and he crumbles to the floor. O'Boyle puts a palm to his face to assess the bleeding. Pulling it away, he looks in a mirror and sees the dire wound. He kicks Charlie in the ribs and keeps kicking him until Charlie stops reacting. Satisfied for the moment, he rushes to the bathroom to pull a towel from the rack and uses it to stop the bleeding. When he returns to the dining room, his target is gone.

Thud! Charlie slams a marble cutting board over O'Boyle's head, and he falls hard to the floor. The board then splits in half, falling on the man a second time. He writhes in pain on the hardwood. Charlie stomps down hard on his back, breaking ribs, and O'Boyle coughs blood.

"Stop," the officer pleads, one hand up in defense while the other nurses his head. "Stop, we can share it."

"How much is in there?" Charlie wonders aloud, panting.

"Six-hundred-thousand," he gasps.

"Is *that* what I'm worth?" He uses the man as a step, and O'Boyle cringes in pain at his weight as Charlie moves towards the sack of cash. "Fuck, money's heavy, huh?" he taunts, lifting the bag.

Not wanting this to be a messy job, O'Boyle refrained from using his firearm but is now rethinking this decision, reaching slowly into his sock to pull out the Ruger LCP hidden there. The shuffling alerts Charlie to O'Boyle's struggle, and without thinking, he pulls another knife from the block and stabs it deep into the officer's back, piercing his heart and ending the fight.

Chapter Ninety-Two
Wednesday, 6:55 am

Standing over the dead policeman, the reality of what has transpired grips Charlie's chest, tightening the muscles around his ribcage and squeezing the air from his lungs. He feels dizzy from the lack of oxygen as each breath seems labored. He sinks to his knees and rests a few inches from the lifeless body, bleeding out all over the light hardwood. He is the third person Charlie's killed; he considers each one worse than the last. He uses this point of view to talk himself down, attempting to breathe at an average pace. Eventually, he crumbles to the floor and stares up at the ceiling. He sees stars dancing along with the stucco and rubs his eyes hard with the knuckles of his shaking fists. As time passes, he collects himself and decides on a course of action. Now he's a *cop* killer, he thinks.

"Jesus," Charlie turns his head to look at Officer O'Boyle's wide eyes staring back at him. This morbid scene encourages him to get up and get moving. The money will be coming with him, he concludes. But what will he do with it? The house phone rings again, injecting renewed anxiety into his spinning head. He has to get out of there, but where to? Then, a whistle blows, and a plan takes shape.

Before he runs, he wipes every weapon with a dishtowel to remove any fingerprints he may be leaving behind. Careful to avoid the puddles, he steps around the corpse.

Charlie throws a jacket over his blood-stained shirt, snaps up the heavy bag, and exits through the back door. Still hidden from sight by the late autumn morning, he jumps several fences bordering the neighbor's homes until he finds the road running parallel to the train tracks. There is a station a few blocks west of his position, and he sprints nearly out of his shoes to get there.

Once inside, he finds lockers running along the north wall and dumps some change into a key slot. Pulling the key free, he stashes the bag into the tight space. Closing the door, he hopes not to have looked too frantic but knows he must. He heads to the public washrooms with the key securely in his jeans pocket to clean up. The water in the sink turns pink as it collects. Looking in the shattered mirror, he sees speckles of blood on his chin and cheeks. He rubs vigorously to remove them and pulls the shirt off his back, tossing it in the wastebasket and covering it with paper towels. Satisfied he is ready to reenter the world, Charlie moves out of the washrooms and heads toward a payphone.

"Brice," the voice on the other end answers. Charlie quickly tells the detective in charge of his case that a man had entered the safe house, killed O'Boyle, and that he was lucky to escape with his life. He asks Brice to pick him up immediately. Brice tells him to get into the first marked cruiser he sees, but Charlie refuses, for reasons he won't share with Brice, insisting he is the one that picks him up. Brice agrees, and Charlie waits.

Fifteen minutes later, Charlie sees the detective's face replace the locker he'd been watching while seated at a crowded bench. Brice leads Charlie out of the building, where two more officers await them. All four get into the cruiser, Brice in the back seat with Charlie. He sees that Charlie is visibly shaken by the experience and tells him that a car had been sent to the safe house moments ago. They'd found O'Boyle and now had cruisers patrolling the area.

"Sounds like he put up a helluva fight," Brice says.

"I heard it but didn't stick around long enough to see it. O'Boyle just shouted for me to run, and so I ran." Charlie lies. Brice has no reason not to buy his story completely. Why would Charlie kill the man sworn to protect him?

"Well, thank God you made it out; it seems we're losing witnesses by the hour right now."

"Molloys are on the defensive," Charlie relates. Brice nods.

"Their lieutenants are dropping like flies. We're rallying to get them all off the street but losing that battle."

"We're still in good shape, though? I mean, we'll take them down, right?"

"We will," the detective says confidently. "They can't kill everyone."

"I need to make a quick stop. I have a letter to drop if that's alright. If I don't make it out of this..."

Brice agrees to Charlie's request, and they stop in front of Tess's building en route to the courthouse. Charlie walks inside the foyer and drops the key into her mailbox. His plan is moving forward.

Chapter Ninety-Three
Wednesday, 10:30 am

"So," Karl announces as he walks Tess to the chaise lounge. "This is our last session before you leave us. What would you like to discuss?"

"Good question," she laughs with a heavy heart. "Do you think I'm going to be alright?"

"Of that, I have no question." He takes his seat as Tess sits on the edge of the lounge. "You spoke with your father last night?"

"Uh-huh, and it was, really, very upsetting at first. Dad told me about how he got nothing out of the act. That Tommy was still gone, had still suffered, and he'd done nothing to stop it."

"A long time for him to live with that kind of guilt. What did you offer him in response?"

"I said he'd stopped the same violence from happening to other children."

"And how did he respond to that?"

"He was full of self-loathing, but I think I got through to him. He was most upset by what Tommy would think, what *I* must think."

"And what *do* you think? Really?"

"Killing is wrong, but for the right reasons, maybe it's not, you know? Maybe some people deserve it. Maybe their lesson is one of violence. Live by the sword, die by the sword, you know?"

"A theory I certainly buy into. So you feel no animosity towards your parents, then? You understand they were trying to protect you, that what you saw you were never meant to see. How do you think you will approach them when you see them?"

"I don't know. I've been thinking about that, actually. I don't want it to be awkward. I want it to be like it was."

"But you understand it won't be like it was, not anymore."

Tess looks up from her hands and stares at Karl. He does not look away. She opens her mouth to speak, but nothing is forthcoming. She shakes her head and returns her gaze to her hands, now hanging over her knees.

"I guess we'll just have to wait and see."

"And do you feel you have begun to grieve over your husband's death?"

"I cry when I think about him. Yes," she nods. "I think I am grieving."

"And your brother? You understand him a little better now?"

She nods again, head lowering an inch, but then a restored memory of Tommy forces a laugh. "He was such a happy kid. Did I tell you how he would dance for us at the dinner table?" Tess is smiling as she relives this once-buried memory. "I will always remember him like that now. Forever."

* * * * *

After her appointment with Dr. Samuelsson, Tess wants to call her parents again, if only to see how Emma is doing. Instead, she decides to wait to see what happens when she sees them tomorrow. Looking at the phone in her hand, she finds Charlie's number and calls him.

"Hi, Tess," he answers with less enthusiasm than intended.

"Are you okay?" she asks.

"Some crazy shit has happened since last we spoke, but I'm okay now. I'm at the courthouse. The trial that was set for tomorrow is going to go through tonight now. The Molloys are gunning everyone down that's going to witness against them."

"Oh, Charlie." Her distress is palpable, and he feels terrible for burdening her with this news.

"Hey, I'm alright; it'll all be over soon." *Then we'll be together,* he wants to tell her but questions the statement's validity. "They're getting me set to witness in a closed courtroom. After tonight, I'll be transferred to a new life in a new location."

"But -" Tess is shaking now.

"Don't worry. They've told me where they're placing me. I'll call you from there on Friday when I'm settled. It's not as far as you'd think."

"No? Okay, I love you."

"God, I love hearing that. Thank you. I love you."

"Just tell me we will be together. That we can make it work."

"We will. I'm working on a plan. When you get home tomorrow, look in your mailbox, will you? There's a key in it. I need you to get something for me with it and bring it out to me. Then I'll explain everything."

"A key? What's it for?"

"I'll explain everything on Friday when I call you from my new location. I think I'll have to ditch this phone, so if you don't recognize a number, pick it up anyway."

"Okay." She feels safe talking to Charlie like this. He's making plans, taking charge. With Sam, she had always been the one making plans. Not because she necessarily wanted to but because Sam never possessed the foresight to bother.

"I love you, Tess."

Her knees go weak at the declaration. She returned the sentiment and headed to the library.

Once at a computer station, she checks on her book. She had decided to offer the book of poetry for free, expecting no monetary gain, only that it be read. Over one hundred downloads have already been processed. Her heart soars.

Chapter Ninety-Four
Wednesday, 7:00 pm

Charlie has completed his civic duty. As relayed by his dying brother and witnessed by Charlie, his testimony has been included in the mounting evidence against the Molloy group.

"Excellent job on the stand," Brice compliments him as they walk to a waiting car in the back of the courthouse. Cruisers surround the vehicle, and Brice hands Charlie a pouch containing his new identity and all the paperwork he will need to convince the world he is Mitch Sanford. The men shake hands, and Charlie is shuttled to his new apartment in a city he's never visited.

* * * * *

Tess visits Tebor in his room at midnight, where Madi waits to discuss Paul's untimely end.

"Can you explain it, Madi? I mean, why -" Madi raises a hand to stop Tess and offers her a seat on the bed. She sits as Tebor closes the door and sits in the corner.

"I was distraught, initially, to hear about Paul's suicide. How are you?"

"I've made my peace with it," she tells her, uncertain if that was true. "I think Paul understood what he experienced and decided to kick-start a new life with this understanding rather than seeing this one through. I think he learned a lot in those last few hours and that what he learned will be reflected in the next life."

Madi opens her mouth to speak, but this time, it's Tess who puts up a hand.

"Right or wrong, guys, that is what I have to believe in making sense of it," she tells them in no uncertain terms. Madi bows her head and folds her hands together.

"What is a child that understands who they are, but a life began where another has ended?" she says quietly to the room.

Seeing the confusion in his friend's eyes, Tebor offers Tess a translation of Madi's statement.

"What we believe, Madi and I, is that someone, like a musical savant, is a child who remembers a life that has ended."

"So, you believe Paul *will* remember?"

"It's not without merit to think so," Madi adds. "Consider an example like Mozart, who wrote his first symphony at eight. How could he have accomplished such genius without remembering a past when he was involved in musical pursuits?"

"It's not a cerebral thing; it's a spiritual thing," Tebor says.

"I like that," Tess tells them. "I *love* that, actually."

"These memories stay with us, all of us. We can see that when we regress, as you did with your fear of being buried alive or Paul's bleeding himself of impurities. They stay with us." Madi offers.

"You can see how stubbornness and disbelief work against us in the present. Understanding our past prepares us for the present and the future," Tebor adds quietly.

"There are thousands of examples of child prodigies in all aspects of human understanding: mathematics, arts, sciences, everything. For a child to understand what would take a lifetime to process offers us more proof of past life consciousness in the present. These people are special in that they can draw on these pasts." Madi stands to start her shift, and Tess takes her hand gently in hers.

"I'm so delighted I met you, Madi. Both of you." She looks to Tebor. "You have helped me make sense of my own life; for that, I will be forever grateful." She squeezes Madi's hand and lingers there a moment. As she released her grip, Madi bent down to kiss Tess on the forehead.

"You've been a very agreeable participant. I believe you can now heal yourself through all you've discovered. I wish you every kindness and every happiness." With this, Madi leaves the room while Tess attempts to alleviate the trembling in her heart.

"I will miss you," Tebor admits, standing to get the door.

"Come join me for breakfast in the morning before I go. My parents are picking me up at ten." She moves towards the door, her heart heavy, thinking she may never see him again.

"I will see you then."

Chapter Ninety-Five
Thursday, 9:45 am

As Tess exchanges numbers with Tebor in the cafeteria, Doctor Samuelsson joins them. Tebor steps aside to give them the privacy he imagines they require in this, their final interaction.

"You've made incredible progress here, Tess. Remember my offer to see you and your parents if the three of you can agree to it."

"I will, doctor; thank you so much for everything." She hugs him tightly, and he hugs her back.

"You take care now."

Tebor walks with Tess, hands in pockets, escorting his friend to the security doors. There, they hug for a long while. Tess pulls back and kisses Tebor on the mouth, grinning through it. Choosing not to draw out the goodbye, she breaks the embrace and walks, bag in hand, to the hospital's foyer. Feeling suddenly apprehensive over stepping back into the world, Tess wonders: can she genuinely do this alone? Did she have to? Charlie will call her soon with a plan to put them together: him, Emma, and her. Signing out at the front desk, she smiles back at the woman who takes her form.

"All the best," the receptionist tells her. Tess nods, thanks her, turns and walks out of the building. In the parking lot, she sees her father, mother, and Emma walking towards her. Her mother waves and Tess puts a hand up. A sudden and unexpected feeling overwhelms her at the sight of them: love. A love for her parents she knew existed but hadn't felt in many years. She feels like a child, their child. Memories of feeling safe in her father's arms and protected under her mother's gaze find her. She feels weepy. The smile that had begun with the receptionist has grown tenfold, and now her parents wear the same. They embrace over Emma in her stroller while Tess feels compelled to repeatedly tell them how much she loves them. They reciprocate, and Tess reaches down for her daughter, pulling her into her arms and hugging her madly, kissing her warm face and breathing her in. The four move toward the parked car and, without another word, drive back to the apartment, enter the building, and sit in her living room to play with Emma. Doug sits cross-legged on the floor with Tess and Emilia while Celeste prepares a lunch.

* * * * *

Hours later, Tess sits with her parents at the kitchen island, each with a glass of wine in hand, cheering Tess's apparent victory over her demons while Emma settles in for a nap. They stare into each other's eyes, sharing the secret between them without a word. Tess raises her glass, and Doug and Celeste follow. She smiles and nods to them both. Doug nods back, tears tracing his strong cheekbones to the deep dimple on his chin. Celeste bows her head, nodding as well. All three glasses clink together in a life-affirming act, and they drink to new beginnings, never to forget but to forgive their shared pasts.

After the first bottle has been put to rest, a second is opened. Laughter fills the house with stories of Tess's childhood and fond memories of her brother. The delight over her renewed memories is contagious. Her parents recount others, bringing Tess to joyful tears.

The phone rings, and Tess rises from the couch to retrieve it.

"Hello?" she answers in a light-headed, approaching drunken voice.

"Tess," It's Charlie. "You sound wonderful," he tells her.

"I *feel* wonderful!" She winks at her parent and walks to her bedroom.

"I'm happy to hear that."

"Did everything go alright at trial?" she wonders, lying on her bed.

"Yes, they've moved me to a new location, a new life. I'm excited to tell you all about it, my name -"

"Your name?" Tess asks louder than she'd meant. "Sorry, they gave you a new name; of course they did!"

Charlie laughs. "Would you like to hear it?"

Tess gives a resounding YES!

"Mitch."

"Mitch," she ponders the name a moment. "I like it, Charlie, I mean, *Mitch*." She giggles, and Charlie feels the familiar tickle in his chest.

"I'd like you to come see me tomorrow if possible, just you, this time. If your parents can watch Emma another day, I mean. I know you've been away from her a while, so if Saturday works better?"

"I can come tomorrow. My parents want to stay the weekend anyway. I have been non-stop with Em since I got home, and honestly, I'll probably have her sleep with me tonight."

"That's great, Tess. I can't wait. But I have a favor to ask of you."

"Ask away!" she says, giddy from the wine.

"There is a bag of mine at the train station downtown. The key in your mailbox, which I mentioned, opens the locker. There is a number on the key."

"Ohhh, very cloak and dagger of you!"

Charlie can't help but laugh. "Not so much, just don't open it till you see me; that's all I ask. You can take the train too if you'd prefer. I'll reimburse you when I see you for the ticket."

"Hmmm, bag in a locker, at the train station, and a train ticket to come see you. All sounds pretty cloak and dagger to me!"

"Just promise me you won't look until I see you. Please keep it safe. Buy it a ticket if you want." He laughs nervously this time.

"So, where am I going?"

Charlie gives her the address, city, and approximate travel time it'll take her on the train. "Bring a book.' he tells her. Tess agrees to everything and promises she'll see him tomorrow, bag unopened. They exchange *I love yous,* and Charlie waits for her to hang up.

Tess floats back into the kitchen and relays her plans for the next day. Her parents are apprehensive at first, but as Tess tells them about Charlie, grinning like a child all the while, they become excited for this new chapter in their daughter's life.

Chapter Ninety-Six
Friday, 7:45 am

Tess finishes breakfast with her family, kisses each goodbye, and tells them she will return late that evening. In the building's foyer, she opens her mailbox and frees the minor orange key from a pile of bills. Cloak and dagger, she thinks and smiles out of the corner of her mouth.

At the train station, she locates the locker and inserts the key. As she turned it, the door opened as the weight of the bag pushed against it. Tess manages to wrestle the oversized item out of its confined space and jumps as it lands with a heavy thud at her feet.

Lifting it, she is immediately tempted to open the bag to understand what is responsible for the weight, but she fights the urge. She has to drag it to the ticket stand, leaving it at her feet to purchase her 10:30 ticket.

As her train is announced, she slings the long strap over her head and lifts it with her back. The weight throws her off-center as she stands, but she finds her footing and limps onto the train and to her seat. Feeling somewhat guilty now, she slides the bag under her legs and pulls out the book she intends to read during the commute. She notices a few looks from the other passengers and feels guilty. But why should she feel guilty, she wonders? It's just a bag, a really, really heavy bag with contents she was asked not to look at. This spikes a bit of anxiety in her, and she feels suddenly like a mule, taking illegal substances over the border or something. Charlie would never ask me to do something like that; she tells herself: He loves me, and I love him.

Charlie's new city is west of hers, which she has occasionally visited with work to attend tradeshows. It's a beautiful city, she remembers. Could she live there? Yes, she decides. She and Emma would make a tidy profit from selling her apartment now. If that is Charlie's plan, the idea of moving in with him is becoming more and more a reality for her. A fresh start. She relaxes into the reclining chair and breathes deeply. Putting the bag's contents to the back of her mind, she focuses on her book and zones out.

Once at the destination, Tess texts Charlie she's arrived, drags the bag to the street, and hails a cab. The cabbie looks suspiciously at her as he lifts the black bag into his trunk.

"What have you got in there? Gold bars?"

"I wish. Files, actually, I have to take them to a friend for tax purposes," she lies convincingly.

She pays the cabbie at Charlie's new residence, and he nearly blows a vertebra, lifting the bag to the sidewalk.

"You going to be alright with that?" he asks.

Tess nods and smiles at the man, telling him she's stronger than she looks. He nods back and drives off, leaving Tess to stare up at the four-story building in front of her.

Charlie then appears at the door and runs out to greet her. They lock in a passionate embrace and kiss each other hungrily. When they pull away from one another, the tickle in Charlie's chest becomes much more as he experiences an uncanny feeling of recognition in Tess's eyes. Tess succumbs to the same feelings and throws herself back into his arms. When she releases him, Charlie lifts the bag to his shoulder and, with his other arm, takes Tess by the hand, leading her into the apartment.

Once inside, they tear each other's clothes off, and Charlie pushes her to the floor, where they make love. It comes easily to both of them, like that night in her car. But this time, they are both completely invested in the other, not just their impulses. They are in love, and it plays out in their lovemaking.

After three consecutive sessions on the hardwood, they lay next to each other, panting and glistening with sweat. Tess is the first to stand, in no way uncomfortable with her nakedness in front of her lover.

"Did you look inside the bag?" he asks her, his voice hoarse.

"I was afraid to," she admits, examining the potential living arrangements were she to move in with Emma. The main room is open and bright, the kitchen a little smaller than hers, two bedrooms and one bath.

Charlie watches as she strolls through his new digs. "Not much to look at, is it?"

"It's not bad."

"Would you go away with me?" Charlie asks without hesitation. "You and Emma, I mean? The three of us." He approaches Tess and takes her hands, the short hair on his chest dripping with sweat. "Witness protection is fine, but I feel like I'll always be looking over my shoulder. I was thinking about South America. Brazil maybe. I know the language."

"You're Portuguese?" She had never considered Charlie's lineage before.

"On my dad's side, it's all he ever spoke in front of us."

"What about your bar?"

"I have a friend who's a real estate agent. I've given her power of sale, and she'll wire me the money when it sells."

Tess unravels their fingers and points at the bag. "So what's in it?"

Charlie looks long and hard at Tess and then to the black duffle bag haphazardly left beside the front door.

"Cash," he admits. "Money for the hitman that almost killed me a couple of days ago; I took it from him."

"Oh, Charlie," Tess puts her hands on his chest. "Did that happen?"

"Yes, but Tess, I killed him. Are you alright with that?"

"As long as you're alright, I'm alright."

Charlie nods and bends to put on his pants. Tess dresses also, and they sit to discuss possible outcomes.

"That'll be another couple hundred grand to me if my bar sells. That's almost a million dollars."

"A *million* dollars?!" Tess exclaims. "How much money is in that bag?"

"I'm worth six hundred thousand dead," he tells her solemnly. "Imagine if you sold your apartment." Tess looks at him. "I know this is all moving very fast, Tess. But that's my life right now."

"We'd have to get visas and scout a location; there's so much to do before we just *disappear* to Brazil."

Charlie doesn't miss that she says *we* and leans in, kissing her.

"What if we took a week's vacation there and found a place to buy? Then I could wait for you."

"I like that."

"I won't go alone. I won't go without you; I'm afraid that if I stay here, they'll eventually figure it all out. I can't put you and Emma in that kind of danger. Brazil would be perfect. We won't tell anyone, the government, or our friends."

"I'll have to tell my parents. They'll be devastated. They'll have to know."

"Tess, they can move in with us, *seriously*. I need to be with you. I can't explain it." Tess presses two fingers against his soft lips.

"You don't have to explain anything. You're my past *and* my present, you and Emma both. Let's make a future."

SAMPLE of THE BLIND AFFECT – By MICHAEL POELTL

2021, February
Jonah at Sixty-One

In time, I've come to believe man is a canvas, brushed by those he's known and those who knew him. Tenderly painted by some or stroked harshly by those he's wronged. While some would include bright hues to offset the dark corners, mine would surely be a thousand shades of gray, save the one black stroke that blankets the only bright spot my canvas ever knew.

As he lies on his deathbed, regret wrenches him into the past. Like a disoriented time traveler caught in a vacuum, Jonah is forced to recount the losses in his life. The loss of innocence, the loss of purpose, the loss of the one person who had made life bearable. It's all very dismal, but the pull is absolute as he relives a plethora of painful memories. Ancient emotions compel him to believe they're happening in the present rather than decades ago. Still, he hasn't lost all sense. He knows these are only memories. But the pain causes his nervous system to live them as though they are real, one final time. The heart monitor spikes next to his head. *Take me.* He begs the universe, hoping this time it's a full-blown heart attack. *Take me.* A nurse rushes in to check the machine and listens to his heart. He senses he is in no danger as she mops a considerable amount of sweat from his brow. Suddenly, she notices something unusual. It is his trademark scent, which he labeled the "pong." Her conditioned smile instinctively fades from her round face, reacting to the sharp waft of body odor. It soaks his gown under the arms. It is an embarrassing trauma he's lived with since he was thirteen, but there's nothing to do about it now. She adds something to the cocktail, feeding his body nutrients with a quick push of a plunger. Jonah feels an immediate sense of calm rush over him. His eyes feel fuzzy. He turns his head toward the windowed wall. Tears escape his glazed eyes over the false alarm. He feels the light touch of the nurse's hand brush his shoulder as she leaves the room, mumbling something reassuring.

The smell of the hospice, midwinter. The food. The cleaning solution. The blood and urine and feces and death. The sweat. It all amasses to a particular scent, he deliberates. *I wanted to die in the summer.* The view outside his window is dismal but fitting. The universe *would* place him in this dreary season at the end of life. Icicles drip from his window where water gathers from a hole in the gutter, freezing overnight and melting during the day. Spring is two months away. He may yet make it to summer, depending on how long he is to suffer. He wishes he wouldn't.

Jonah shifts slightly in his bed, careful not to dislodge the tubes, keeping his sixty-one-year-old body tethered to the present in a morphine dream. The burn of addiction enters his chest as the scent of tobacco lingers in his room. Some of the nurses smoke. In another hour, he would be wheeled to the open-air balcony by Mav, who would join him for his twice-daily constitutional. It was nowhere near enough for his addiction, but it was about all he could manage in his current state. The hacking cough that assails him for the hour to follow is most unpleasant.

He hates being chained to this existence, waiting for death. His mother drank herself to an early grave while his father worked himself there. Both were dead before ever facing old age. Perhaps there was some dignity in it - dying before they'd been given a chance to choose. *Choose or lose.* But with today's treatments and medications, a person could easily outlive their usefulness by decades, it would seem. Jonah remembers when he'd turned fifty. "*For what,*" he'd asked himself.

No matter. He's no one to visit him at sixty-one, no one to care. He has made sure of that. He's been hard on himself these last fifty years, and that kind of internal torment is his friend, his partner, his child.

It's not how he imagined it in his youth, dying. He'd envisioned children and grandchildren gathered around his deathbed. Or no, maybe he'd track a slow walk as he follows his family out of the driveway after a Thanksgiving to remember, waving goodbye. In this universe, he blows a kiss, and there it is, the image they remember of him: a happy man who had lived a full life and had loved and been loved in return. That even he would die in his sleep with a smile. But that's a fairy-tale ending reserved for those worthy of such an end.

"You can't do that." His mother meant to protect him, of course. After his twin died in childbirth, he was it, and his mother at first seemed adamant he would survive. He couldn't climb a hill or walk across a stony creek without an ever-scrupulous eye. Everything boys did, everything that seemed normal, was off limits. *Nothing* was safe. Everything was terrifying to his mother. He hadn't even learned to ride a bike. Still, he had loved her through all of it. He had felt confined but protected.

Later, he understood her sickness; reality was unbearable. She'd mistaken him for his dead brother, and he'd corrected her and was slapped so hard his glasses flew across the room. He was startled. She was never the same after that. A few weeks later, strange men started accompanying her home from the bar. This was when he considered his first drink. At thirteen, he found one of his mother's hidden bottles of vodka and forced himself to drink. It was awful, but drinking it made him feel closer to her. The burn in his abdomen made him feel safe and

287

warm. The delirium, the pain, the vomiting, and the rush of love. He now wished he'd never brought up her alcoholism.

And now, at the end of a life unlived, one born of sadness, dragged along on the coattails of depression, Jonah waits to close his eyes for good.

* * *

Another day breaks. He's never been a morning person. He's always hated mornings. But to function in society, one must have a job to go to, like it or not, or so one was told. Money earned to afford the life everyone else wanted for you. Jonah didn't want for much. He would have been quite content to avoid life altogether. People especially. Morning people the most. Now, there is no job and no reason. The start of another day begs the question of whether it is even worth the effort. Should he just pull the IV out of his arm and let nature take its course? The IV is for the pain, hydration too, he'd heard them say. Jonah doesn't deal well with pain. *Why go out in pain?* He'd lived in pain.

He glances at the tattoos on his left forearm. Each is a reminder of an event in his life. His skin is still smooth. He reaches over his narrow frame to run a slow finger over one of the words imprinted on his flesh. *FORGIVENESS*, in Beyond Wonderland font. He coughs out an ironic laugh. He remembers his mother's voice urging him against the 'dangerous' practice of inking. "*Not in this lifetime, Mister,*" she would have said. She was dead so soon, long before his first, but still, her voice rang true in his head. He often whispered this mantra to himself when he sensed a choice might take him in a direction his mother would disapprove of—the woman who had robbed him of adventure.

Jonah had always wished he'd been named Jack rather than his twin brother. Jack was a name used in so many nursery rhymes and fairy tales. Not all had happy endings, but Jonah always imagined himself in their place. Jack and Jill, Jack Sprat, Jack and the Bean Stock, Jack B. Nimble, Little Jack Horner. Jack wasn't even a real name. It was a nickname. As though his mother naming him something unreal had created his destiny. Maybe if Jonah had been named Jack, his life would have been fuller, less dull, or shorter.

Christ, I could use a drink. "Clean" for three years. No alcohol, and still, he gets struck down with this. Sepsis. *How many organs are failing right now? Did they say three?* Two weeks in the hospice and still not dead. *Why do I linger?* Meanwhile, they've carted four bodies out of the place. He has a spectacular view from his front room window as the ambulances pull up, lights on, but no sirens. Too late. But that's the idea behind a hospice: to die in plain sight of those being paid to wait you out. He swore he could make out singing or humming and whispers to the dying in adjoining rooms before the declaration of death was handed out. **DO NOT RESUSCITATE.** It was a choice he'd made after his latest trip to the hospital when he'd received the grim news. The kidney infection had led to sepsis, and any odds of surviving seemed to deteriorate daily as symptoms worsened. The short-lived series of antibiotics further damaged his kidneys and liver. The news would almost have had Jonah smiling if it weren't for the pain in his abdomen. He took the doctor's recommendations, finished his Will, and checked himself into this hospice. It's nothing close to luxurious, but it had an opening. He had his lawyer arrange for a local charity to pick up his worldly belongings and rent his apartment to someone else. Just like that, he'd never existed. He imagines that's how he will leave the world, too. His story lost to the larger lives being lived. Someone will pick up the rent where he left off. Someone will eventually fill this bed, too. His body will soon be ash. *Who will spread his ashes? Who cares?* Just throw them into the wind in a celebratory "*Hooray.*" Like a handful of confetti, his final farewell to a world he'd never been a part of.

1970

The Suburbs

It was a difficult pregnancy. That's how his mother described having Jonah and his brother Jack in her womb. "The two of you were always play-fighting in there," she explained, her slender hand motioning to her now trim waistline, her tone more cheerful than usual. "It was very uncomfortable, but I put up with it. I told you both to get it out of your systems before I came in and smacked you." She placed her cigarette on the edge of an empty beer can and picked up a glass of something more potent than beer. She took a hard swallow, picked up the smoke and sucked the end, held the smoke in her lungs a moment, then exhaled, the sadness given room by her escaping breath. Jonah watched the smoke fill the kitchen. He liked how it swirled around and even how the smoke continued to fall out of his mother's nostrils. He could take or leave the smell, but everything he wore smelled like his mother, which was comforting. The little breakfast nook was lit by the sun pouring through the kitchen window and the white lace valance that made oblong circles on the floor. His mother picked a rogue bit of tobacco from the end of her tongue and studied it. *Spirit in the Sky* by Norman Greenbaum came on the radio. The radio was always on at a low volume. It kept her from thinking too much, she'd said. She turned it up. A smile and a far-away look accompanied her, humming the song.

"How long was I in there?" Jonah asked, seated on a wooden chair, pulled close to his mother's, their knees practically touching. She looked at him disapprovingly. "You were *both* in there nine months, Jonah. You *and* Jack." She never forgot about Jack. Jonah forgot on purpose. He wanted his mother to himself. She always brought up stupid old Jack. Jack, Jack, dead old Jack. "*He's dead!*" He wanted to scream this in her face as if she didn't know. Wasn't it enough they visited his grave every Sunday, took a picnic, and stayed there for three stupid, wasted hours at a time? Meanwhile, Jonah couldn't do anything right, and he certainly wasn't allowed to do anything fun. Homework at the green laminate table, pencil sharpening's, and eraser bits dotting the swirly pattern. Then, less lucid, T.V. and dinner, mostly shoveled down or scraped away. Then, the inside of his room, the escape. The posters on the wall are the only spark to his imagination and the only essence of the outside world. He was real, but he didn't feel real when she was alone with her glass, and he was alone, alone. He would sneak peeks at the street beyond the window and see boys racing their bicycles up and down the road or maybe climbing the large maples that lined the boulevard. A world of fun and exploration awaited anyone bold enough to venture outdoors. *What if I fell out of one of those trees? What if the wheel came loose from the bike? What if, what if, what if, what if.* It was exhausting to think about. But she was his mother, and he loved her for many other reasons, like when she would trace her fingers along his small face, ending at the tip of his petite nose, telling him what a handsome little man he was. That was a favorite for him. He felt loved and safe and warm under her playful eyes.

Jonah's mother had been like this for as long as he could remember. Frazzled. It made him anxious for her, and he wanted to help her but sometimes didn't see how. He had been home-schooled for the first few years until she enrolled him in grade four at the school three blocks from their home. She'd told him she couldn't teach at that level. He felt scared to leave her alone but excited at the possibility of having friends outside the house. By the following year, he still hadn't made any. He didn't know how to make friends when he didn't feel normal. He couldn't have them over to his house or play after school. His mother didn't mingle with the other mothers at drop-off or pick-up. And her behavior was becoming his behavior. He kept to himself in class, not participating in group activities, and never raised his hand even if he knew the answer. He stayed in his head with his thoughts, where he was safe. His daydreaming was becoming an issue with his teacher.

"The school wants you to take a test, Jonah," his mother told him, lighting another cigarette. Her fingers were like gold where they held the filter. (Jonah found this appealing. Imagine having golden fingers! *What were they worth?*) "They're concerned about your progress."

"I do my work. I'm just not as smart as the other kids." He watched the smoke slip out the open window. It was spring now. The last snow had melted into a gray sludge on the lawns and the road.

"You have to try harder, Jonah. You have to *talk*. Just say *something* once in a while." A long drag, a disinterested look, a frown on her forehead. She might yell, but he hoped not.

"It's okay, mommy. I don't need friends. I've got you." His mother laid a hand on his and squeezed.

"I love you. But I've got things to worry about, things you wouldn't understand. I'm not your friend. I'm your *mother*." He nodded up at her. She was a pretty woman, he thought. Short, dark hair framed a pale complexion. Full lips and wide eyes blinked away the smoke as it caught up in her lashes. He lifted a small palm to his mother's cheek. She leaned into it and stubbed out the cigarette. She wrapped her golden fingers around his hand, and Jonah instantly felt richer.

"You're my friend, Mommy. My *best* friend." His smile was genuine.

She didn't smile. She looked away.

"Is Grandma coming tonight?"

"Soon, actually, Mommy is helping Daddy at the pub again," she said. She loved to get out and help at the restaurant. Other than him, Jonah thought it was her favorite thing. He liked seeing his mother happy, though he occasionally wondered whether she was happy to leave *him* or happy to get out of the house.

After dinner, Grandma rang the front bell, and Jonah rushed to let her in. A big hug. She smelled of flowers, lemons, and something else he couldn't place but was probably just an old lady smell. They would play board games, and she would let him stay out of his room until late. Jonah's mother kissed him on the top of his head and slipped on her high heels. He couldn't understand why anyone would wear such ridiculous shoes. Grandma didn't. His mother looked extra pretty every time she went out of the house. Make-up, hair and nails done, and a dress he thought she might suffocate in. A fur coat completed the ensemble. *Why didn't she go out like this in the day, only at night? What happened out there?* It was a world he would never see, which made him jealous.

"I'm just going to have a chat with your mommy before she goes, Jonah. Why don't you pull out a few of your games and get ready to lose at Monopoly," Grandma said with a wink. Jonah nodded enthusiastically and headed for the living room, but he knew he'd be listening to the conversation. A clue to the mystery of his mother.

"This is becoming a habit. *Every* night? You're turning into your father, Lucinda."

There was a pause. Jonah felt the tension.

 "I'm going to help Luca - my *husband* - at the pub. I'm not just sitting at the bar drinking wine." His mother's voice was terse.

"Be sure you don't. They say it runs in families; you know." Now Grandma's words were short and staccato.

"I'm doing my best, mother. But being home all day and night with just him is not easy. I need something else."

Jonah sat down hard on the carpet. He heard his mother stumble to the door,

"Look at you. You've already been drinking! And around *Jonah*." She lowered her voice and turned to point at the living room. Jonah sat stock still. He didn't think he was even breathing.

"Thank you for coming to watch Jonah." His mother slammed the door shut. Jonah jumped a little in his skin. So, this was all his fault. Now he understood. Grandma probably knew this, too.

"Be a good boy, Jonah. Just let me sit for a while." Grandma lowered herself slowly onto the couch and let out a sigh. The television was playing a western, and its light cast a cruel shadow over her face. She suddenly looked mean and sad, not loving and kind. It was his fault his mother was how she was; everyone knew it and hated him. "We all *love* you, Jonah. We want the best for you." *Lies.* The western made loud, banging sounds.

1973

The Sting of Love

A week after turning thirteen, Jonah sat on the front porch, watching men cut down a dead tree. They were sawing and hacking with relish at the misshapen branches. The old relic stood askew under the electrical lines running miles along the sidewalk. It was July, and school was becoming a distant memory. His mother had left him to run errands, so he sat in the noisy chaos of chippers and saws, awaiting her return. There was the sweet smell of fresh sawdust in the air.

The metallic blue '69 Chevy Nova squealed into the driveway, and his mother emerged, hair electrified, dress sideways, arms flailing, screaming terrible words. She grabbed him by the collar of his shirt and dragged him into the house backward. Jonah stumbled and fell on the laminate floor, banging his head hard. His mother's behavior dumbfounded him. She continued to scream at him even as she kneeled to tend to his head. Jonah thought she must be as shocked at her actions as he was, but it was difficult to tell. She began to replace the screams with sobs and moved her small body into a ball beside him. A paper bag, clinking with bottles, rattled under her head, where she had somehow managed to set them carefully.

"Why would you do that, Jack?!"

His head pounded. He knew yelling back at his mother didn't help. Yelling, "I'M NOT JACK," would only make it worse. Slowly, gently, he reached for her. Her golden fingers no longer fostered the innocent curiosity they once had. He knew now they were tinted yellow from habitually drawing the foul-smelling nicotine into her lungs. He sat in astonishment, looking at his mother with new eyes. One hand rubbed at the pain exploding from the back of his head. The other hand steadied him as he rose to his feet.

"W*hy* can't I sit on the porch?! They're a *hundred* feet away!" His voice cracked with the apparent signs of puberty and his crumbling sense of self as he pointed at the men and the noise through the open door. He was angry. It was a culmination of things. He was lonely. He was afraid. He was sick of being safe.

His mother reached out to him with trembling fingers, shaking her head. "I'm so sorry, baby," she said, her voice now soft from the screams and the realization. "I didn't mean for you to fall." Her face was shiny and wet with tears.

"Yeah, well, I don't *need* you to protect me anymore. I'm *thirteen!* Jonah pulled his hand away from the warmth collecting on his palm at the back of his head. Bloodstained fingers. His mother cried out and leaped to her feet. Jonah backed away instinctively, and his mother burst into tears again. He didn't like seeing her like this, but enough was enough. The increasingly erratic behavior had come to this. He was bleeding, and it was her fault, not his.

He knew how much she'd hate herself now, how sorry she'd feel, how bad it was. A pang of sympathy entered him and then just as quickly fled.

"Just calm down," he said. She was shaking. He helped her up and brought her to a chair.

"I've tried so hard to keep you safe," she began. "You're the only thing in my life that makes sense, Jonah. I *need* you." She held his hands, which were becoming red as she entwined her fingers in his and kissed them. She had his blood on her lips. The scene disoriented Jonah. He felt weak. He felt sick. Nauseous.

"Can you look at my head?" He knelt at her feet and bent his head to rest on her lap. Her fingers carefully navigated his thick, brown hair to inspect the damage. "It's just a small split," she whispered. "I can fix this for you." She released his hair and looked Jonah in the eyes. "I love you, Jonah." The words, the fingers in his hair, and the look of desperation on her face were too much. Jonah stood and feigned a smile. She stood, too, and picked up her bag of bottles. "I'll get you a wet cloth, and we'll clean you up." She slinked down the hall to the kitchen. Jonah heard the lid twist off one of the bottles. Then the tap ran as he sat, wanting to be sick. A damp tea towel. He took it from her without touching her hand. She gulped thirstily from the cup.

"You're not so breakable after all."

She turned on the television. They sat in silence for an hour.

2020, May

Severn at Fifty-Nine.

Severn hates how an event can be tracked so easily back to that one decision or experience as if life were something so wholly unchangeable. As though that distinctive moment where your action or inaction - already written in the stars - would inevitably play out a specific event. Are our lives simply destiny? Does everything have a beginning, middle, and end? It's the middle she labors over.

Severn's life to this point has been anything but rosy. Her 12-year-old self could never have predicted that this would be how it would end up. From thirteen to thirty-one, she had no real memories to hold onto. They were essentially gone. She'd visited psychiatrists for years, but something was keeping those memories locked away. Something kept them from surfacing and, perhaps, causing her enormous grief. That's how Dr. Sturgis described it to her. But now was apparently the time to get them back. Let the chips fall where they may, she thought.

"Severn, are you ready to experience your lost memories?" Dr. Sturgis, a woman of retirement age herself, opened today's session frankly.

Severn flinches, hands folded in her lap, seated on the worn, leather couch. The room smells of lavender, as it always has, meant to promote calm. To Severn, today, it wasn't having that effect.

Severn looked at the woman before her and thought she must have been striking thirty years ago.

"I ask because I no longer want to dance around the subject. We've done everything we can to manage your day-to-day concerns. You've done remarkably well with your cognitive behavioral therapy, but forever avoiding the real trigger is keeping you from experiencing a full life. I liken it to someone who a dog bit at a young age. They avoid dogs altogether, feeding their anxieties, fearful of a potential run-in with a dog at a park or when out for a walk. Soon, they don't leave the house because of their fear of dogs and their anxiety around the thought spikes. Seems a little irrational, right?" Severn nods reluctantly. "But that's learned behavior from a traumatic event. Knowing where the fear is coming from is easy in this case: the dog bite. Your case doesn't offer us a point of reference to your issues. When this person avoids dogs, they avoid the fear but build the anxiety around it. What's driving your fear is a mystery to you. So how can you ever truly free yourself of it and its consequences?"

"Knowing?"

The doctor raises her eyebrows, places her clipboard down, and removes her heavy glasses. "Right, your thoughts feed your feelings, which create the behavior. Your thoughts just so happen to be buried at a subconscious level. There are ways to access them. It's been seventeen years, and I want to get to the root of your symptoms. You're so anxious over knowing your lost past that you've backed yourself into a corner. Tell me again, what's stopping you?"

"I just... I get *blocked*. I can't access memories from that time in my life. Also, I made promises."

"To yourself?"

"No, to Mary, my friend, and my mother." Severn feels a chill travel up her spine.

"The only person you need to make promises to is *yourself*, Severn. Promise yourself that you will get better."

"I want to get better."

"Then let's begin." Dr. Sturgis leans forward, pressing the subject. Severn had been to therapists before her. None of them did anything but try to treat Severn's immediate issues. None ever sought to visit her event horizon. "What do you recall from 1974?"

Severn takes a deep, trembling breath. Maybe this time, it will all come back to her. Maybe she can handle it.

"My mother... my father had died... and my mother was a wreck." Severn's brow tightens as she struggles to remember.

"And what about your mother in 1994, twenty years later; what do you remember about her then?"

"Not a drunk. Not anymore. She was constantly calling me after I moved out. I was thirty-four."

"Did she never mention your life from '75-'93?" Dr. Sturgis was baffled by this. She knew what had happened to Severn when she'd agreed to take her on as a patient. She had worked with her for seven years. They had made progress with her related issues, but now she felt it was time to get to the root of it. "Others know what you were doing, even if you don't."

"Everyone walks on eggshells around those two decades. They always have and still do," Severn explains calmly. "As I mentioned when we started, I was originally counseled to leave it alone for fear of what it would do to me. They said I had forgotten to protect myself."

"You've enjoyed a purposeful life since then. A career in social work. A house of your own. A relationship with your mother. By all outward indicators, you have a *normal* life."

"So why would I want to ruin that by knowing?"

"Because holding trauma back, even hidden in the most secure places in your mind... it's still *in* you. You can't always see the damage it's causing, but there it is, influencing you negatively."

"I'm happy." Severn nearly chokes on the phrase. "Excuse me." She picks up her water glass and drinks. Severn's face hints at the missing decades: the frown lines, the damaged skin, the tired eyes. She had been through something awful. The stress had turned her once blonde hair into a nearly translucent grey. Still, she was a pretty woman.

"Your life has been manageable through the work we've done, but our progress could disappear altogether if we don't break down those walls and recover your memories. I won't press if you don't want me to, but I think you have the tools you need to cope now, and so I feel my work with you is nearly done unless we press on further."

"No, please!" This revelation visibly shakes Severn. "I *love* coming here."

"And I enjoy your company, Severn, but there is a waiting list of people to see me, and I can't help them if you and I are just going to reaffirm the work we've done."

Severn remains seated in silence at the shock of the doctor's statement. What would it do to her to unravel the mystery of eighteen years unaccounted for?

The question has weighed heavily on her mind for years. She takes a deep breath and calms her mind. "If you think I need to do this, then... okay."

Dr. Sturgis leans forward to address Severn delicately. "You're a courageous woman. You've been brave for a very long time. I have a simple technique to draw out your memories. It should start to happen within moments of our beginning and will take as long as it takes. Your subconscious mind will reveal itself to me under hypnosis. I will give you time to process what we find in a safe environment. Whatever it is, Severn, we'll get through it together."

1974

The Fox & Ferret

Severn gripped her mother's hand as they crossed the busy intersection. She was twelve and dressed in her Sunday best. The light on her milky-white face forced her eyes closed while her high cheekbones and forehead took the brunt of the July afternoon sun. Her mother maintained her quick pace as Severn's much shorter legs scrambled to keep up. High heels were far from Severn's favorite choice of shoe. She could barely balance on them standing still, and being hustled across a crosswalk when the hand was blinking for her to stop was altogether ridiculous. "I can see the sign, Mommy," Severn complained, nearly biting her tongue as she navigated a pothole.

"Okay, then, get a wiggle on, young lady!" They reached the sidewalk, narrowly escaping a delivery truck's determined attempt to make the corner.

The Fox & Ferret was Severn's mother's favorite pub to visit after Sunday service. The moment they entered the double doors, she asked the hostess for a glass of chardonnay.

"Thirsty? Could you have ordered me a soda while you were at it?" She sat abruptly and removed both shoes to stretch her toes. She knew her mother was an alcoholic. Everyone did. Though Severn wasn't entirely sure what this meant, she was certain it wasn't good. Her mother had repeatedly forgotten to pick her up at friends' homes. She hadn't gotten up with Severn to get her ready for school in over two years. She hadn't cooked a meal in just as many. Severn had heard the whispers. After her father died, she found her mother slowly disconnecting from everything. A massive life insurance payout had kept the family in good standing. Severn still went to a private school, and someone who was hired made sure the kitchen was always stocked, and they kept their handsome home. Severn felt they went to church to remind the congregation that everything was fine. It was all an illusion. She knew it. Her mother knew it, but the liquor seemed to dull her mother's senses. Liquor was awful stuff. Severn had sampled it at her friend's house one weekend at a sleepover. She couldn't imagine drinking it at the rate her mother went through it.

"Good afternoon! You ordered a chardonnay?" The pub's owner, Luca, passed the large glass to her mom and winked at her. Severn's mother's cheeks colored slightly. Severn liked him. He always doted on the two of them. He produced a 7up for Severn from behind his back, complete with lemon and lime wedges. She smiled and accepted the treat with gratitude.

"Let me guess," Luca said, feigning confusion. He pointed at Severn first. "Grilled cheese with tomatoes and a side of fries." She nodded with a grin. "And for the lovely mother... a Cobb salad."

"Just a small one, please, Luca," she reminded him. "Thank you." Luca nodded and navigated the growing crowd to place the order.

"Isn't he a lovely man?" Severn's mother put the smudged glass to her lips. She looked at Severn without really looking. Severn wondered if Luca was married. Maybe having someone like Luca in her mother's life might help her.

"Do you come here on days other than Sunday?" Severn drank from her 7up and burped. Her mother seemed to take exception to the question and the burp.

"So, what if I did?"

"Just a question, Mom," Severn returned. "Don't get so *offended.*"

"Adults are allowed to do whatever they want, Severn." She took another long sip of her wine. "So, yes, I come here without you occasionally."

"For what? Lunch?" Severn narrowed her eyes at her mother.

"Yes, sometimes I come for lunch while you're at school." Her tone softened. "Sometimes, if there's someone to talk to, I stay until you come home from school."

"Sometimes longer," Severn said spitefully. She'd been a latch-key kid for the last year, taking herself to school and home and preparing meals. It was getting old.

"Don't be *horrible*, Severn," her mother replied harshly. "Do you think that I can just sit at home all day? I don't have any help. It's not like I have a husband.

It's just me. I have a lot to do. And I need adult company sometimes." She drained her glass.

"Well, if you can sit here all day, then I guess you could sit at home." Severn asserted, having never spoken to her mother this way before. She questioned why she was doing so now.

"I won't be interrogated by my twelve-year-old." Her mother put her face in her hands. She rubbed her eyes. Was she crying?

"I'm sorry. I don't know why I said that." Severn knew full well why she had said that. She was tired of having lost a father *and* a mother to the same accident. She was tired of being alone. Thankfully, the moment was broken by the arrival of Luca with their food. He unceremoniously placed their food in front of them. They both smiled appreciatively at him and, without speaking, began eating.

When they finished their lunch, Severn was delivered an ice cream sundae with a wink from Luca while her mother went to the bathroom. It was probably the fifth time she had made this trip in as many lunches. Severn allowed it. Luca was nice. Her mother should date him, she thought. A song by Barry White played over the pub's noisy diners. She liked this one: *You're the First, The Last, My Everything.* His voice reminded her of her father's, deep yet soothing. Severn sipped at the dregs of her 7up, staring into the sea of people moving through the pub's door, her body reacting to the music while her mother enjoyed her time in the bathroom. She picked up her napkin from her lap and wiped her face. She suddenly realized she'd spilled strawberry syrup on her white dress. Her mother would be upset. Lifting her dress to see how far the stain went, Severn noticed a larger stain on her underpants. It was much redder than the strawberry syrup. She felt the humiliation rise from her neck to her cheeks in a crimson heat. The shame hurt physically. Panic set in quickly, and Severn surveyed her surroundings. How much blood would seep out of her? *Would it collect on the floor?* How would she get out without everyone staring? What could she wrap around her waist? Where was her mother? It was hardly a surprise she was absent for this. Severn hoped against hope that her mother would have a simple fix for this unannounced event. *Why in a pub, of all places?* She peeked again under her dress, lifting it cautiously. The blood had stained the back of her dress where she sat. She would be exposed both front and back. Her mind raced. *Please come back, Mom, and don't fuss about it.*

A moment later, her mother had returned with a suspicious glow to her cheeks. That would have to take a backseat for now. Severn leaned over the table, ushered her mother forward with a frantic wave, and explained the event. Her mother looked around at the crowded tables and stood to pull on her light jacket. For a brief, terrifying moment, Severn thought she would leave her there and spare herself any embarrassment. Then, her mother carefully lifted Severn's jacket from the chair back. "Stand up, and I'll cover you." Severn obeyed, and her mother quickly placed the coat around her daughter's waist. Suddenly, Severn felt a rush of love for her mother. It had been a while since this feeling had invaded her body. It felt both comforting and unfamiliar. It reminded her of simpler times. She loved her mother, not as the drunk she had become, but as the woman who had once made her a priority. It saddened her to think this moment would vanish like other good memories.

"You ladies are leaving so soon?" Luca caught up with them at the door, and Severn noticed his face was also flushed.

"Emergency," her mother explained. "Sorry to rush off, Luca. I'll see you tomorrow."

1973

Grandma Anne

At thirteen, Jonah had made one friend, and when Grandma Anne came to watch him on Friday nights, he was allowed a guest. This was Mort, an awkward kid whose primary interests were model airplanes and insects. Mort and Jonah had little in common except for their lack of friends. Still, this was progress in his grandma's eyes, and she was happy for him.

Grandma Anne often nodded off after a board game under the hypnotic drone of the television. On this particular night, Jonah surveyed the house for his mother's stash of booze and cigarettes. Mort was an impressionable kid who only wanted to please Jonah and would do whatever that took. Jonah would be fourteen soon. Mort was already fourteen. He was overweight and wore too-tight T-shirts. He seemed unfazed by his apparent weirdness, and instead of feeling embarrassed, Jonah was proud of his friend.

"What is *vodka?*" Morty asked as he took another swig from the bottle. His round face went sour as the alcohol filled his virgin mouth. His nose shrank back into the shadows of his cheeks, and his eyes squeezed shut. Then he coughed.

"Well, it's booze. My mom's favorite." Jonah accepted the bottle back. He put it down quietly and lit a cigarette for both of them. The kitchen was dark, save the streetlight dimly illuminating their secret. Jonah took a drag and blew it out, handing the smoke over to his friend.

"My parents don't smoke," Mort said matter-of-factly. "I'd be kicked to kingdom come if they ever found out." Mort had confided in Jonah before that his father wasn't afraid to let his son know who was in charge. Jonah had seen the bruises, but they didn't talk about it. It explained why Mort treasured his time alone, putting models together or pinning new insects to his board. He knew more about bugs than anyone. Mort took a long draw of the cigarette, and the smoke slipped down his windpipe, forcing him to cough again.

"Don't inhale it, Mort." Jonah took the butt from his friend. "Just let it hit your tongue and blow it out." He'd done this twice now and remembered the ordeal of inhaling. He pushed another swig of the vodka down and felt suddenly ill. His stomach churned, and his throat opened. The vodka, his dinner, and other stragglers in his digestive system suddenly burst from his mouth in a torrent. It splattered all over the linoleum floor. Mort pulled back, but too late. The hot sick dripped from both of his feet. The smell was enough to make him suddenly gag. Mort's stomach rumbled, which quickly elevated into an unstoppable force. The foul, fiery liquid spewed from his mouth with fervor. With Jonah still doubled over in front of him, Mort tossed hot chunks all over the back of Jonah's head and neck. The scene would have been comical to both of them if they'd seen it on T.V., but this wasn't fiction. It was real, and it was disgusting.

Mort's face grimaced as they gathered their wits and surveyed the damage. He stood on rubbery legs and lifted his feet as if pulling away from a spider's web. His socks squishing.

"I need a shower," said Mort with a flat voice. Jonah just nodded and pointed to the stairs.

"Jonah!" Grandma Anne stood at the threshold between the living room and kitchen and glared at him. Her eyes were red around the edges. Jonah looked up as fear took its place next to nausea, and he quickly put out the cigarette.

"Into your mother's *"stash?"* Her tone was accusatory, and her fists were clenched. "Damn, fool, kids!" Mort ran the rest of the way to the bathroom, leaving a trail of footprints along the linoleum – slipping once. Jonah tried to stand, stretching the tired muscles in his stomach.

"I'm sorry, Grandma," he said, vomit dripping from his chin. "I didn't know what it was."

"You knew well enough to sneak off to drink it, though!" He wasn't going to pull the wool over her eyes. "I take a cat nap, and you two proceed to drink... what is this?" She picks up the bottle and reads. *"Vodka. "*Another hard look in Jonah's direction sends his stomach turning. "This is *poison,* Jonah! *Poison!"*

Was she being serious? Had he actually mistaken poison for his mother's *favorite drink? Poison! He ran to the bathroom to join Mort, who was* running the shower. He climbed in with his friend, both fully clothed, and they rinsed their sticky bodies and muddied minds.

"Your grandma scares the shit out of me, Jonah," Morty confided while gulping air into his lungs. "I'm staying in here." He toweled off his head and nearly crashed into the sink while Jonah did the same.

"We can't stay in here forever, Mort. We'll have to go to bed." Jonah opened the door just enough for the boys to watch as Grandma Anne's arm thrust them each a housecoat.

"Come out when you have these on. Hang your wet things on the shower rail." Her voice was no-nonsense. They were in real trouble. Jonah knew he had disappointed her. The boys changed and emerged from the steamy bathroom in short order.

"Please don't tell my parents, Mrs. Gilchrist," Morty begged, his wet head still dripping on his housecoat. Grandma just pointed to the couch for the boys to sit on.

In the living room, they listened to Grandma Anne's rant as she paced the length of the couch. *"No excuse"* was repeated often. That and *"What's gotten into you, Jonah?"* When she'd finished, the boys were ordered to Jonah's room to sleep. *"Never again!"* they heard her affirm as Jonah softly closed his door.

1974

The Love Letter

Severn was becoming concerned over her mother's self-isolation in November of 1974. In November of 1972, Severn's father had gone away. It was a car accident; the details of which Severn was never really made aware and tried hard not to imagine. A horrible image would sometimes pass through her mind on sleepless nights, but she quickly tried to quell it with mundane thoughts of boys or movies or stories from school. November, that cruel month where winter-like cold began to settle into your bones, would forever be an unwanted shift; gain becomes loss, happiness becomes melancholy.

Severn had loved her father for his gracious manner, comical faces, and loving way he put her to bed when he was home. A book, a story, and a few minutes lying next to her as she dozed off after a smattering of questions designed to keep him with her longer. Their relationship was nothing short of perfect in her young mind. She missed him more than she could stand some nights, and while her mother sat in front of the television, finishing her wine, she ached to sit with her and talk about him.

"I know you miss him, baby," her mother would say when Severn crawled onto the couch and laid her head on her mother's lap. Her fingers would gently stroke Severn's long, blonde hair. "I miss him too. We're managing, though, aren't we?" Severn's head would nod. "We'll be alright, Severn. He made sure of it. Daddy made sure of that."

But Severn knew something had changed in her mother. The drinking had taken on an epic nature. Severn would sometimes come down dressed for school, and her mother would watch static on the TV screen with a glass of wine still firmly in her grasp. That scared her, but she didn't know what to do about it.

It was rare they would cry together over their shared loss; Severn could count on one hand how many times it had happened. She had lost count of how often she cried herself to sleep over losing her father. The absence of his presence was felt in every room and through every proud moment she experienced. Not being able to share these with him was crushing. Not to find him in his study when she walked past on her way to bed was eerie. She would tell herself stories he had once told her at bedtime to fill the void, sometimes hearing his voice in hers. She would kiss her stuffy, imagining it was him, and accept a kiss from the brown bear. It was tragic, but her counselor had recommended she do this to keep Daddy in her heart and her memory.

Luca, the man from the pub... Severn wondered whether he might love her mother. Maybe he would leave his wife and come live with them. She wasn't prepared to replace her father but was willing to allow it for her mother's sake. She considered many scenarios where the charming man rang their doorbell and entered with a bouquet for her mother, a box of chocolates, and a wink and a smile for her. Severn's heart raced at the idea. But her mother was in no shape to date anyone. Whatever was happening at the pub was one thing, but to present herself as the woman she was outside the pub or church might be impossible for her mother.

Still, it was worth a try.

Severn rifled through her mother's purse on the front table while she watched the evening news with that faraway look in her eyes. Severn was searching for a card or coaster with a number to the pub so she could call it, ask for Luca, and explain her intentions. It scared her to speak on the phone to a man, but she thought if her heart were in the right place, he would take it as a compliment and her approval of what they were already doing. Clearly, he wasn't happy at home, and God knew Severn's mother wasn't happy.

As Severn searched the deepest depths of her mother's messy purse, her hands encircled a small bottle she had brought into the light. The label read *Valium*, and she wondered if her mother was sick. Severn placed it on the table. Next, a crumpled note appeared between Severn's fingers, and she carefully pulled it free of the cluttered contents. She watched her mother a moment, still motionless on the couch, while the T.V. glared back. Severn flattened the note on the front table and then retreated to her father's study to read it. The note was from her father. Her heart skipped a beat. She felt she shouldn't read a letter from her father to her mother. It seemed wrong. (*But he was her father every bit as much as he was her mother's husband. With that reasoning, she read on.)*

It was a love letter. He told her mother how much she meant to him - how much he loved their life together and their daughter. Severn smiled at this. He reminded her that the following weekend would be their eleventh anniversary and conveyed his plans. The letter was dated the week before he'd died. Severn's hand covered her mouth.

Her mother had carried this letter in her purse for over two years. The thought made her cry. Had she been too hard on her mother? Had her father's death destroyed her? She knew it had been difficult, but after reading about the love they'd shared, plans for the future, and how happy they were together, her mother's pain seemed amplified.

"Oh, Mommy," she whispered, folding the crumpled paper gently. She returned to the hall and slid it back into the purse. She watched her mother for another moment and then joined her on the couch. She laid her head on her mother's lap and hugged her. The fact was her mother had been very strong for her and herself. She drank too much, but maybe that would change.

"I'm so sorry, Mommy," she said, squeezing her around the waist more firmly. Her eyes shut tight. Perhaps no man could replace her father as a husband to her mother. "I love you."

Her mother didn't respond save a soft hand on her head. She began to stroke her hair, and this was enough for Severn, for now.

1975

The Happening

At 11:30 pm, Friday night, Severn awoke to her mother pounding on their front door. This was beginning to happen more and more lately. Her mother often left her keys at the bar or dropped them along the way. They were on her seventh set of keys for the house in six months. Severn had sworn she wouldn't let her mother in the next time this happened, but it was a cool May evening, and the sky threatened rain. *But wouldn't she deserve that?* Wouldn't she deserve the humiliation of having the neighbors find her on the front porch, soaked through and passed out?

Instead, owing to her forgiving nature, Severn opened the door to her mother's incoherent blathering. There was a thank-you buried among it somewhere. She sat her mother on the foyer bench and helped strip her of her footwear and light jacket. Then she proceeded to walk her upstairs and drop her on her bed. She pulled the unkempt bedding over her mother and placed a glass of water at her bedside.

Immediately after, she called her friend Maribel. It was late, but Mary's family were night owls, and she knew it wasn't any trouble calling after ten. Mary picked up the phone.

"Mary, it happened again," Severn began, "I just put her to bed."

"I'm sorry, Severn," Mary replied earnestly. "You're doing great. You'll be a great mom one day." Severn could make out *Someone Saved My Life Tonight* by Elton John on the other side of the call. Fitting, she thought, Mary had always been her saving grace.

"I'm getting worried about what people might think," Severn continued. "Do you think if other adults knew, they might call child services?"

"You just need to get through high school, and then you'll be an adult. Do you think you can do that?" Mary always tried her best to find solutions.

"That's six more years," Severn said, her hand rubbing her forehead. "I'm afraid she'll be found out, and someone will come to the door and take me away."

"No one's going to take you away," Mary assured her. "Just keep doing what you're doing, and everything will be fine."

There was a moment of silence between them, and Severn admitted, "I'm worried about her. It hasn't been getting better. If anything, it's worse than ever." Severn's voice cracked as she cried into the receiver to her best friend.

"Do you think you would want to live with me?" Mary asked. "With my family?"

Severn hadn't dared to consider such a solution. "That would be amazing, wouldn't it? Best friends and roommates and we could get bunk beds and share a room."

"And we could talk all night and share clothes!" Mary joined in on the fantasy. "Could you do it?" Mary's question was the end of the dream, however, as Severn realized her reality. Leaving her mother to fend for herself seemed insensitive in light of her inability even to manage her keys.

"It's a nice thought," Severn replied, reluctant to let the fantasy die altogether. "Would your parents agree to it?"

"If they knew what we know about your mom, I think they would."

"Because it's not like she's abusive..." Severn realized she was defending her mother and stopped herself. "Or maybe she is, I don't know,"

"Let's just pretend like maybe this *could* happen," Mary replied, leaving Severn open to the idea while still considering her mother. With that, they said goodbye for the night, visions of something better dancing dangerously in Severn's head.

* * *

The following evening, thirteen-year-old Severn had been invited to a party. With no one to ask whether she could or couldn't go, she decided to attend. There would be older kids there, she knew that, which made her nervous, but she would have two friends with her, Alicia and Maribel. The event had been hyped up as the party of the year, with absent parents and all that. She called Maribel and planned to meet her and Alicia at the corner.

"Do you think there will be alcohol there?" Severn wondered nervously over the phone. "Or drugs?" She knew she would never try anything like that after seeing the effects.

"We don't have to join in if there is, Sev. Let's show up so people know we came. If we don't like it, we can always come back here and watch a movie."

Severn agreed and promised to relay the same to Alicia. They would meet at the corner of Sherborne and Main, just two blocks from the party and twelve blocks from Severn's home.

Severn showered and feathered her long, blonde hair in the style of Cheryl Tiegs, who had recently graced the cover of her mother's Bazaar magazine. Rooting through the makeup boxes in her mother's vanity, Severn applied a bright coral lipstick labeled "Abstract Orange" on the smeared label on the bottom of the sticky black tube and a robin's egg blue eye shadow. At the last moment, she streaked a dark red blush across her pale cheeks. It left two lines of crimson in a way that made her appear far more like her mother than she'd ever observed before. She blinked into her reflection, feeling even more adult than a moment before. All of this was going to help. There was a good chance Chuck may be at the party, the boy she'd suddenly felt an aching attraction to. A grade older. She'd decided she would like to experience something with him. A kiss or a touch. Something that made her feel akin to being alive and cared about and loved or just liked or nice to look at or anything noticeable.

So many changes that she couldn't account for or discuss with her mother. Her breasts required more than a training bra. They had grown plump, and the nipples had become dark and sensitive. They billowed out of her flat-chested support and created lines and creases in her shirts. It embarrassed her that her breasts might be noticeable. Still, she didn't know whether she should hide them or give in to the attention they occasionally garnered. She was as tall as most of the boys in her class but inevitably forced into the *"cult of likeness"* too shy to return their glances. What she wanted was what most girls wanted. She wanted someone to like her in that attraction-and-love kind of way. Not the creepy way she felt she was being ogled in. Boys who still pinched her and threw dirt at her didn't make her feel good about herself. And there were still plenty of those. She wanted someone to make out with her. She wanted someone to tell her they liked her. Someone more mature. She wanted handholding and phone calls. She knew her feelings that went beyond the innocent version she was told of boy-girl relationships was something to hide. Still, she often imagined someone making her feel that feeling she had created in private. But she had no grasp of how this would ever be real with no one to tell and no one who would comment or care. She somehow feared none of it would feel real unless she could tell her mother. Her mother wouldn't ask, so there was nothing to reveal, and even worse, her mother's version of anything like this made her feel like it was wrong and dirty. The usual separation in the understanding of love and attraction between the generations was trumped by a mother who had presented a version of complete detachment. The simplicity of being told it was normal but to watch out was missing. The careful attitude that came with the knowledge someone was watching and cared about the outcome didn't exist. A tear ran down Severn's cheek as she pulled on her sneakers, cutting a line through the newly applied blush. Severn wiped at it, not realizing it would leave a trace of her maturity being compromised with a child's simple gesture.

In the family room, she looked at her father's portrait and leaned into the photograph, placing her lips on the kind face that stared back at her.

"Love you, Daddy," she told him. "Wish me luck."

It was almost 8:00 pm, and the twilight sky was transitioning to dark. Severn embraced the evening air with a deep breath as she stepped out the door. The damp warmth hit her face as a momentary breeze moved through her hair. She had ten dollars, her school ID, and her house keys in her small, over-the-shoulder purse. She felt this weight on her hip as she strode purposefully towards her friends. The streets seemed quiet - as if whispering her presence without wanting to awaken her surroundings. To wander through the dark, completely unknown, was the dreamlike quality of adulthood she longed for in the moments she knew she was no longer a child but, as of yet, unable to control her destiny.

To say this was a quiet and predictable neighborhood was, without fail, the only way to define it. Severn had been out alone many times in daylight, and her mother had allowed this. So, when she noticed a van in front of the park, she told herself to stop being stupid and move on. It was strange how the park looked menacing tonight. The van sitting idle in front of the tennis courts offered a jarring juxtaposition to the playground she had frequented only a few years ago. She was just being dumb. Just because it was dark didn't mean anything was wrong. She could do this herself. She didn't need her drunken mother to drive her to a party. So stupid. Just the same, Severn picked up her pace, moving quickly past the dark van, a sense of unrest filling her stomach with nausea.

She just kept walking. *See? Nothing.* Several cars drove past her, crawling along the residential street. She flinched slightly as each approached from behind, but they passed unceremoniously. *Only a few more blocks. So stupid.* The purse bounced more rapidly against her side. She grabbed it and held it still. The fake leather felt soft, almost like a hand, and she felt safer—another car. Expecting to see her shadow move across the passing lawn as it had with the other vehicles, Severn realized this one had no headlights. With a sudden, quick response, she strode up the front walk of a random house to appear as though she were home. The vehicle passed, and as she turned to look, it was obvious it was the same van she'd passed moments ago.

She forced the rising anxiety she was experiencing from her mind. *Who was this little girl? Who was this child who couldn't walk a few blocks without being afraid of the Boogeyman? She* was the one who took care of things. *She* took care of herself and her mother and their outcome. Severn returned to the sidewalk with this assertion and continued her path to meet her friends. Tonight was going to be a *good* night.

All of this rapidly drained away. At the next stop sign, she froze in terror. She saw the van parked on the cross street from the corner of her eye. It seemed alive with a malicious focus. Why did her body stop? Why did she know? How did she have the instinct? It could have just been a van. A driver lost. A tire flat. Parked for the night. She managed to summon the strength in her legs to cross the street, continuing her path until she connected with her friends. *It's just a van, silly.* But she knew.

On the other side of the street, two men emerged from behind a line of shrubs. *Why were they in the shrubs?* She couldn't see, as dusk was now dark. They were faceless. Big. Surprising. One was grabbing her as if hugging her. He held her, and her face was tight against his jacket. It felt rough, like old wool. She didn't have time to fight before there was another body behind her. Encircled. There wasn't any sound. Suddenly, something was in her mouth. No way to scream. She kicked a little but somehow also knew it was fruitless. It was only a moment before they were under her arms and legs. It was bad, and no one would know, and no one would care. She was going in the van. And somehow, she blacked out.

Pick up The Blind Affect today and discover Michael Poeltl's back library.

More books by Michael Poeltl

A.I. Insurrection – The General's War
Armageddon (Book 2 of the A.I. Insurrection series)
Exodus (Book 3 of the A.I. Insurrection series)
Waning Metaphorically (Short stories)
The Judas Syndrome
Rebirth (Book two of The Judas Syndrome)
Revelation (Book three of The Judas Syndrome)
West of Noreaso (Young Reader Fantasy)
An Angry Earth (Children's Book)
If a Tree Falls in the Forest...
E=ME
Available on Amazon

About the author

Website: www.mikepoeltl.com
Goodreads: Michael Poeltl
Twitter: @mpoeltlauthor
Facebook: Michael.Poeltl.author
Amazon Author Page: Michael Poeltl Amazon

Acknowledgements

Rose Keefe – Editor - www.rosekeefe.com
Thanks again to my editor and friend, Rose, as she continues assisting me in my journey. Re-edited February, 2021